STRANGERS
ON THE BEACH

A Novel

Josh Pahigian

STRANGERS
ON THE BEACH

A Novel

Josh Pahigian

ISLANDPORT PRESS

Islandport Press
P.O. Box 10
Yarmouth, Maine 04096
www.islandportpress.com
books@islandportpress.com

Copyright © 2012 by Joshua Pahigian
First Islandport Press edition published October 2012

ISBN: 978-1-934031-83-4
Library of Congress Card Number: 2012934447

Book jacket design by Karen F. Hoots / Hoots Design
Book designed by Michelle Lunt for Islandport Press
Publisher Dean L. Lunt

To Heather, who walks the beach beside me

Part One

Chapter One

A Late-Night Swim

"Sevigny," she cried. "Sevigny!" Her strained voice conveyed the warble of an accent Roger could not identify. That one word, again and again, *Sevigny, Sevigny, Sevigny,* her voice desperate, strange, and beautiful. In hearing the three syllables repeated, Roger almost wondered if this were the only word she knew. Yes, he might have wondered that if he'd stopped to wonder anything at all. But he didn't. He just reacted, bursting outside and into the fog, trudging through a tidal pool, diving into the first breaker, and then swimming. And swimming.

While the rest of Pine Point Beach slept, Roger Simons had heard her cry through his open window, allowed it to infiltrate his dreams, and heeded its call. It was one or two o'clock in the morning, and he was in the midst of doing the most heroic thing he'd ever done. He didn't stop to wonder at the fact that he was doing something brave; nor did he pause to observe that the cold, dry sand he pressed with hurried footprints spilled out for so many unseen miles in either direction, or that the sea before him churned beneath a moonless sky. He merely heard her voice and awoke, and before his head had left the pillow, or so it seemed, he was in the water.

"Sevigny," she cried. Roger cringed at how much farther he still had to swim. A moment later, he realized her voice had been stifled by a swell, lifting and dropping her, pulling her under. When he next heard her call, he knew he'd veered off course. He put his head down and swam.

"Sevigny . . ." She was drifting away. He drove his arms through the water more ferociously and surged into darkness. He twisted to redirect himself. "Sevigny!" He tasted the salt of the sea. He thought he could see her splashing—yes, he could. "Sevigny . . ." And all at once he was upon her.

"Sevigny," she gasped as her cold hands clung to him, as they both struggled for air. "Sevigny," with a sob, during the long, slow swim to shore.

Roger swam half on his back and half on his side, holding her against his chest with his left arm while his right arm worked with his legs to propel them through the water. The beach seemed immeasurably farther away than he had ever imagined it could be. As for the woman, she wrapped both arms around him and strained to keep her mouth above the water, just below his chin. After a time, she began to help in the cumbersome work with legs that fell into rhythm with his. Twice, she nearly slipped away, her head sliding lower and lower into the circle of his bent elbow and curved wrist. Both times they stopped, floated briefly, without panic, without words, and repositioned themselves. The third time, she anticipated the breach and kicked more forcefully, and wriggled her waist and shoulders until she'd pulled herself higher onto him, so they could continue without losing momentum.

When the breakers began to crash on them, Roger knew they had made it. After just a few more kicks, he lowered his feet into a stutter against the ocean floor and tried to set her free, before realizing she had no intention of relinquishing her grip. He slid a hand down the smooth curve of her back, over her hips, then halfway down her legs to find a fulcrum from which to lift. With his feet touching the sand and his hands touching her body, Roger noticed for the first time that she was naked, or very nearly so. He felt her breasts pressing against his body as he carried her, and wondered what strange creature he'd plucked from the ocean. When they reached thigh-deep water, his tired arms were suddenly struck by the weight of her lithe body. His legs too began to buckle, and he no longer noticed her near-nakedness.

High above, the moon was breaking through the clouds. The fog was dispersing. Before him, the wet sand glistened, waiting to be reclaimed by the tide. A bit farther ahead, the gentle slope of the beach rose toward its plateau. For several steps Roger squinted to locate the outline of his cottage in the shadows beyond the dunes, but from the water's edge, he could see only rooftops. Despite the reviving moon and his familiarity with the terrain, he couldn't get his bearings.

He staggered up the slope and gently dropped her when he felt the loose sand beneath his feet. He fell beside her and they both gasped as the adrenaline drained from their bodies. Then, when they had recovered slightly, he lifted her shivering body and began to make heavy footprints in the sand once more. By the time they had reached the dune grass, he'd given up on finding the path. They'd drifted farther than he would have guessed, and were at least a dozen lots down the beach from his, probably in front of the Plantes' or the Labbes'. It was only mid-June, and most of his neighbors hadn't yet arrived for the summer. Given the circumstances, he didn't think they'd mind if he stumbled through a backyard or two.

He paused only briefly as the first licks of wispy grass caressed his legs. He wondered if he might put her down to walk beside him. But, in that moment, as the moon finally overpowered the clouds and lit up the Plantes' patio, Roger turned first to look at the glistening depths from which they'd just emerged. He scanned the horizon, or as much of it as he could see. His mind was beginning to work again. He was starting to wonder how this underwear-clad woman had arrived in the waves in such a state, on such a night, when there were no boats or other signs of life upon the water. He gazed into the heaves and sighs of the ocean and held her close. Finally, he lowered his eyes to her face and studied it in the half-light. Behind the sand, strands of tangled brown hair, and beads of seawater, he found her eyes, and saw that they were fixed somewhere far away.

"Sevigny," she said one final time, but in a whisper so faint that Roger couldn't be sure later whether he'd heard it or merely seen it on her lips, as they'd parted and closed three mournful times.

Chapter Two

A Sleepless Night

Billy Carter tried not to listen. He'd awoken to a man's voice talking about the lackluster motel reservations, telling his mother that tourism would be down, saying the Pier might still draw a crowd on a Friday night, but that his friend at the Chamber had said to figure on a 20 percent drop overall. The T-shirt sellers and clam-shack owners were already griping about a lost season, even though summer was still a week away.

"Doesn't matter," Billy's mother said. "Last year all we got was Canucks anyway. Canucks who didn't tip worth two shits."

"Canucks . . . that sounds naughty," the man replied, in a voice that made Billy's stomach drop.

"Oh, I've known some naughty Canucks all right," Billy's mother said. She laughed a laugh Billy had hated all his life. "But they still didn't tip worth a shit."

"Shucks, Brandy," the man said. "You've met some Canucks who sure suck."

There was silence. Then, Billy heard his mother say, "Come 'ere," and the man moaned "Uh-huh," in a throaty, guttural way. A moment later, Billy heard the *thwack-thwack-thwack* of the sleeper sofa's metal skeleton unfolding in the living room. He heard his mother say, "Not yet, baby." He heard her quick footsteps, then the *whoosh* of his bedroom door closing. Then he heard their bodies fall onto the mattress, their rustling, and other noises.

Outside, the air was damp but warm for June. Down the hill, closer to the water, Billy knew it would be cooler. After he had lowered himself out his window and slipped through the rusty fence that enclosed their yard, he tried to focus on the sidewalk, on the cars parked along it, on the houses. He knew better than to let his mind return to the living room and his mother and whichever man she'd brought home tonight.

He made his way down the long, gradual slope of Atlantic Avenue, toward West Grand. A scattering of porch lights lit his way, illuminating a stretch of sidewalk that Billy was capable of traversing even in the dark. Still, it was nice to see some lights. They meant that not everyone had moved away. At fifteen, Billy was becoming rapidly aware of the larger forces in the world that were decimating his neighborhood. Not long ago, the Hill District had been a bustling part of town. Now, there were only a few families left.

While the grown-ups complained about the layoffs at the B&M Baked Beans plant in Portland and the shuttered storefronts at the Maine Mall, Billy lamented that his two childhood friends had both moved from town midway through their freshman year, leaving him a man without a tribe at school. Even Mrs. Webber, who used to give him Table Talk pies and chat about the Red Sox, had disappeared one day without saying good-bye. One by one, nearly everyone had left, taking with them the markers that had differentiated their small yards and weather-beaten homes from the rest—the towels draped over porch railings, or sprinklers spraying water onto the sidewalk. Yellow eviction notices and orange-and-black FOR RENT signs had replaced those signs of life.

At the bottom of the hill, Billy walked past the much larger homes on West Grand, still awaiting the return of their summer inhabitants from wherever it was they went during the "other" ten months. Several of the houses remained boarded up from the winter, but before long they would all be open. Even if the motels downtown had trouble filling their rooms, Billy knew these regal estates would soon be occupied. They always were. As he crossed West Grand, he felt as though he were stepping into a different town. Behind him were the small rental houses on either side of Atlantic, with their dented aluminum siding and porches that seemed perpetually in need of repair. That was the world to which he belonged. Before him lay the sprawling mansions with their "front" yards facing the ocean, their floor-to-ceiling beachside windows, their pillars, and brick patios. This was the Old Orchard Beach portrayed on the postcards and in the magazines, the one famous for its white sand, bustling Pier, and hopping nightlife.

Billy walked down a driveway that led between two of the mansions. When the pavement turned to sand and gravel, he kicked off his sneakers. Continuing along the path, he felt the tips of the long, thin blades of dune grass nibbling at his legs, then the soft sand of the beach between his toes. He walked toward the crashing waves and then shivered for the first time when he reached the flat, wet sand. He hopped over a rivulet draining toward the sea. The stream told him by its very narrowness that the tide would be turning soon, or perhaps already had.

Within five minutes, Billy had passed the Brunswick Hotel. Within ten, he'd slipped between the tall, dark stilts of the Pier. Within fifteen, he'd passed Surf Six and the other nightclubs north of the Square. When he reached the first of the six towering condos that rose every few hundred feet up to the Scarborough line, he veered to his left, onto the dry sand, and sat down. He pulled his legs up against his chest and wrapped his arms around his knees. He stared into darkness. "It's not fair," he said quietly.

As Billy sat in the sand and tasted the salty tears trickling down his cheeks, he gave voice to an outrage that had been festering within him all his life. He parted his lips because if there were a God, Billy wanted Him to hear and be ashamed. "It's not fair," he said, in more than a whisper. "I hate her. And I hate this town." With each word, his voice grew a bit louder. "I hate it." He slowly rose to his feet and turned to glare at the dark spot where he knew his town to sit on the swell of land that rose behind him. "It's nothing to me," he said. "I don't need it."

Billy looked heavenward and glowered at the halo of yellow obscuring the moon. Then, as he stood there, the clouds began to disperse. The orb broke through, clean and white, and as it lit up the beach, Billy addressed his grievance to it, unsure of whether, in its newfound luminescence, it meant to mock or acknowledge him. "I hate it!" he yelled. "All of it! And no one can make me stay!"

To Billy's surprise and horror, a voice answered. It was a quiet voice that spoke slowly, which seemed to hint as much at the person's reluctance to speak as his inability to bear silent witness to Billy's testimony any longer. "Do you really mean that?" the voice asked.

For a fleeting instant Billy thought it was the voice of God speaking to him, but as he processed the words, he realized they had come from behind him, not above, so he spun away from the moon and with a quickening pulse turned to face the dunes. Just ten feet away there stood a man, obscured from the waist down by dune grass. His shirt, like his black hair, clung to his angular body. Billy realized he was soaking wet. He gazed at Billy with a strange mixture of disdain and curiosity.

Billy fell back a step, then another, before regaining his balance and standing to face the stranger.

"I'll help you," the man said slowly. "But first, you'll need to help me."

Chapter Three

Bountiful Sea

Sally Fiddler arose at dawn each day to emerge from the tall condo building abutting the Scarborough line, where Old Orchard Beach converged with Pine Point Beach. She traced the water's edge nearly every day of her life, except for the very worst days of winter when the weather prevented her from traversing the three miles south and three miles home that constituted her march. Even then, Sally suspended her efforts only because others had pressured her to exercise more caution. On a blustery morning in 1998, police officer Ernie Sabo had ventured into the teeth of a savage nor'easter to lead her to safety after she'd become disoriented in the blowing snow. After that, she'd promised Ernie to stay inside whenever the snow was so severe that she couldn't see the pink house from her bedroom window.

There were no worries about snow today; it was nearly summer, the busy season for Sally, who, although she received little praise for her efforts, saw her toil as a way of repaying the town for its kindness. Her father had drowned when she was thirteen, and two summers later her mother had run off with a tourist, never to return. Ever since, Sally had lived at Seaside Heights as one of its only year-round residents. She drew a small stipend from the condo association in exchange for sweeping the stairwells free of sand and turning the lobby lights on in the morning and off at night. She also received a small allowance from the town. Despite the divide between Old Orchard's working poor and deep-pocketed seasonal residents, the locals always took care of their own. And when it came time to hash out the municipal budget each spring, the town council never waffled when it got to the line dedicated to the mentally challenged girl, who was, in fact, no longer a girl, but suspended in a sort of perpetual childhood even as she reached the middle years of womanhood. Sally, the good people of the town understood, was aware, but not *too* aware, of the world around her. Some said she couldn't speak. Others swore they'd heard her utter perfectly formed words in moments when the mood had struck her. In any case, she was different and vulnerable, but the town accepted her just the same.

Sally began her duties with greater zeal than usual on this morning. The warm sun suggested summer had arrived, and for Sally, who enjoyed this season most of all, that was a wonderful thing. With her wagon in tow, she hurried through the dry sand, then across the damp sand that had been molded by the tide. When she reached the smooth sand along the water's edge, she turned toward the Pier and began her trek. It was five o'clock and the tide was still coming in, which meant Sally had to gradually veer closer to the dry sand with every step she took toward Surf Six, the Pier, the Brunswick, the Sun Dial, and the little river where she'd turn around.

After fifty paces Sally paused to excavate a sand dollar partially covered with sand. She flipped it over with her metal ski pole and, seeing that it was intact, raised the pole and dropped its point onto the shell. It wouldn't be long before the shellers returned. They were the scourge of a delightful time of year when watches, rings, coins, bills, balls, Frisbees, keys, and all sorts of other things were left on the beach for Sally. The shellers tried to make small talk. They slowed her down. They took things that didn't belong to them.

She crushed a few more shells before pausing to inspect a piece of driftwood that had been caught in a tidal pool near the pink house. She decided it wasn't worthy of a place in her wagon; maybe it would be after a few more months of tumbling. Next, she encountered a mesh clamming bag that she scooped up, along with a wayward buoy.

But these were common things. What Sally encountered next was uncommon. She had just passed the Royal Anchor Inn when she saw it. The waves of the incoming tide had just given way to the calm of high tide, and she saw something lying half-covered in the sand. She flipped the item over with her stick, then stooped, rinsed the sand from it, and stood up. It was a black hood that reminded her of when Mrs. Munson came and dressed her up and took her to look at pumpkins in the Square. Yes, it would be a perfect mask, if only it had two more holes. She would have to cut eyeholes into it, or maybe Mrs. Munson would. Maybe she would mend the bottom, where it was ripped, and cover the squiggly lines that looked like words. Sally laid it carefully at the bottom of her wagon.

As if this discovery hadn't made for a special-enough morning, after Sally passed the first condo and then the long yellow expanse of the Copley Motel, something else caught her eye. She squinted into the wet sand that shimmered beneath the climbing sun and was practically trotting by the time she reached the outermost edge of a fifty-foot stretch where various objects were tumbling in the gentle waves. It looked like someone had dumped a wardrobe, pantry, and dresser into the sea.

Sally began scooping up whatever she could and ferrying items of interest to higher ground. She would have time to sort through the bounty later. First, she needed to safeguard as much of it as possible against the tide. Here was a woman's shoe. There, a bobbing water bottle. A lantern. A pair of pants. Another shoe. An orange vest. A sopping book. A plastic container. Pants. Shirts. A black dress.

Sally's wagon was already brimming by the time she lifted a small leather case from the sea and located the zipper that wrapped around three of its sides. She unzipped it and was surprised to find dry pages inside. It was a book, full of words written in pretty looping letters that meant nothing to Sally. She flipped through several pages and was about to throw it back, when she came upon a picture. It was a sunset on a beach, with palm trees. It had been drawn in pencil but Sally could fill in the color at home. Flipping ahead she found more pictures. She zipped up the book, carried it to her wagon, and wedged it tightly against one of the sides, pushing it down so that it would be safe at the bottom with the Halloween mask.

But Sally still had one more thing to find, the most special thing of all—a small wooden box that she noticed bobbing twenty feet from shore. She waded out and waited for a wave. Then, in the lull before the next surge, she trapped it against her legs. She stood in knee-deep water and traced with pruned fingers the two letters on its top. Then she fumbled with the clasp before finally figuring out how it worked. She flipped up the lid and gazed into the box with amazement. She stared for thirty seconds at the sparkling prize inside. Then she closed the lid, fixed the clasp, and hurried to shore.

She had not yet completed her route; in fact, she had not even reached the Pier. But she turned her wagon and headed for home, clutching the little box tightly in her hand. She did not see the dark figure watching her from the dunes.

Chapter Four

The Call

Ernie tried not to stare. The new girl was old enough to look at in that way, and maybe ten years ago he would have, but it didn't feel right. Still, it was hard not to look if she was going to wear a top like that, and lean over the register like that, and smile like that as she took his order. She was young enough to be his daughter—and besides, he thought he recognized her. Yes, she'd been one of Jen's friends, one of her teammates on the softball field or basketball court.

"You went to school with my daughter," Ernie said, taking his change from her hand.

"I didn't think you recognized me, Mr. Sabo," she said, before correcting herself. "I mean, Officer Sabo."

"Ernie will do," he said, puffing out his chest. "I recognize you all right." He squinted, and studied the contours of her face.

"It's Carrie," she said, smiling over her shoulder as she turned to get the bagel he'd ordered.

"You're Nikki Tibbet's daughter," Ernie said, when she returned to the counter.

"That's right," she said. "How's Jen?"

"Good," Ernie said. "Jen's good. She lives with her mother."

"Oh," Carrie said. "Is she still at UNE?"

"No," Ernie said. "She transferred to Northeastern."

"I'm home for the summer," Carrie said, "so tell her to come by. I'm here every day."

"I will," Ernie said, though he doubted he'd see his daughter anytime soon.

She smiled and leaned to one side to see the next person in line.

"Well . . . I'll probably see you tomorrow," Ernie said awkwardly, and he turned to go. But before he reached the door, the click of his radio stopped him. The voice came through nice and clear so that the people on the stools along the window and in the booths took notice.

"Officer Sabo, copy?"

"Gotcha," Ernie replied, trying to sound hip like one of the cops on TV. He was aware that he had an audience. He only hoped Debby wasn't radioing for him to bring back a bear claw or muffin. Debby's voice hurriedly said, "The Coast Guard's reporting a wrecked sailing yacht down at the marsh. Chief wants you to see if anything washed up. Maybe visit Sally to see if she found anything interesting this morning."

"I'm on it," Ernie replied.

"Hey," Debby said.

"Yeah?" Ernie answered.

"You ain't at Beach Bagels, are you?" Ernie lifted his eyes from the receiver in his hand and looked at the girl behind the counter. She smiled.

"No," he lied. "I'm in the cruiser."

"Never mind," Debby said.

"Gotcha," Ernie replied. He reholstered the receiver, surveyed the shop full of eavesdropping customers, and announced to no one in particular, "Probably just a sloop that drifted off its mooring. We don't see big boats like that up here." Then he hurried out the door.

Chapter Five

Beach Walk

Roger awoke to the sound of helicopter rotors. Before he could recall
what seemed like the most vivid dream he'd ever had, the noise passed.
He slipped into sleep once more, even as he noted that the sun had
grown bright against his bedroom window and that he'd slept beyond
the hour when he usually began his day. At the sound of the second
chopper, he sat bolt upright with his elbows locked beneath him on the
mattress. Before his spent muscles could plead for leniency, he leapt
unevenly to his feet and stumbled into the living room. It had been no
dream. The beautiful young woman he'd rescued the night before lay
sleeping on the couch.

Roger tiptoed through the kitchen, opened the sliding glass door,
and stepped onto the deck. He peered southward over the dunes, squinting against the sun. The first helicopter was already fluttering over the
Pier and continuing around the bend toward the Saco River's mudflats.
The second was growing smaller, whizzing over the condos and toward
the Pier. Meanwhile, down on the sand, a crowd was in the early stages of
exploring some joint discovery. It was hard to say from such distance, but
Roger surmised there were twenty or thirty people on the sand near one
of the brightly colored hotels. He wished he'd bought the telescope he'd
been meaning to purchase ever since he'd moved in. Like a lot of things
he'd meant to do when he'd bought the cottage, it had never happened.

If it were a week later, such a crowd would have hardly attracted his
attention. In-season, the beach was always overrun with people, and it
was not uncommon for them to gather in sprawling multigenerational
groups. But in the off-season, even its dying days, such crowds were rare,
and suggested a beached whale or injured harbor seal had come ashore.
Roger was under no illusion that the present crowd was gathering to

gawk at any such creature; rather, he had a sinking feeling that the activity on the beach was somehow related to his houseguest.

Walking the beach a minute later, he made a concerted effort to stroll as if it was his habit to do so every morning, although it was not. Anyone who knew him would have known that he spent the better part of the day sitting in front of his computer screen. If he got outside at all, it was for a jog at dusk.

Fresh out of college, Roger had spent nine years on Wall Street and had made a small fortune by the time the market crashed in 2008. He'd gotten out just in time to ensure a comfortable existence for himself, and had picked a sufficiently scenic place to begin his life of leisure. But it felt wrong to be retired in his early thirties, and weird to be living year-round in a neighborhood of summer homes. It hadn't taken long for him to fall back into his old ways. He'd started day-trading the same energy sector he'd once analyzed for Nomura. It was a hollow pursuit—he certainly didn't need the money—but he didn't know any other way to pass the hours.

On this sunny Thursday morning, though, Roger Simons was down on the beach, tracing with nervous footsteps the two miles of ebbing shore between his home and the swelling crowd just before the Pier. After twenty minutes, he reached the assembly just as an Old Orchard Beach police officer was unfurling a roll of yellow tape. Finding no trees or other fixed objects upon which to tie his tape, the officer had to rely on the goodwill of onlookers to set his perimeter. Roger realized this only too late.

"Hold this," the officer said, thrusting a handful of the tape into Roger's gut so that he had no choice but to accept it. "Don't move," the officer said. Then he moved on to find another placeholder ten feet away.

"Sucks to be you," a man beside Roger joked.

"Don't even think about crossing this line," Roger said, forcing a smile.

Inside the yellow crescent, which extended some fifty feet along the water's edge, Roger spied nothing more than a mess of soggy garments and other items of little apparent value. He had been half expecting, and fully dreading, a waterlogged body, but there was only debris. For a spectacle it didn't seem like much.

As Roger stood holding the tape and trying to make sense of the commotion, a brave seagull swooped down into the evidence field, prompting the officer to temporarily abandon his perimeter-setting exercise to shoo it away. When it lifted off, the crowd emitted a mock cheer.

"Hey," Roger said to the gawker who'd teased him. "This is just trash?"

The man frowned. "Could contain a treasure," he said, "or a wad of cash." Then, sensing that Roger was confused, he asked, "Ain't you seen the news?"

Roger shook his head.

"It was on channel eight," the man said. "And six. And they had it on CNN. They're already down the marsh." He gestured to the south, where Roger could see three helicopters now hovering.

Before Roger could pick the man's brain further, the police officer, having completed his initial task, began to address the crowd from the center of the debris. "Listen up," Ernie Sabo said. "We have another officer on the way. I need you to respect the boundary until he gets here. There's been a wreck, and . . ."

Just then, another gull swooped down into the forbidden zone and started to pick at a soggy box of what appeared to be pasta. The officer took a threatening step toward it, but the bird only hopped a few feet away to another potential food source. The officer reached down toward his hip and for a second Roger thought he was going for his firearm, but when he raised his hand it held only his CB. "Paulie, get down here with those bags," he barked. "We've got a beach full of people and a swarm of gulls." Roger counted just the one gull on the ground and two circling above, and despite his lingering unease felt slightly reassured.

After he'd coerced the bird to join its brothers in the sky, Officer Sabo continued. "We've got a situation," he told the crowd. "Coast Guard says Ferdie Sevigny's yacht's down the marsh, and he ain't washed up yet. So this is an evidence field. Anyone removing anything will be persecuted to the fullest extent."

"Prosecuted. You mean *prosecuted*," a voice piped up from the crowd.

"That's what I said—*prosecuted* to the fullest extent of the law," Officer Sabo said.

Roger knew that Ferdinand Sevigny was a wealthy Australian—an oil tycoon or a media magnate or something, with more money than God and not the slightest idea of what to do with it. He'd spent the last decade or so piloting single-engine airplanes, flying hot-air balloons, sailing around the world, setting one ridiculous record after another. *Guinness World Records* loved him, and so did the tabloid media, even though Roger thought he seemed like little more than a rich guy caught in a midlife crisis. So, *her* Sevigny was *that* Sevigny. It hadn't even occurred to him.

"Here," Roger said to the man beside him. "Your turn." He thrust the police tape into the man's chest, but the man stepped back and shook his head. Roger turned to the next available person, a man in a T-shirt that read I'M A BUD MAN.

"Bud man," Roger said, "you're it." After saddling the man with the responsibility, Roger turned and headed back toward Scarborough.

Chapter Six

Covert Operation

Billy tried not to attract attention, which had been his goal ever since his two friends had moved away. On this morning at OOB High, that meant feigning surprise and curiosity like the others when word began to spread that there had been an accident at sea.

When his classmates went rushing to the windows to see the news copters fluttering overhead and the fire trucks rumbling out of the station, he did too. The red engines were a common-enough sight. The choppers were not, and gave credence to the whispers that something big was afoot. Further corroborating this suspicion, in the first five minutes of third period Miss Hastings had received no fewer than five text messages on the phone that sat ever-present on her desk. It was mid-June, and apparently she no longer saw any need to be discreet. Finally, when her phone vibrated for the sixth time as she stood at the blackboard, still working on the same algebra equation, she told the students to close their books. She hurried to her desk and feverishly thumbed a reply. Then she raised her head and said, "Sometimes things happen in life that are so important, you need to pause, no matter what you're doing, to *live* them. And that's what we're going to do, because this is one of those moments. We're going to *live* it."

She walked over to the television monitor mounted in the upper right-hand corner of the room and raised a hand to click it on. She hit the channel button a few times until she found CNN, and then asked the students to be quiet and pay attention, presumably so they could "live" the moment. There were three days of school remaining, and neither the ninth graders nor their teacher believed they could learn much more in such a short time, anyway. The developing story in their town was a welcome excuse to take a morning off, and of course, they were all curious to learn what was causing the ruckus.

A wide-angle shot of the beach appeared on the screen. Although this was a familiar backdrop for most of the students, it seemed to glow with new significance. More than a few of them flushed with pride as they saw the site of their summer volleyball games and winter snowball fights sparkling in so many pixelated inches. So mesmerized were they that they scarcely noticed the scrolling letters along the bottom of the screen that read LOST AT SEA: BILLIONAIRE ADVENTURER FERDINAND SEVIGNY DEPARTED NOVA SCOTIA LAST NIGHT ON SOLO TRIP ACROSS ATLANTIC. BOAT FOUND IN SACO, MAINE. COAST GUARD SEARCHING MAINE WATERS.

Augmenting the scrolling message and the image of the town's brilliant beach, the voice of a female anchor was explaining that technicians "on the ground" were setting up a live interview with a local policeman, who was one of the first responders. She said the feed would be ready momentarily. In the meantime, she described the "Down East Drift," an offshore current that directs objects at sea into Casco Bay and carries them parallel to shore for several miles before depositing them at the mouth of the Saco River. It was this ocean effect, she explained—the same one that had been known to carry off swimmers who ventured too far from shore at Old Orchard Beach—that had brought Ferdinand Sevigny's sailing yacht, the *Wind Dancer*, into the Saco marsh. While she discussed this relevant tidbit of oceanography, a swirling graphic replaced the image of the beach on-screen, showing how the current spun like a hurricane in the bay.

Next, the woman began to eulogize the missing man. She said in a somber voice, "Ferdie Sevigny set sail alone, as was his custom, from a remote Canadian port. He was ready to face his greatest challenge yet—crossing the Atlantic, blindfolded. But in the dead of night his trip was cut short off the rocky coast of Maine. Long before Sevigny could face more-perilous obstacles, his trip ended . . ."

As the report continued, the picture cut away from the swirling graphic back to a wide shot that panned from the Pier to a crowd outside the Copley Motel. The teacher and her students offered *oohs* and *ahhs* as landmarks they knew well shimmered in a new light. They were more than just a bit peeved when the picture cut away a moment later to show a loop of still shots featuring the missing man. There he was, a distinguished gentleman with a thick salt-and-pepper mane, an even thicker beard, and an expression of supreme confidence in nearly all of the photos that ran during the melancholy narrative.

There he was, smiling broadly and giving a thumbs-up as he prepared to leap from an airplane; and there, standing solemnly atop a mountain, embracing a Sherpa. He was perched atop the mast of a boat; shaking hands with Brad Pitt, his other arm draped around Angelina Jolie. In another shot, he was bowing before the pope. Now, he was standing blindfolded on a dock with a gathering of befuddled Canadians observing, and there was that thumbs-up shot again aboard the airplane. The loop continued.

Billy sat with a blank expression on his face. Deep inside, however, he was smiling. Throughout his childhood he had remained largely ignorant of the worldwide celebrity and cottage industry that was Ferdinand Sevigny. Like most of the fifteen-year-olds in the room, he barely recognized the name, but unlike the others, he recognized on the screen before him a certain glimmer in the adventurer's eyes. It had been dark the night before, and Billy had been in quite a state when he'd met the stranger on the beach, but he was almost certain this Sevigny was the same man who had stood before him, soaking wet—who had walked beside him up the hill, promising him a new life. Now, as he learned more about his prospective benefactor, Billy felt lucky to be in league with such a man. He felt lucky to be the only guardian of Sevigny's secret.

Billy studied the man's face as he watched the footage loop through the same eight pictures one more time. He recalled that *his* Sevigny had been clean-shaven and had had darker hair. And he couldn't remember whether his Sevigny had smiled the way this one seemed to, in every single photo. Billy remembered him as frowning throughout their encounter. It had to be him, though. Yes, there was that same glint in his eyes. And it added up: a shipwreck, a dripping refugee, an Australian accent.

"May I be excused?" Billy asked.

Miss Hastings nodded absently toward the manila folder on her desk that contained the bathroom pass. The interview with Officer Sabo was just beginning.

Walking down the corridor, Billy heard the televisions in the other classrooms similarly mesmerizing the other ninth-grade teachers and students. He found this reassuring as he dug the list out of his pocket and quietly opened his locker. He emptied his backpack, then found his Latin notebook. He ripped out the first twenty pages that were full of notes, leaving them in his locker, and then put the notebook in his pack. He dropped in two pens. OOB High had an open-locker policy, meaning no one could use a lock. Everyone was made to observe the "honor system," in the name of ensuring students didn't conceal any sort of drugs or weapons in the school. This policy made what Billy had to do next much easier than it might have been otherwise. He crept a few feet down the hall to Nick Balbone's locker. He opened it, slipped his hand into the pocket of Nick's windbreaker, and extracted Nick's cell phone. This, too, he dropped into his backpack. He stood there for a minute, considering things, then reached back in and removed Nick's windbreaker entirely. He balled it up and crammed it into his pack.

After removing these and other select items from the long stretch of lockers in the East Wing, Billy headed to the cafeteria. Tenth-grade lunch was in progress, but Billy figured that with so few days left, no one would mind his arriving ten minutes before the rest of his class. His assumption proved correct. Miss Manthos merely nodded and gave him a smile as he made his way to the counter.

Billy showed his free-lunch card, took a plate of tacos from under the heat lamps, and then, when he reached the rack of potato-chip bags, placed one bag on his tray and took two more and dropped them into his pack, which he carried at his hip. In this manner, he also pilfered two plastic bottles of apple juice, two granola bars, and a stack of chocolate-chip cookies wrapped in cellophane.

Billy deposited his tray on an empty table at the far end of the room, dropped the bag of chips, apple juice, and granola bar from his tray into his pack, and then added a few napkins. He checked to make sure Miss Manthos was looking the other way, and, leaving his uneaten tacos on the table, headed for the gym locker room, where he knew he'd find towels, soap, and hopefully a pair of Mr. Brogan's sweatpants.

Billy was starting to enjoy his mission. It was nice to think that he had a secret related to the event captivating his classmates and teachers. Most of all, it was nice to know he would soon be leaving town.

But he was getting ahead of himself. He remembered what the stranger, who he now thought of as "Mr. Sevigny," had told him. *I just need to be patient and do whatever I'm asked. Then I'll be rewarded.*

Chapter Seven

Sea of Opportunity

By the time Ernie Sabo had secured the crime scene and done live interviews with CNN, MSNBC, and all three of the locals out of Portland, the sun had climbed high in the sky. FBI agents had arrived, ordering him to step down. He was neither surprised nor dismayed by this turn, as it had only taken him a few minutes to conclude that the debris on the beach was just that—debris—too inconsequential to be termed evidence. There was nothing important amid the flotsam, nothing to suggest what had damaged the boat or imperiled its captain. And there was no body.

Ernie knew that finding the body was the key. Just because he was handing over jurisdiction to the feds didn't mean he wouldn't beat them in the end. In each interview, the reporter had asked him to speculate as to the whereabouts of the body. He didn't know, but he'd find it, he'd told them. As he'd repeated those words, the idea had crystallized in his mind, narrowing his thoughts into a sort of longing. *The body, the body, the body*. He wanted nothing in the world more ardently. Finding it would guarantee a run on the morning talk shows, a spot on the nightly news. *The body*. But where was it? Maybe still at sea, taking longer to wash up than the rest of the debris. Maybe weighed down by cinder blocks. Maybe down in the marsh, getting nibbled by crabs.

Ernie tramped the warm, dry sand with his pant legs still rolled up to his knees and his boots in his hands. He watched the scurrying feds in their fancy yellow jackets. He wondered what he might be able to see that they would miss. Old Orchard Beach was his town; it had been, for his whole life. It seemed only right that he be the one to find the body, to see his name splashed across the headlines.

He was nearing an age when he had begun to think about his life's work and how it would be remembered. He had a few years left on the force, he figured, but probably not too many. Most of his twenty-nine years had been unremarkable—domestic disturbances, Friday-night fights, kids acting stupid—but he'd had his moments, too, when fate and quick thinking had thrust him into the spotlight. He'd savored those times, although not enough, he realized now. They came too infrequently. Perhaps he'd enjoyed greater-than-usual action early on, and it had unduly inflated his expectations.

He still remembered almost reverently the days when he'd patrolled the Square on a twelve-speed as a summer rent-a-cop, and his rookie year after that, when he'd been the first to the Pier on a steamy August night when an after-hours poker game at the Pier Pub had gotten out of hand and sent the crackle of gunfire into the air. He'd run down the long, dark corridor of the Pier, past the slumbering tattoo and snow-cone stands, the T-shirt and jewelry counters. When he'd first started running, he had seen a small, single light five hundred feet away; he realized soon enough that it was a motorcycle, and it was coming right at him. As the roar of the engine shook the wood beneath his feet and the light nearly blinded him, Ernie reacted. He tackled the bastard right off the motorcycle as he tried to barrel past. When it turned out the perp had an outstanding murder warrant, well, Officer Ernie Sabo was suddenly a name people recognized all over Maine. The truth was, in all his years, this remained his sweetest memory.

Now he sensed another once-in-a-lifetime opportunity. Finding the billionaire's body would be a nice legacy.

The feds were already crawling all over the beach, and more would be arriving soon. He needed to think fast. He needed to use his knowledge of his bay and his beach to his advantage. But the clock was ticking. It wouldn't be long before one of the agents stumbled upon a clue that would lead to another. As Ernie looked out at the water, wondering how to capitalize on his last, best chance to do something profound, his gaze fell upon the sandy banks of Bluff Island. The narrow parcel, less than two miles from shore, rose gradually from the sea before giving way to a patch of stunted pines and beach plums. It was uninhabited, except for the sandpipers and seals that nested there. *Maybe . . . just maybe,* Ernie thought. He raised his binoculars. There was no boat setting anchor there. *If this guy made it to the island, he might still be alive.*

At the footpath that wended through the dunes and led to East Grand, where he'd left his cruiser, Ernie reached for his radio. "Paulie," he said. "You copy?" He stood barefoot in the sand, waiting for an answer, his head vaguely nodding as his mind lurched ahead.

"Gotcha, Ern," a crackly voice replied. "I thought you were right behind me. You still down the beach?"

"Yeah," Ernie said. "Listen, did the Coasties check out the island?"

"No idea. Must have done a fly-over. Nothing in the sand?"

"Nothing," Ernie said.

"How about Sally Fiddler? Anything?"

Ernie's eyes shot instinctively up the beach toward Scarborough, to where the last tall condo building stood. "Shit," he said.

"I can put a call in to the feds," Paul's crackly voice said.

Ernie lifted his binoculars and saw that all was quiet up at the town line.

"No," Ernie said. "She didn't find anything. I'm coming in."

Ernie cursed himself for forgetting about Sally. If he went to check with her now, he'd technically be interfering with a federal investigation. He could always plead ignorance, say he was just visiting a friend. And if he happened to notice that she'd found something, well, what was he supposed to do, say he wasn't interested? He cursed himself again, though, for forgetting that she'd probably sifted through the trash long before anyone else. Sally was one of those sources that he would need to tap if he wanted to beat the feds.

He brushed as much sand from his feet as he could in a few seconds, then slipped on his boots and tied two loose knots. He slid behind the wheel of his cruiser and thought about turning on the blues and reds before deciding against it.

Two minutes later, Ernie pulled into the parking lot of Seaside Heights and saw immediately that something was wrong.

Like all of the condos, Sally's had been constructed on large concrete blocks that were a built-in safeguard against the once-in-a-generation storm that would wash over the dunes and onto East Grand. The front door was located between the blocks, on the patio beneath the first floor.

Ordinarily, Sally kept this entranceway free of sand and clutter. Over the years, other residents had learned to pay the simpleminded woman the respect of leaving their beach chairs and umbrellas along the wooden fence abutting the dunes, rather than bringing them onto her immaculate concrete. That was where Sally's wagon was parked today—over by the fence, neatly packed with her morning's haul.

But that wasn't what concerned Ernie. His eyes were drawn to something on the patio: Sally, crumpled, lifeless, facedown on the ground.

Chapter Eight

Inscrutable Guest

Even if he had glanced at Seaside Heights as he'd walked past on the beach, Roger Simons wouldn't have seen Sally's prone body waiting to be discovered by Ernie Sabo. The patio was concealed by broad blocks. And besides, Roger had noted very little of his surroundings on his way back to Scarborough.

So immersed was he in thought that Roger barely noticed the bartender swabbing the deck at Pirates' Patio, the painters slathering a fresh layer of aquamarine on the face of the Royal Anchor, or the investigators and reporters scurrying onto the sand. His mind was elsewhere. *What exactly had she said when he'd reached for the phone?* He tried to remember. He tried to replay the hazy, exhausted hour they'd shared on the kitchen tiles, shivering and gasping, after the adrenaline had drained from their bodies. Roger had been propped against the refrigerator, feeling the warmth of its exhaust on his back, while she had sat against the stove with her knees pulled up to her chest, beneath the tablecloth he'd wrapped her in as he'd lowered her to the floor.

When the pounding in his chest had subsided, he'd raised his hand for the phone, pulling it off the counter. It was then that he'd looked at her and almost allowed himself to think what a shame it was that he had to give her up. It wasn't often that he found himself on his kitchen floor, in the middle of the night, with a woman wearing nothing but panties— not to mention the fact that she had such emotive black eyes and golden-brown skin, *and* owed him her life.

But there was only one thing to do. He began to dial. She spoke decisively with only slightly stilted diction. "Don't," she said. "No police."

Roger held the phone in one hand. The kitchen light illuminated the woman's face. He could see now that she was younger than he'd realized, probably in her early twenties. "Don't," she said, shaking her head resolutely enough to bring a strand of tangled hair across her forehead. "He will come for me . . . unless he's dead—but he can't be. He will come . . . they mustn't know."

Roger tried to make sense of her reluctance to do what people normally do when they've suffered trauma. But possessing too little information from which to form a theory, he simply asked, "Are you okay?"

"Only cold," she said.

"What's your name?"

"Marisol."

"I'm Roger."

She forced a smile that quickly faded.

"What happened, Marisol?"

"I was on a sailboat."

"And there was an accident?"

She stared at him blankly.

"There were others?" Roger asked.

"One," she said. "A man."

"Sevigny?" Roger said.

"Yes," she confirmed, eyelids fluttering.

"Then we need to call for help, Marisol," Roger said. "They'll come with lights, and boats—to search for him." He began to dial again, thinking that perhaps her English was not as good as he'd assumed; maybe his benevolent intentions had been misunderstood.

"No," Marisol cried, struggling to push herself away from the stove. She lurched forward as if to wrest the phone from him. He turned away, avoiding her, and that was when she ended the debate. She began to cry—quietly at first, as if she would have preferred to contain her tears, but then her sniffling became full-blown sobs. Her exhalations were interrupted only by muted pleas for mercy.

As she buried her pretty face in her hands, it suddenly no longer seemed to matter who she was, or where she'd come from, or whether her friend—or lover, or accomplice, or whatever he was—might be struggling for his life in the ocean. Calling for help became so far removed from the realm of possibility that Roger was surprised when he looked down and realized he was still holding the phone.

"It'll be okay," he said. "Don't worry."

Now, in the light of day, Roger had learned that her companion was renowned adventurer Ferdinand Sevigny. Why Marisol hadn't told him this the night before, he did not know. And furthermore, he couldn't fathom why she had insisted they not call for help, to potentially save the life of a drowning man, for whom she'd shed so many tears. With these thoughts swimming in his head, Roger opened the sliding glass door of his deck and stepped inside.

He found her awake, still wearing the oversize pajamas he'd lent her. Sitting on the couch, half wrapped in a blanket, Marisol glanced cursorily at him, then returned her eyes to the television, which was tuned to one of the news channels. The screen was split so that one side showed the events unfolding two miles away on the beach and the other showed a partially capsized boat being towed through a channel that Roger quickly deduced was the Saco River. He could see from the streaks on her face that she'd been freshly crying, but had then composed herself.

"I looked for you on television," she said flatly, without looking up.

"I left just as they were setting up," he replied. "They haven't found him?"

"No," she said. "They won't."

"Well . . . ," Roger began, before noting the certainty with which she'd spoken and leaving his thought unfinished. "Why not?" he asked.

"Because Sevigny is not ready to be found," she said.

33

Chapter Nine

Her Story

Roger settled awkwardly onto the couch beside his guest while CNN continued its coverage of the breaking story. The intimacy he'd shared with her during their joint struggle for survival had dissolved, giving way to the discomfort that lack of familiarity occasions in unlikely house-mates. Roger felt it in the silence that hung between them as they sat three feet apart.

But then, unprompted, Marisol began to speak.

"You don't know Sevigny," she said quietly. "If you did, you would understand why we could not call the police last night—why *I* could not. And why I wait. You would understand that he might find me today, or never, but that I must never go looking for *him*. He is a great man, but even he is not as great as he wishes to be. He would hate me, disown me—who knows?—if I did anything to harm his image." She spoke in a soft voice, and though Roger could see that she was making an effort to look at him, every time she raised her eyes to meet his, she just as quickly lowered them.

"How do you know he's alive?" Roger asked.

"Because he *is*," she answered quietly. "Sevigny would not die in such a way. He is a man who crossed the African jungle, from one side to the other, without a map or compass, only a machete. He's climbed mountains. He's swum the English Channel. He's survived the cold of Alaska, the red sand of the Great Victoria. Sevigny is alive."

"Then where is he?" Roger asked, before adding, "Wouldn't he have introduced himself to someone on the beach by now?"

She smiled and slowly shook her head, as if the very naiveté of his question amused her. "That would bring him dishonor," she said. "Sevigny doesn't crawl for help. He doesn't admit defeat."

"They're sweeping the bay for his body," Roger said, amazed by the depth of her denial.

"They won't find him," she said. "He set out to sail the ocean with a blindfold over his eyes, and that is what he'll do. Sevigny finishes what he starts." She laughed, then added, "That is where they'll see him next—floating into Casablanca, probably right on schedule."

"His boat is full of water, getting towed right now," Roger said incredulously, gesturing over his left shoulder in the direction of the Saco marsh and then toward the television, where a stout Coast Guard tug could be observed sending plumes of black smoke into the sky as it pulled a battered sailing yacht a hundred yards behind. "Maybe he'll use a different boat," she said. "Or the *Wind Dancer* will disappear one night from wherever they take it. Tomorrow, maybe, it will be gone. And in two months it will show up in Morocco, and Sevigny will have quite a story to tell. He'll probably still be wearing the blindfold."

"That's another thing," Roger said, growing weary of her unyielding devotion to the idea that Sevigny could be so infallible. "CNN says he was sailing blindfolded and *alone*. How do you fit in?" The question was something less than the full query he had in mind, which might have been phrased, "So just how long are you planning to sleep on my couch, and how in the world do you expect this guy to find you in the unlikely event he's even alive, especially if he's wearing a blindfold? And, umm, *who are you?*"

Though Roger had kept his frustration mostly in check, the young woman seemed to understand that his patience was wearing thin, and that a more-thorough explanation was necessary.

"My position is complicated," she said. She stared vacuously at the television. It occurred to Roger that she might again be on the verge of tears. "It's complicated," she repeated, with more resignation than self-pity. "Without Sevigny, I am no one. And when I'm with him, it is the same."

After another pause, during which Roger was sure she would break down, she continued. "Until I was seventeen," she said, "I lived with my mother and father and brother and sisters, on an island off the coast of Tobago. I grew up ignorant to the ways of the world, mending my father's nets, singing with the children of the village. I was not dissatisfied, because it was the only life I knew. In the spring I ran through the sugarcane fields in bare feet. In the summer, we would hide in the orchard. In the fall, my sisters and I culled coffee beans until our fingers turned red. In the winter, when it rained, we sat beside our father and ground sorghum while our mother baked."

As Marisol detailed the simple pleasures of a life she'd apparently left behind, Roger observed a deep melancholy overtaking her. She spoke softly, while her hands remained folded in her lap as if in prayer. With each sentence Roger felt as though he were bearing witness to a confession. It made him uncomfortable.

"We lived by the sea," she said, raising her eyes to his, "as you do. On our eastern shore there was a cliff, and as a child I would climb it with the others to dive into the Caribbean. We would take turns, one after another, until we knew we were too tired to follow the trail back up even one more time. Then we would lie on the flat rocks so the sun could dry us before we returned to the village. Later, I would go to the cliff alone to wait for the masts on the horizon. I would walk back to the village and meet my father on the dock. It was from that cliff one afternoon that I saw a boat unlike any I'd ever seen. Its masts were so much higher and sails so much larger than any that belonged to the boats of our village. It was then that I first began to wonder about the world beyond our island, Little Tobago."

"It was Sevigny," Roger guessed out loud. Marisol nodded.

"His boat reached the dock an hour later. And by the time our fathers had come in, Sevigny had already traded our women anything that wasn't tied to his deck. At first, he showed them exotic spices and kitchen tools, exchanging them for drinking water and papayas. He was generous. I remember him walking down the dock and disappearing into his cabin, and when he came back he had a big pot like the kind our women used to boil crabs.

" 'Here's the next item,' he said. 'It belongs to the first woman or child who can bring me a red melon.'

"Then when the bearer of such a piece of fruit arrived, before handing over the pot, Sevigny reached in and pulled out a neatly folded tablecloth. 'Here's the next item,' he said, holding it up with his arms spread apart. 'A tablecloth from India.' He made several trips down the dock. He traded whatever he brought back for far less than it was worth. It seemed to bring him pleasure to order a cooked chicken, or a bag of coffee beans, or a salted fish, and to have it promptly delivered.

"How we worshipped him, and not just the women, but the men too, when they made port for the night. Even the proudest fathers treated him as if he were a king. They took turns standing beside him, smoking cigars and drinking wine in the village square. They praised his boat and the goods he'd traded with their families. They were amazed by the idea that a man like Sevigny would come to their village. He spoke fluent Spanish, and we all listened as he talked about his adventures on the seas and across the continents. Some of the men were more aware of the lands beyond our island than I was, and they asked question after question, eager to show off the little knowledge they had of his world. Of course, I'd seen plenty of Englishmen before; we all had. But not like him. We'd seen crabbers and oilers and coffee traders, but never a man like Sevigny. His stories moved from the skyscrapers of New York to the sands of the Sahara, to the people of distant lands.

"Like the mothers and fathers, the children also showered him with attention, approaching in small groups to perform dance steps or offer melodies before their parents shooed them away so they might more fully enjoy Sevigny themselves. I was no longer a child by then, but I too was full of wonder at this new creature that had stepped into the center of our world. My poor father . . . I'd always idolized him, doted on him, but suddenly he seemed small and simple. And the other fathers did too. They seemed like scarecrows beside this man of the world."

Roger studied Marisol's face as she spoke, and observed her downcast eyes, so full of sadness. *Yes*, he thought, returning to the notion that had struck him a few moments earlier, *it's almost as if she's giving confession.*

"While the children scurried about and the parents huddled around him at the table in the square," Marisol continued, "I sat off to one side on a stone wall, with a girl my age. We tried to figure out what the existence of such a man could mean to us.

" 'Tomorrow he will sail away on the ebb of the tide that brought him,' Anabella said.

" 'And what of us?' I asked. 'Our fathers will return to the dock and our mothers to the fields. And we to mending nets.'

" 'That is our life,' Anabella said.

" 'It is a happy life,' I said, as if speaking the words would make them true.

"And so, as a red sky gave way to night, we spoke that way. We were both ashamed but did not say it. We left it beneath our words.

"Eventually, the mothers lit lanterns and hung them on the posts and in the doorways, and then, later, they began rounding up the children and husbands and leading them to bed. When the time came, I listened to my mother, though I did not feel like sleeping. I wished Anabella good-night and turned my back on our visitor and on the villagers who remained by his side. But my mind was already racing.

"Three times I had noticed Sevigny looking at me, and the last time, right before my mother called us in, his eyes had lingered long enough for me to know."

Chapter Ten

The Rest of Her Story

She stood now with her back to Roger in the small living room with her gaze fixed somewhere on the shimmering blue ocean just beyond the glass door and swaying dune grass. And for a moment, she lingered there silently. Roger had been as surprised by the content of her story as by the detailed manner in which she'd delivered it. He wondered if she would say more or if she would leave the rest unsaid. And he wondered, too, at what had caught her attention upon the sea. Perhaps the tug they'd seen on TV had finally come into view. He figured it was headed toward the South Portland Coast Guard station, but he didn't get off the couch to see if that was what held her at the window. He sat and waited, and then finally said. "You don't have to say anything more. I think I understand." For some reason, that prompted her to resume her tale.

"I was young," she said quietly, without turning from the window. "But not too young. I knew there were ways for a woman to convince a man. I also knew Sevigny could have any woman he wanted; a simple island girl like me had little to offer him. But I had to try. I had to hope he would pity me, as he'd pitied the mothers when he'd made one preposterous trade after another.

"As I helped put my sisters to bed, my mother told me that the next morning we could cut in half the set of linens that had spilled from Sevigny's bounty. We could sew the two halves into smaller sets for the children's beds, including the one I still shared with my youngest sister.

" 'Yes,' I told her. 'That is something we could do. We could rip these beautiful sheets in half to fit our tiny beds.'

" 'Marisol,' she said, 'is our life so terrible?'

" 'No,' I said. We said nothing more.

"Father stayed out, but eventually came in to sleep. Lucinda, lying beside me, was too young to realize what Sevigny's visit meant. She quickly fell asleep. But I waited, and waited, and then waited some more. Then I crept from our bed. I could not risk waking anyone, so I took nothing with me. I slipped outside wearing only my nightgown, holding my sandals in my hands for fear they would scuff a stone on the road that led through the square, past the school, and down to the water's edge.

"When I reached the dock I put those sandals on my feet because then I *did* hope they would betray me as I stepped onto the planks that led past all of the village boats, and to Sevigny's at the end. I did not want to come upon him unaware for fear of what he might do to an intruder in the dark. My heart pounded and I shivered as I walked down the dock. I walked toward the shadows of his magnificent sailboat while my village slept on the hill behind me.

" 'You have come,' he said from somewhere in the darkness. 'To slit my throat and take the few valuables I have not already given your people. Or you have come to beg me to take you away.'

"His voice startled me, and as I tried to locate it, I suddenly realized he was sitting in a chair on the deck, not sleeping in the cabin as I'd expected. Before I had even reached the dock, I had begun to work out answers to what I had imagined his objections would be. I would remind him we were poor. I would tell him there was an eagerness in me to learn new things and see new places, a spark that the simple school of our village had kindled but not satisfied before the teachers had run out of things to say and had sent me home to help my mother in her field. But somewhere in the darkness, I'd lost my breath, and when I spoke my voice was thin and able only to utter a few short words. 'I do not wish to slit your throat,' I said.

"He laughed. Then he said quietly, 'Yours are a good people. I doubt anyone will come for that . . . but someone might. It would not surprise me either way.'

"I did not know what to say. I merely stood there, struggling for air.

" 'How old are you?' he asked.

" 'Twenty,' I said.

" 'You should not lie,' he said, 'so soon after I compliment the good nature of your village.'

" 'I'll be eighteen in October,' I said, this time exaggerating by only a few months, speaking in a voice that again surprised me by how small it sounded. I tried to remember the different arguments I'd prepared as I lay beside Lucinda, as I'd walked through the village and down the hill, but they had vanished.

" 'What's your name?' he asked, and I told him.

" 'That's a pretty name,' he said, staring at me in my nightgown.

" 'It means 'sea' and 'sun,' ' " I said. *'Mar y sol.'*

" 'Yes,' he said. 'I know.'

"I remember noticing something I hadn't seen in the square but which I saw on the dock, even in the darkness. I knew he was looking at me, but it seemed as if he were looking *through* me. For an instant, it seemed as if I were looking at a blind man. I think that's why I was so surprised by what he said next. He said, 'We would have to leave early.' Then he added, 'Or perhaps we have enough wind to raise sail right now.' " She turned away from the window and faced Roger for the first time since she'd risen to her feet. "That was six years ago," she continued. "Sevigny has been good to me. He helped me to improve my English. He hired a tutor to travel with us. Then in Melbourne—where we live most of the time—he brought professors to the house. He introduced me to history, art, science. We've also visited his other homes around the world. I've eaten at La Coupole, stood beneath the Sphinx, wandered through the Met. He's shown me the world, but kept me hidden from the cameras that follow him. He takes me on his adventures, but he's never given me anything to call my own. He's never given me a chance to use the knowledge I've gained."

Roger nodded. He tried to think of a delicate way to ask the question that had been percolating within him for some time, but finding none, lurched ahead anyway. "So are you more like his . . . umm . . . daughter, or, umm . . . girlfriend?"

"I am not like a daughter to him," Marisol said demurely. "Though at times he treats me like a child." She looked down. "It was not too many weeks after I joined him before I began sleeping in his bed. It was my choice. I went to him. He did not pressure me."

Sensing Marisol's discomfort with the turn the conversation had taken, Roger said, "So, getting back to this latest trip: I knew it was impossible to sail the ocean blindfolded. At least, blindfolded and *alone*."

"Maybe for some," Marisol said, "but Sevigny could do it."

"But he was cheating," Roger said. "You were along."

"I was not helping with the sails or navigation," Marisol said flatly. "I was there to keep him company. He hates to be alone; it depresses him. It drives him to madness."

Roger did not reply.

"You're right, though," she said. "If people knew Sevigny has had company on his 'lone' adventures, they would not be kind. Some of his records would be taken away, and that would bring him shame."

Marisol looked at Roger, and it struck him that her eyes contained something of that same distant quality she had described in her benefactor. She stared at him so intently that it almost seemed as though she might be gazing into the teeth of a bottomless fog.

"Do you understand now," she asked, "why I cannot go to your policemen? It would ruin him. And if he didn't come forward, who knows what they'd do? They might send me back to Little Tobago, where the shame would be mine. I would have to face my mother. So you see, I am trapped between two worlds. I can never really belong to Sevigny's, and I can never return to the one I left."

"I'm sure your mother would forgive you," Roger said.

"You don't understand," she said, shaking her head. "I abandoned her. I ran off with a man I hardly knew. I left my people."

Roger was not unmoved. And she must have read this softening on his face because she added in quickly strung words, "It is the life I've chosen, I know."

Then, she surprised Roger. With a quiver of doubt rising for the first time in her voice, she asked, "If he *is* gone, what will become of me?"

Chapter Eleven

A Change in Plans

When school let out, Billy walked past the buses that were waiting to bring home the students who lived farther away than he did. He passed the skate park and the fire barn. Instead of crossing Union and heading toward Atlantic, he stayed on the school side of the street and turned onto Cummings. It occurred to him that he should make certain no one was following him, so he glanced over his shoulder. This wasn't a road he usually walked, and though he didn't think any of his schoolmates still lived at Ocean Yard, he didn't know for sure. For a while, he remembered, some families had covertly remained in their trailers after the banks had posted the eviction notices. Some had even left, amid a fair amount of drama, only to quietly return a few days later. Eventually the courts and police had swept them away.

All the same, Billy thought it wise to be certain none of his classmates were heading up Cummings to the trailer park that had devolved from neighborhood to wasteland in his own short lifetime.

Content that he was indeed alone, Billy continued along the half-mile stretch of wooded road leading to the abandoned slab of asphalt that gave rise to two dozen neatly arranged but severely dilapidated trailers. Twice he stepped into the seclusion of the woods when he heard automobiles approaching, and both times he managed to remain unseen. There was not much beyond the abandoned plot—only the town dump, and the filling station where the public works department fueled its plows and sanders in winter. That was why Billy thought it wise to remain unnoticed. There was no reason for a boy his age—or anyone, really—to be straying into this forgotten part of town.

After ten minutes, he turned into the trailer park's driveway and wended his way through clumps of weeds and grass that had sprouted through the tar. He complimented himself again for choosing such a fine place to stow a castaway seeking seclusion. His pride swelled further at the idea that while the entire town was talking about the disappearance of the famous Ferdinand Sevigny, only he knew the secret of his location.

When Billy reached the sixth trailer on the right, the first one they'd come upon the night before that hadn't been padlocked, he knocked twice and turned the knob. "It's just me," he called, stepping inside.

Billy saw the note in the middle of the floor just beyond the threshold. On a scrap of paper, in precise little letters, it read: "Finding accommodations unsuitable, I am leaving in pursuit of more agreeable lodging. Will still find the items you've gathered useful. Meet in the same place as yesterday, at the same time, alone." It was unsigned.

Billy's heart sank. Perhaps the hideout had not been so wisely chosen after all. His secret seemed diminished; he'd been the only one to know of Mr. Sevigny's whereabouts, and now he'd lost that. Standing in the trailer, he sighed and thought that it looked shabbier than it had the night before, with its stained carpet, piles of abandoned laundry, and tattered drapes. He stepped outside, reread the note, and tried to reassure himself. It was still a secret. Only he knew Mr. Sevigny was alive and in town; he just didn't know exactly where he was anymore. And there was still the deal they'd made.

Arriving home at 3:30, Billy stashed his backpack in the bottom of his closet and covered it with a couple of sweatshirts that he ruffled into a pile. It was unlikely his mother would come into his room, much less look in his closet, but he took this precaution just in case. Then he lay down for a nap as the sleepless night finally caught up with him.

When Billy awoke hours later, his room was dark and his door was closed. He had slept longer than he'd intended, but not so long as to miss his appointment. As his senses returned, he realized his mother had come home with a guest.

"You should have seen the gash on her forehead," a male voice said. "I was ready to call Old Man Morton."

Mr. Morton owned Morton and Sons, the only funeral parlor in town.

"That bad, huh, baby?" Billy's mother said. Billy hated the tone of her voice.

"Next thing I know, she's on her feet, refusing to say what happened," the man said.

"She probably just lost her balance," Billy's mother replied in a slurred version of the voice she used in regular conversation.

"She *can* talk," the man said. "I know she can. Ginny Munson swears she can. I wish she woulda just told me what happened."

"Come on, baby," Billy's mother said, giving her seductive voice another try. "Why talk me to death?"

"Why?" the man repeated. "Because you're too drunk to remember in the morning."

"You're lonely," Billy's mother said.

"You don't understand," the man said. "I—"

"Shhh," Billy's mother said. "What did you come here for?"

"You don't understand," the man blurted out. "After I got her inside and called Ginny to come clean her up, I found something in her wagon."

"The junk from the beach?" Billy's mother said, evidently referring to something he had said before Billy had awoken. Billy now realized it was the cop, the one who came twice a week but hardly ever did the things with his mother the other men did.

"Yeah," the cop said, "down at the bottom—only it wasn't junk. It was a hood, like the kind you'd put on someone you kidnapped. And it was stained with something . . . maybe blood."

"Baby?" Billy's mother said uncertainly.

"The guy didn't have an accident," the cop said.

"So they're looking for a suspect now?" Billy's mother asked.

"That's just it," the cop said. "I'm the only one who knows about the hood. I hid it at Sally's. When Ginny got there I said Sally had fallen and asked her to look after her. Paulie was radioing, saying Chief was getting worried I wasn't standing down, so I had to head in. But tomorrow, after I head to Bluff Island to see if my hunch is right, I'm going back to Sally's. Ginny will be gone by then. I'm gonna piece it together. If the guy's alive, I'm gonna find him."

There was a pause.

"Brandy?" Billy heard the cop say. "Brandy, you awake?"

Billy heard the man sigh, and then a minute later he heard the kitchen door open and then quietly close.

Chapter Twelve

Useful Information

Billy had a sick feeling in his stomach. It hadn't been there when he'd walked beside the man the night before. It hadn't been there when he'd trekked to Ocean Yard after school. But it was there now, as he stood on the beach in the dead of night. Maybe it was just the uncertainty of meeting such a strange man in such a remote location—or maybe it was more than that. Maybe what the cop had said was true. Maybe Mr. Sevigny *had* been the victim of foul play. Maybe someone was still after him.

Billy remembered what the cop had said about the hood being stained with blood, and thought he would check to see if there was any cut or scab on the man's face when he arrived.

After a while, Billy started to wonder if he was in the wrong spot. It had been dark the night before, and the emergence of the dripping man from the dunes had given him a start. Maybe he hadn't returned to the exact place where he'd been when the quiet Australian voice had startled him. He lifted his backpack off the sand, slung it over his shoulder, and began to walk slowly toward the Pier. As he swung a stick, knocking down the tender wisps of dune grass that lined the high side of the beach, he tried to steel himself for the instant when Mr. Sevigny would emerge. He wanted to appear brave and confident.

After fifty yards, he stopped, stared left and then right down the dim beach, then began to retrace his steps. Only then did he hear the call; instead of taking the form of a voice rising from the dunes, it came as a whistle. Billy became conscious of it gradually, hearing it faintly at first and disregarding it as nothing more than some nearby homeowner coaxing his cocker spaniel inside after a midnight pee. But by degrees it grew louder and sharper, until Billy realized it was coming from the water.

He walked toward the surf and soon heard the beat of a paddle against the groan of the waves. His eyes followed the sound until a dark figure came into view, gliding atop the surface in a slender sea kayak. All summer long, a couple dozen of the crafts sat in formation, a small armada on the sand in front of the Royal Anchor, chained and waiting for the hotel guests to use.

"You haven't waited long," the man said, after riding a final surge of foam onto the beach and standing to face Billy. He hauled the kayak up the incline and lowered it to the sand. Before Billy could speak, the man explained. "I had to be sure you were alone."

"Are you staying at the Royal Anchor?" Billy asked.

"No," the man said, as if amazed Billy would ask such a stupid question. "Bloody hell."

"I thought—" Billy said, pointing at the kayak.

"This?" the man said. "I borrowed it from my temporary accommodations." Then he looked at Billy and said, "You haven't told anyone?"

"N-n-no," Billy said. It was a habit he'd kicked, or thought he'd kicked—the stuttering—and even here, despite his anxiety, he was able to check it. "Not a soul."

"Good," the man said. "I believe you."

But something about the way he said these words left Billy thinking that maybe he didn't. For Billy, who wanted so desperately to please this mysterious stranger whom he'd come to see as his savior, this measure of doubt was nearly unbearable. He was ashamed without even knowing why.

The man in front of him was small, yet he stood in such a cocksure way that he seemed more imposing than his stature warranted. His closely cropped black hair clung to his head, matted by droplets of seawater, above a narrow face in which his sharp, dark eyes and perpetually furrowed brow stood out as dominant features. His face was the very portrait of disdain. Even in borrowed clothes and twenty-four hours into exile, everything about him said he was a man who expected to have his way, and who wasted little time in making sure he got it.

Billy did not see any wound on the man's face that could have been bleeding recently, and he temporarily allowed himself the relief of disregarding the troubling information the cop had shared with his mother. He began to unveil the items he'd pilfered. While the day before he had enjoyed a measure of authority during their interaction—leading the dripping refugee to Ocean Yard and scrounging some clothes for him from one of the trailers—on this, their second meeting, the dynamic was different. Billy had arrived with his pride already wounded by the man's rejection of the trailer hideout, and now, as Billy removed each item from his backpack to an indifferent response, Billy's desire to please only grew more desperate.

The cookies "would do." Mr. Brogan's gym pants "smelled like they could use a wash." Nick's windbreaker looked "a little small." And so on. Finally, as Billy became aware of his acquaintance's impatience, he realized a complete review of the bag's contents was neither necessary nor desired. He stuffed the items he hadn't yet revealed back inside and hastily stammered, "Everything else is here, too. The phone even has a camera."

The man shook his head. "A camera?" he said. "What would I do with that?" He took the bag. Then he said, "Billy, there's something more important I'm hoping you can provide for me, and that's information. They've been searching . . . have they found a boat?"

"Yes," Billy said. "We watched it at school."

The man nodded, pleased.

"You're pretty famous?" Billy said, half asking. *His* Sevigny still seemed quite a bit younger than the one he'd seen on television. He wanted some confirmation. But the man merely said, "There's no such thing as *pretty* famous. Either you are or you aren't."

"And you are," Billy said.

"Tell me," the man said, ignoring Billy's comment, "has a body washed up?"

"No," Billy said. "I don't think so."

"They didn't say anything on TV about a body?"

"No," Billy said.

"How about . . ." the man began, but then he paused, as if debating whether to continue. "What about a woman's body?"

"I don't think so," Billy answered.

"You don't *think* so?" the man said sharply.

"They didn't," Billy said, "B-b-b-but—"

"But what?"

"I haven't watched the news since school," he said. "I fell asleep."

"I see," the man said, disgusted. He plopped the backpack into the kayak, picked up the paddle, and began dragging the vessel down the slope.

"I hope . . ." Billy started to say, but fell speechless. He didn't know what he hoped. He only knew his efforts had been inadequate. It was a feeling he was used to, and in many ways, it was the feeling he most wished to leave behind when Mr. Sevigny, or whoever this strange man was, made good on his promise.

"If you can be of further help," the man said over his shoulder, "I'll meet you here in two days."

But something in the way these words were spoken made Billy certain, as the man paddled away, that he would never see him again. For thirty seconds, his mind and heart filled with despair. It was over, his dream of escape. And then, out of the depths of misery, something occurred to him—later, perhaps, than it should have, but before hope was lost. "Wait," he cried. "Wait!" He was afraid that the drum of the waves would drown out his voice, so he barreled into the water, pants and all. "Mr. Sevigny," he cried. "Mr. Sevigny!"

Billy watched as the kayak slowed, then began gliding back to where he stood in the water.

"Are you crazy?" the man growled after he'd come within a few yards of Billy. From his place on the water, he stared down at the shivering boy with malice in his eyes. "Don't you understand I can't be discovered?"

"But *I do* have information," Billy announced. "One of the cops told my mother he's going to the island in the morning. He said everyone thinks you're dead, but he knows it's not true. He found evidence you're alive."

"Evidence?" the man said. In the moonlight his face seemed to grow white. "What evidence?"

"Of foul play," the boy said. "And he's gonna prove it."

"Prove what, exactly?" the man sneered.

"He's going to the island in the morning," Billy said, "and then he's coming back to prove you're still alive."

"The island?" the man said.

"He thinks you might be there," Billy said.

"He thinks Sevigny's there?" the man said. "Alive?"

"Uh, yeah," Billy said, confused.

"Are they looking for . . . for a suspect?" the man asked.

"Not they," Billy said. "Only the cop. He didn't tell anyone; he wants to break the case himself."

"He's the only one who knows?"

"Yeah," Billy said. "He told my mom, but she fell asleep."

"Asleep?"

"She'd had some drinks," Billy said, lowering his eyes.

"I see," the man said. "But you overheard."

"Yes."

"And he's going to the island in the morning. What island?"

"Bluff Island," Billy said, gesturing to where the parcel of land sat on the dark horizon. "I didn't know if that was where you were going, so I thought I should warn you."

"How far out is it?" the man asked.

"Less than two miles," Billy said. "Our school takes a field trip there every year."

"And it's uninhabited?"

"Yes. The cop's going there first thing. He thinks you're stranded."

"Well, then," the man said. "Maybe I am."

Chapter Thirteen

Surprise Accomplice

An hour before dawn, the cutter anchored at the mouth of the Saco began to bustle with activity. Soon, it would lurch into gear. The Coast Guard had thoroughly canvassed the bay the day before and had discovered no hint of the missing man. The FBI had led the effort on the ground, inspecting the *Wind Dancer* and the items that had washed ashore, but they'd found little to answer the riddle of Ferdinand Sevigny's whereabouts. Neither agency was ready to accept that the man would not be found, but both were beginning to consider the possibility. The ocean had a way of swallowing its secrets. In the name of due diligence and good form, however, the cutter began to chug up the coast to where two rescue choppers would search a wider grid than they had the day before, and the federal agents in town began to file out of their motel rooms into the sun.

As Sally began her daily march, the tide-swept sand looked just as it did on any June morning, save for some police tape that remained staked in front of the Copley, and for two people, a man and a woman with matching metal detectors, sweeping the wet sand ahead. Sally paid them little mind.

Meanwhile, up the hill on the gentle rise overlooking the Square, Carrie arrived at Beach Bagels to open the door and start the coffeepots Mrs. Munson had loaded the night before. The baker's truck would be arriving soon. She leaned her bike against the building and dug her fingers into one of her pockets for the key.

As for Ernie Sabo, understanding that his orders were to stand down, and that Chief White would have it no other way, he radioed Dispatch at four that morning complaining of a headache, saying he'd sleep it off and make it to the station by ten. He hardly ever called in sick, and didn't feel guilty about it, especially since he was only doing so in order to go above and beyond the call of duty, which was what he'd signed up for in the first place.

Forgoing his morning coffee and the ordinary dictates of protocol, Ernie arrived at the Scarborough co-op before first light and observed several shadowy figures lurking on the docks, readying their vessels. He walked through a corridor of damaged lobster traps, piled twenty high, until he reached a slip that belonged to his friend Ronnie, a lobsterman, who was already out on the water judging from the empty spot where his rig was usually docked.

Ernie was borrowing a twenty-footer with an outboard that he and the boys sometimes used when they felt like casting for stripers or just blowing off steam. He knew the rescue choppers had hovered over the bay the day before, but he hadn't observed them taking any interest in the island. For some reason, his gut was still screaming *Bluff Island*. Maybe it was a genuine hunch—he'd had a few in the past—or maybe it was just wishful thinking. There was only one way to find out.

He used the key Ronnie had given him sometime back to open the little metal drop box on the post. He reached inside, groping for the key to unlock the boat's tether, and then nearly jumped out of his skin when a voice nearby said, "It's not there."

"What?" Ernie cried, realizing someone was already in the little boat he'd intended to commandeer.

"Thought you could use some company," the voice said, and though Ernie couldn't make out the face in the shadows, he recognized the speaker.

"Paulie?" he said. "You scared the shit out of me."

His fellow officer Paul Mason was at the stern, filling the engine with one of the fuel hoses that appeared every thirty feet along the dock. "Couldn't let you go alone," he said, "and have all the glory to yourself."

"But how'd you know—" Ernie began to say, wondering if Paul had read his mind, which had happened more than once in the decade they'd been working together, but also wondering if Paul had found out another way. He hoped it was the former.

"The way you were rattling on about the island yesterday," Paul began, "I thought, I'll be damned if he isn't going to call in today . . ."

Ernie stared at him as his eyes slowly adjusted. The truth was, he didn't mind the company. "Island?" he said, playing dumb. "I'm just going to watch the sunrise. I suppose if you want to come along, that's fine . . ."

They both laughed.

A few minutes later, as Ernie steered the boat through the marina and along the jetty, he noticed a look of concern on his partner's face. "Hey, Paulie," he said. "What's eating you?"

"Nothing," Paul said over the hum of the engine, but after Ernie gave him a dubious look, he began to talk rapidly about the bane of his existence, that crushing condition against which he'd often railed in his friend's presence: gout.

"I drink one beer," he said, "and the next morning I can't get my boots on."

Ernie nodded in a way that he hoped would be perceived as sympathetic.

"I split a shrimp cocktail with Millie, and by the time we get home, I can't . . . perform," Paul continued, his voice trailing off.

Ernie didn't really know what to say, so he pulled on the throttle to make the engine roar and the boat surge ahead.

Ten minutes later, as they approached Bluff Island, Ernie pointed to the cutter a few miles south. Paul's eyes followed the gesture with a glint of unease.

"Bet those boys sleep past ten," Ernie yelled.

"They probably spent the night at Mr. Goodbar hitting on Brandy Carter," Paul said, in a way that struck Ernie as almost too cheerful given the topic. But Ernie forced a smile. In a moment of weakness and inebriation a few months back, he'd confessed to Paul more than he'd meant to about his sessions with Brandy. His moment of indiscretion had been prompted by Paul's admission that he occasionally visited Brandy's living room. Paul was a married man, and his surprising disclosure as they'd sipped longnecks at the bar had taken Ernie by surprise. He'd felt obliged to offer some secret of his own in return. His own trysts with Brandy, who was down the other end of the room clearing a table, had come spilling out. He'd thought it would be a relief to get it off his chest, especially after learning that a devoted family man like Paul might sometimes avail himself of Brandy's services too. But as soon as Ernie had volunteered the information, he'd regretted it. It was the kind of thing that could come back to bite you, no matter how trusted your confidant.

Now, in the light just before sunrise, he wondered if that was how Paul had known he'd be heading out to the island. He wondered if Paul had visited Brandy after he'd left, and if she'd told Paul his secret. But she'd been drunk and passed out. She couldn't have told him anything.

A few hundred feet from the little rise of land, Ernie cut the engine.

"I haven't been out here since last fishing season," Paul said.

"And you probably haven't stepped ashore since grade school," Ernie added.

"Neither have you," Paul said.

"Who do you think's been feeding the sandpipers?" Ernie replied.

Paul smiled. It was true that the entire front slope of the island, the side that faced the mainland, was covered with piper nests. They sat like gray baskets amid the thin grass that sprouted fifty feet from the water's edge, where the sand gave way to darker soil. The adult birds, meanwhile, scurried back and forth along the water's edge, picking at whatever morsels the sea had dredged up. Beyond the sand and dune grass, the land rose to form a rocky butte where scraggly pines and prickly beach plums grew. Counting a sandbar that extended like a thumb off the southernmost side, the island measured barely a half-mile across.

"Let's circle around—" Ernie started to say, lifting a pair of binoculars toward his face. He paused, though, before the magnifiers even reached his chin. He'd spotted something, and when he glanced at Paul, he realized his friend had seen it, too. With his right arm Paul pointed at the same colorful piece of cloth that had caught Ernie's eye. It was tied to the trunk of a thin pine just beyond the grass. At the base of the tree there sat a pile of . . . something—it was hard to make out exactly what it was. Ernie raised the binoculars and peered through the lenses. "Let's check her out," he said.

Chapter Fourteen

The Worried Host

After Wednesday night, when he'd awoken from a dead sleep to pull a drowning woman from the ocean, and Thursday, when he'd learned that the woman was at the center of an international news story, Roger would have hardly thought it possible that when he next laid down his head he would wake to discover anything quite so startling. And yet, on Friday morning, he emerged from his dreams to face a new conundrum.

After Marisol had finished telling her story and explained that she could only wait for Sevigny to find her, Roger had told her he needed some time to think. He'd gone out on the deck with his laptop, shut the slider, and left Marisol watching television. He'd watched the boats trolling the bay and the investigators making their way up the beach, searching for something, anything, that might provide a clue as to what had happened at sea, a topic his guest had steadfastly avoided.

He had looked at the men and women on the sand, earnestly trying to make sense of things, and didn't like the feeling their presence gave him. He was harboring a witness who surely possessed information that could have aided in their search. He didn't like being part of something clandestine, and he felt sick when he imagined that his inaction might be further imperiling a man who could still be alive, at sea or on land, and in need of help.

He also didn't like having Marisol in his house. If Sevigny were dead, as Roger suspected, that meant the man wouldn't be arriving to take her away. And Roger would be left to either convince her he had perished, or to help her plot her next move when Sevigny's body eventually turned up. If he were alive, as Marisol maintained, what chance was there that Sevigny would be able to locate her? Barring some supernatural capacity within the adventurer, it seemed unlikely he would find his way to Roger's door.

Roger had spent the better part of Thursday afternoon leaning against the railing on his deck and gazing down the beach, then sitting and watching the boats, then standing again, then flipping up his computer screen and searching for anything online that might better inform his thoughts, wondering all the while how he'd gotten himself into such a mess in the first place, and how he could get out of it.

Inside, he'd heard the whirr of the bathroom shade being drawn down, followed by the gentle patter of the shower's spray. She was a beautiful girl, that was undeniable, and it was impossible not to imagine her golden body standing beneath the water. He'd held that body in his arms just the night before, had touched her smooth skin, had felt her round breasts against his chest. He couldn't help but think of her in the way a man sometimes thinks of a woman.

After her shower, he hadn't heard any noise inside the house for a time, and it was almost possible to pretend the last day hadn't happened. Perhaps it had been a vivid fantasy, nothing more. However, the commotion on the beach said otherwise.

Later, he'd heard the whoosh of the fan above the oven, and had looked through the glass door to see her standing over the stove. Initially, he'd found this image of her making dinner, presumably for the two of them, endearing. Midafternoon was giving way to evening by that point, and he hadn't eaten all day. But then, before the scent of whatever she was frying could reach the deck, the gesture seemed out of line. Who was she to make herself that comfortable in his kitchen? As she leaned over the stove with her back to him, he'd caught himself staring at her through the glass, and that had only made him resent her more.

After a dinner eaten in awkward silence, Roger had come right out with it.

"Tomorrow morning," he'd said, "I'll take you to buy some clothes, and I'll give you some money. I'll drive you wherever you want to go." Her face had dropped, but in a way that led Roger to believe his ultimatum was not entirely unexpected.

"You can't stay here," he had continued. "My neighbors will be back any day. Our yards are close together, and everyone keeps their windows open. I don't want to lie to them."

"But there's nowhere for me to go," she'd said.

"I'll take you to the bus station or the airport," Roger had suggested. "I'll buy you a ticket."

"And without my passport or identification, what good would it do?"

"There must be someone you can call," Roger had implored. "How about in Melbourne, or one of the other cities you've traveled to? There must be a butler or a—"

"No," she'd said petulantly.

"I know," Roger had persisted, as he suddenly remembered something she'd said earlier. "How about the tutor he hired for you? Can you call him and explain—"

"No," she'd snapped.

Roger was unyielding; the thought of her becoming someone else's burden was suddenly too appealing to abandon. "But that's someone who knows you, and knows Sevigny," he'd said.

"Sevigny's nephew was my tutor," she had said curtly. "And he is the *last* person I would call." She had pushed out her chair, stood up, and stomped from the room, leaving Roger to do the dishes.

That night, Roger had dreamt of a new ending to the tense evening they'd spent together. In his dream, he was still adamant that she must leave, and she was still a sulking child, only this time, as he'd stood over the sink washing dishes, she'd come up behind him and wrapped her arms around him, reaching with desire.

When he woke at first light on Friday morning, he couldn't decide if he was relieved or let down that it had only been a dream, but by the time he'd climbed out of bed and allowed his head to clear, he knew it was best this way.

He walked into the living room with resolve and was surprised to find the blankets neatly folded on the couch, the room deserted. She was already gone.

Chapter Fifteen

Footprints in the Sand

The two officers approached the tattered orange distress signal with a mixture of exuberance and trepidation. Before even making land they'd debated the merits of the two paths before them—not in the abstract, as when they'd set out, but in real terms. On the one hand, there was the prudent course that would have them radio Chief White with a report that they'd discovered—accidentally, they could still maintain—evidence they believed was related to the current search. The chief would no doubt tell them to sit tight until the feds arrived. On the other hand, well, they'd already come this far, and the feds had had a day already to search the island if they'd wanted to. Making the case to continue most compellingly was the shimmering piece of orange fabric tied to the tree. It bid them to come ashore in a way that proved, ultimately, irresistible.

In truth, Ernie Sabo had already chosen which path he'd follow the moment he'd lowered himself into Ronnie's boat. But for Paul Mason, who had tagged along ostensibly for no other reason than to be a good friend, the decision appeared to be more difficult.

"I don't know about this," Paul said for about the fifth time as Ernie raised the propeller and allowed the momentum to carry them the last fifty feet. They were approaching on the south side, from which they could still see a narrow sliver of their town and its beach on their left, while the open ocean glistened on their right.

"You don't know about what?" Ernie asked, even though he knew full well what his friend meant.

"We should call it in," Paul said.

"We came out to troll for stripers," Ernie replied. "But before we could throw a line, your gout kicked up, and you got the runs. We made land so you could take a dump. While you were stinking up Mother Nature, I couldn't help but notice a bright orange cloth tied to a tree right in front of my face. So we checked it out. That's it. Nice and simple."

"But—" Paul said, fishing for the best objection he could muster, "but gout doesn't give you diarrhea."

"Chief doesn't know that," Ernie scoffed. "That's the kind of thing you tell someone and they don't ask questions. It's a non sequitur."

"A what?"

"Take your socks off."

"Anyone could have hung that there," Paul persisted. "Fishermen last season, or some kids out for a joyride in Daddy's boat."

"Exactly," Ernie said. "So there's no reason to call Chief until we know for sure. C'mon, hop out and pull us in."

"We'll radio if it's a lead?" Paul said hopefully.

"Yeah," Ernie said, "probably. Come on, I don't have an anchor—"

"Why do *I* have to do it?" Paul whimpered. It was still early, and out at sea it was cooler than on the mainland. He didn't look forward to getting his legs wet, but he rolled up his cuffs, took up the tether, and lowered himself into the knee-deep water. He towed the small boat until its belly scratched the sand.

"Look," Ernie said as he hopped out. He was pointing at a trail of footprints not far from where they'd landed. They led from the water's edge, through the dry sand, and into the dunes. A matching set appeared just a few yards from the first trail, heading back to the water. The tree with the tattered orange fabric and pile of objects against its trunk stood on the other side of the dunes on the same trajectory as the prints.

"They look fresh," Paul said, stooping to study what appeared to be a size-ten sneaker imprint.

But Ernie was already hurrying into the dunes. "C'mon," he called over his shoulder. Paul lingered over the prints for a moment before following his partner.

"You're not going to believe this, Paulie," Ernie said, when his friend reached the outermost bounds of the shabby forest. "I think we found our man."

At the base of the scraggly pine was a small pile of clothing, still soggy with seawater: a shirt, a pair of trousers, a sweatshirt, a notebook. But most intriguing of all was what looked to be a small wooden jewelry box, with an "M" and an "S" engraved on top. It was held shut by a brass clasp. Ernie tried to open it but found the little lock unyielding. He decided not to smash it; not yet. It was evidence, after all. And besides, there was the notebook, which he'd already begun to investigate. He opened it to the first page and realized that soggy and smeared though it was, it contained a note written in blue ballpoint ink, in flamboyant looping letters that looked almost like calligraphy. It read:

I have suffered an accident at sea, but not far from shore. The mast rope slipped and the crossbeam struck my head and knocked me overboard. I am bleeding and weak, but will attempt to swim to the mainland. In the event that I do not make it, please convey my love, and these few items I had on my person when I fell overboard, to my nephew, Rupert.
Sincerely,
Ferdinand Sevigny

"I guess he didn't make it," Paul said soberly.

"That would be the easy answer," Ernie replied.

"What do you mean?" Paul asked.

"Whoever left this made one mistake—actually, two," Ernie said, standing up out of his crouch and looking down at their boat. He nodded. "He made two obvious mistakes."

"You mean Sevigny?" Paul asked.

"No," Ernie said. "I mean the person who wants us to think he's been here, and to think he's drowned. It could be Sevigny, I suppose, but it could also be someone else."

"What do you mean?" Paul asked uneasily.

"The footprints," Ernie said. "What did you notice about them?"

"Size ten, I'm guessing," Paul replied. "Probably sneakers."

"Paulie, have you ever fallen out of a boat?" Ernie asked.

"I've jumped out," Paul said.

"What's the first thing you did?"

"I swam to where I was going."

"Did you ever jump out of a boat with your shoes on?"

"No," Paul said, starting to see his friend's line of reasoning. "But I jumped off a bridge once, that time on Route 9, when I pulled the lady from her car."

"Did you have to swim to her?"

"Yeah."

"Did you take your shoes off?"

"No, but I should have. My boots filled up—"

"Paulie," Ernie said, "if Sevigny swam to this island with his sneakers on, why would he leave with them on?"

At some point during the exchange, the blood drained from Paul's face and his eyes narrowed into small black dots. Ernie noticed this change, but wasn't sure what to make of it. He repeated the question: "Paulie, why would Sevigny swim off the island with sneakers on his feet but leave his clothes in a soggy pile here?"

"The set of prints heading to the water should be bare feet," Paul said.

"He left in a boat. And he came in one, too," Ernie said. "A small one—that's why he didn't need to take his shoes off when he got to shore, like we did. He scooted right up onto the sand."

"So what's the second thing that doesn't check out?" Paul asked, with something approaching dread in his voice.

"The note," Ernie said. "Where did this guy get a dry notebook?"

"He didn't. It's pretty wet," Paul said unevenly.

"It wasn't when he wrote the note," Ernie said. "Look at how little the ink has smeared. And look at how the pages in the middle are dry. I think this note was written, then the book was dunked in the water to make it look wet."

Ernie returned his attention to the little jewelry box. He turned it over in his hands, held it to his ear and shook it. He fidgeted with the lock. Then, he made a decision. "Find a rock," he said. "Let's smash this sucker open."

Chapter Sixteen

What the Seagull Heard

Sally had been relieved to see a familiar face when she'd regained consciousness the day before. She had recognized Ernie immediately and had felt reassured. She did not understand the decisions he had to make concerning what had happened to her, and what to do with the items in her wagon, but she intuitively trusted that he would do whatever was in her best interest. She had allowed him to lead her inside, sit her in her chair, and call her friend, Mrs. Munson, to come look after her. She'd nodded when he'd told her to leave the Halloween mask and other things beneath the lobster traps until he returned. She'd nodded when he'd said not to show them to Mrs. Munson.

Sally did not understand the error in judgment the officer had made. She did not understand his mistake in assuming that what was transpiring on the beach was unrelated to what had happened outside her door as she'd dug her key out of her pocket. It was not his fault. She did not even try to explain what had happened to her, because, in fact, she did not fully know herself what had happened—only that something had. She was beginning to get it, however, as she set out the next morning.

As Sally approached the spot in front of the Copley where she had found so many treasures the day before, she saw a woman waving a metal wand over the sand, tracing the perimeter of the yellow police tape. The woman was not anyone Sally knew. Ordinarily she did not like people she didn't know; she usually turned her eyes away when they passed. But this time she approached the woman, and as she did the stranger reached up a hand to remove the headphones from her ears.

"Yesterday," Sally said.

The woman looked at her for a moment and smiled. "Yes," the woman replied slowly, encouragingly, as if she were talking to a child. "That's right. There was a big to-do, wasn't there?"

"It happened yesterday," Sally said.

The woman nodded. "Weren't there a lot of policemen and reporters? And did you see the helicopters?" she said.

"Yesterday," Sally said.

"That's right," the woman replied. "Are you here all by yourself, dear?"

"Yesterday."

"You live nearby?"

"Yesterday," Sally repeated. And that was all she could say, no matter what the woman asked, no matter how much more she may have wanted to say.

Eventually, the woman shrugged and wished her a good morning. Then she gave Sally a pat on the shoulder and returned her headphones to her ears, leaving Sally to pull her wagon along the beach. Before very many more steps, Sally encountered a man who had a device just like the one the woman had. He was doing the same thing.

"Hello, there," the man said, removing one of his headphones.

"A man pushed me," Sally said flatly.

The man furrowed his brow. He quickly turned and scanned the beach until his eyes found the woman with the device like his. She was about two hundred feet away. "Who?" the man asked. "Where is he?"

"A man," Sally said. "He didn't think I saw him, but I did."

"That man?" the man asked, pointing with his metal detector at the only man he could locate on the broad sweep of beach, a fellow in green sweatpants throwing a tennis ball for a golden retriever.

Sally shook her head.

The man looked relieved. "A man pushed you?"

"He pushed me," Sally said.

"I see," the man said, and he studied Sally, paying special attention to the Band-Aid on her forehead and the bruise that extended beyond its borders. He studied the frustration on her face. "Why would someone do that?" he asked.

"He pushed me," Sally said.

"Who?" the man asked. "And why did he push you?"

"He pushed me," was all Sally said. The man shrugged, and Sally continued to make her way down the beach. She came upon a scallop shell, which she crushed with the butt of her stick. Then, with her astute eyes, she found a shark's tooth; she tucked it into one of her pockets. Next, she found a piece of smooth green sea glass, which she laid in her wagon. She continued her march.

After many such discoveries, Sally happened upon a big brown gull standing menacingly over a dead crab. The ugly bird raised its head so that it extended skyward, as if it were a chick rising from a nest for nour-ishment. *Caw, caw, caw*, the gull said. Then it lowered its head and looked at Sally, tilting its head left, then right, then left again, as if won-dering why this latest intruder did not retreat as had its peers.

"He took it," Sally said. "The man."

The seagull looked at her.

"He pushed me down and he opened it and closed it and took it," she said. "He didn't think I saw him, but I did."

Caw, caw, caw, the bird replied.

Chapter Seventeen

Fast Friends

As the sun appeared on the water at the bottom of the hill and sent light trickling through the front window of Beach Bagels, Carrie greeted the locals who reported for their morning coffee. She was on her own for the first hour, as Mrs. Munson was running late. Carrie had no trouble keeping the java and the banter flowing. It seemed everyone wanted to gossip about the crazy day before, and to speculate about where the Sevigny investigation would lead. Carrie liked having such an easy conversation starter close at hand. It was much more interesting than chatting about the weather.

Later in the morning, the Sevigny mystery served as an icebreaker between Carrie and two new girls who had just arrived in town. Usually she was not one to strike up conversations with their type. Like most townies, she understood and appreciated the money outsiders brought to town, but she also carried an unspoken resentment toward them. They were, after all, intruders, yet they expected to be treated with deference. If the customer was always right, then clearly, these tourists saw themselves as consumers of the town for the summer, and they expected the locals to make their stay as pleasurable as possible. After a while, it wore thin.

But these girls were different. They weren't "pasty basties," as the daughters of Old Orchard Beach referred to the pale-skinned Canadians who slathered themselves with sunscreen, nor were they "prissy missies," the silly young teenagers who came to OOB with their rich families. They were college girls, like she was; these two were between their sophomore and junior years at Boston College, and had come to Old Orchard looking for summer work. Their first appointment—after their double mocha iced cappuccinos—was with the landlord at Beach Villas, who had placed an ad for discount lodging in their school newspaper. Then they were heading to the Square to see what they could score for employment—hopefully waitressing gigs at one of the restaurants near the Pier, or if that didn't work out, counter jobs at one of the pizza joints or T-shirt shops.

"You know," said the tall blonde, who had introduced herself as Sam, "as long as we make, like, enough to pay our rent and our bar tab, it beats being at home."

"Yeah, one more summer at home and I would have freaked," the other girl, Mandy, said.

Carrie did not tell them that she lived with her parents. She just said, "I hear you." Then she suggested a few places that were always looking for seasonal help. There was Pier Fries, where they'd accumulate greasy rashes from standing over the fryer; Rita's Smoothies, where they'd pack on fifteen pounds of empty calories; Jenna's Hennas, where they'd get hit on by sweaty biker dudes. There was also Palace Playland, where they'd get puked on by brats stumbling off the Pirate Ship ride. Carrie told them that unfortunately, most of the restaurants had only bussing and dishwashing slots left; she knew this because she'd started her own search at their doorsteps two weeks before.

"So, it must be, like, so cool to live here," Mandy said. "There's a zillion bars, right?"

Carrie explained that there were actually eight, and that Mr. Goodbar was the only one that stayed open year-round. She didn't tell the girls that she'd never set foot in any of them because she'd only recently turned twenty-one, and had known better than to go drinking underage in a town where everyone knew her name. Nonetheless, she spoke with authority about the town's watering holes, further impressing her new friends.

"So, you know, like, which ones will serve us?" Sam asked, lowering her voice. "We're twenty."

Before Carrie could answer, another customer, who'd apparently entered without Carrie noticing, cleared his throat, expressing annoyance at the delay. Sam and Mandy stepped aside so that Carrie could take his order, retreating to the stools along the window. They chatted and sipped their drinks, but before they headed out to find jobs, they returned to the counter.

72

"Like, it's Friday night," Mandy said, even though it was, in fact, ten o'clock in the morning. "What are you doing?"

"Want a tour?" Carrie asked.

"That would be awesome," Sam replied eagerly. "We can hit some clubs."

"Cool," Carrie said, even though she knew Mr. Goodbar was the only place open, with the start of the season still four days away.

Chapter Eighteen

A Glimpse Inside

The jewelry box was made of an unusual wood. It wasn't as light as balsa, but wasn't as dense as pine. It appeared to be handmade. It was about the size of one of the cardboard boxes Ernie retrieved from the ordnance closet on the first day of every quarter, when it came time to freshen up the bullets in his weapon.

"Somebody carved these letters into the top," Ernie said. "Then they put it together and finished it with lacquer."

As the sun lit up the morning, he crouched beside his friend and fellow officer, turning the box over in his hands, admiring it, and coming to terms with the fact that in a moment he would smash it to pieces with the stone in Paul's hands.

"What's eating you?" Ernie asked. He could tell something was bothering Paul.

"M. S.," Paul said, snapping out of whatever had been distracting him. "Mr. Sevigny?" It was the third or fourth time Paul had guessed at the meaning of the fancy letters chiseled onto the cover.

"I don't think so," Ernie said. "Maybe Mrs. Sevigny. Wasn't this guy married?"

"I don't know," Paul said.

"Me neither," Ernie admitted.

"So what's inside?"

"A class ring," Ernie said. "Or a pin from the Queen of England. Or cufflinks from the Super Rich Shoppers' Club. Or maybe another note. It feels pretty light." He took the rock from Paul's hands and placed the box on the ground before him. "What do you think?" Ernie asked, weighing the rock in his right hand against the look on Paul's face.

"It *is* evidence," Paul said. "And it's not our case. And technically, I'm on duty, even if you're not."

Ernie didn't mind that they were operating outside the realm of their jurisdiction, or even that they were ignoring the usual investigative protocol, which, he'd learned through the years, was the best thing to do when his gut said expedience should overrule proper form. Rather, he was reflecting upon the beauty of the box, on the obvious care with which it had been constructed. It seemed a shame to destroy it.

"We should call Chief—" Paul began. Then he added, oddly, "But we already figured out the footsteps. We know something's fishy . . . Chief won't believe it . . . Unless we wipe them out."

"What?" Ernie asked, not following his friend's line of thought at all. "Wipe out the footprints?"

Paul stood up abruptly. "Listen," he said sharply. "I don't like this. The guy's dead. I don't care if he was wearing sneakers or goddamned L.L. Bean hunting boots. We should call Chief."

"Paulie?" Ernie said, still in his crouch.

"Goddamn it," Paul said. "You're making me do this."

"Paulie," Ernie said, "I'm gonna level with you."

"Level with me?"

"Listen," Ernie said. "Yesterday when I told you I hadn't found anything on the beach, I lied. Sally Fiddler *did* have evidence—good evidence that only I know about. The guy didn't have an accident."

"What do you mean?"

"I found a hood in Sally's wagon, like an executioner's—like the kind you'd put on someone you were kidnapping. At least, that's what I thought at first. Then I saw the news and the picture of this guy wearing his blindfold. That's what I found—the blindfold he was wearing."

"So? That doesn't prove there was foul play," Paul said.

Ernie smiled. "Inside the hood," he said, "were stains. It looked like blood."

As he spoke, Ernie observed that Paul's lower lip had begun to tremble. Ernie thought his friend might be about to cry, and he wasn't sure why.

"Listen, Paulie," he said, "did you see Brandy this morning? Did she tell you I found something—is that why you're sore?"

Paul shook his head.

"I understand if you're pissed," Ernie said. "That's what I get for spilling my guts to the town whore. But listen, I was planning to cut you in. Whatever glory there is, we'll share it."

Paul didn't answer; he just stood there. Then, finally, he said, "Just wait one minute, okay?" He lumbered, as quickly as Ernie had ever seen him move, down the little slope, through the dunes, across the sand, and to the boat.

Still crouching over the box, Ernie watched his friend with a mixture of amusement and affection. He realized before Paul had even reached their borrowed vessel that he was probably going back to retrieve a tool—maybe the razor-sharp gaff they used to lift fish out of the water—from the compartment on the starboard side. Indeed, such an instrument would be useful to pry open the box without destroying it. At worst, they would break the clasp.

Sometimes Paulie can be a real asset, Ernie thought. As headstrong and gung-ho as he knew himself to be, Paul was more uncertain but more methodical, and though his plodding attention to detail sometimes caused him to miss the forest for the trees, it could also come in handy.

These warm feelings for his friend were mixed with the special rush he'd come to savor whenever he was on a case. He was on to something big, and he knew it. His body pulsed with the thrill of the chase. His mind became more and more narrowly focused on unraveling the mystery, so that his usually fragmented thoughts became a unified force, like a laser beam fixed on a target. He felt better than he had in years. The looming prospect of another summer spent citing drunks seemed far off. His town, which he could see in the distance now as Paul started to make his way back up the hill, seemed somehow close by and welcoming. It was an imperfect but lovely place, full of goodhearted people, even if they were a bit rough around the edges.

In that moment, before Paul had returned with the tool to open the box, Ernie knew he was doing the right thing. He knew his good work would not go unappreciated, even if he were bending the rules. He thought of Chief with his silly sayings. He thought of the new girl at Beach Bagels who had been a friend of his daughter's. He breathed in the joy that came from knowing he'd spent his life's work—as mundane as it sometimes was—doing for others, not himself. He realized his joy would

only grow if he could just unravel the mystery of Sevigny's disappearance—if he could break the case before the feds did; the feds, whose cutter had already given up on the waters immediately off the coast, whose
agents had been asleep when he'd started his day.

Even if he wound up losing his badge for it, his most reckless breach
of procedure yet, he believed the respect and goodwill he'd earned
through the years would carry him gracefully into whatever came next.
He was seizing his chance to make a difference, which was the reason
he'd signed up for the police force, for this way of life, in the first place.
Going out his way, on his own terms, was preferable to sitting around
the station signing parking citations and drinking coffee with the chief,
as he'd watched other senior officers do.

Ernie stood up from his crouch when he realized Paul had returned.
He smiled at his friend and reached out a hand to take whatever Paul had
retrieved from the boat. But Paul wasn't holding a gaff in his hand;
instead, he held his pistol, and before Ernie could say or think anything
beyond the warm feelings he'd been experiencing, Paul discharged his
weapon. Once. Twice. Three times. The shots echoed across the quiet
landscape, dissolving into the sand and sea and sun that were the only
witnesses. Then the sounds of the island slowly, gradually, returned: the
lap of the waves, the chatter of the pipers.

"Why'd you have to get hung up on those goddamned footprints?"
Paul said, breathing heavily, his eyes brimming with tears. "Why
couldn't you leave well enough alone? Why couldn't you call Chief like
you were supposed to?"

Paul stood over his friend as if he expected him to answer. He
watched the blood spread across Ernie's shirt, then spill into the sandy
soil. He wondered how things had gone so terribly wrong. Then, retrac-
ing his steps, he headed down the hill.

Chapter Nineteen

The Brunswick

The Brunswick Hotel had opened in 1902, four years after the original Pier was built, and five years before the embers of that long wharf had crashed into the sea. Many locals believed that Old Orchard's near-apocalyptic fire was a sign the town shouldn't have welcomed outsiders in the first place. And yet, the town's evolution as a vacation hub was merely delayed by the disaster. In part, this was because as devastating as the flames had been, they had spared the largest hotel along the shore.

According to local lore, the inferno had crept right up to the Brunswick's doorstep, had even licked its shingles, some said, but had passed it by, despite decimating the other beachfront lodgings. Through the generations, the notion that a man named Eben Staples had preserved the Brunswick had been accepted into Old Orchard's oral history. Eben had been a stable hand of limited mental capacity—so the story went—hired by Martin Drake shortly after the Brunswick opened. Eben fed the visitors' horses and saw that they were properly exercised while their owners lounged on the beach. There were no visitors, or horses, at the Brunswick on the night of the fire, however; nor was Eben at his post. It was a frigid December night, and the hotel, like the town, was slumbering through one of its first off-seasons.

Just the same, at the first hint of smoke, Eben had run down the hill and begun hauling buckets of wet sand from the beach. While the rest of the beachfront burned, Eben poured bucket after bucket around the Brunswick's plot, beginning near his beloved stable and continuing until he'd formed a foot-wide, shin-high crescent that resembled a giant horseshoe as it wrapped around the ballroom, the front gate, and the guest quarters. Over the course of the next two hours, while Mr. Drake and the other brave men of the town's early days fought a losing battle on the fire's front lines, as one building after another perished, Eben methodically went about his work, carrying two pails at a time, dumping them, and then returning to the beach. According to the story, when the fire eventually encompassed the hotel, Eben disappeared behind the flames, only to be discovered hours later, after the fire had passed, huddled in the stable.

With his heroic deed, Eben Staples forever altered the town's trajectory and etched his name onto its heart. After the ashes had stopped smoldering, the lone building remaining on the beach was the Brunswick, and the town rebuilt itself around this regal estate. By the boom-time following World War I, Old Orchard was poised to become the premier East Coast vacation destination. Duke Ellington played the ballroom at the Brunswick, along with Rudy Vallee and Guy Lombardo. The Roaring Twenties brought politicians, pro ballplayers, and other members of America's elite to town.

Ironically, when railroad tracks were laid between Boston and Old Orchard Beach in 1911, and when a light rail was constructed to ferry visitors from Portland to the new Pier a year later, Eben became obsolete, and Martin Drake turned him out. On a sad night in August, as guests danced in the ballroom, piled in and out of trolley cars out front, and made love in the quarters, Eben said one last good-bye to his lonely stable and then sneaked up to the Governor's Suite, which Mr. Drake kept as his own. There, high above the raucous crowd, Eben Staples hanged himself from the crossbeam above Mr. Drake's empty bed.

In its heyday, the hotel was decadent and opulent—and all those other words used to describe landmarks that have outlived their prime but still stand to honor an era that was probably not so glamorous or glorious as now supposed. In fairness, the Brunswick of the twenty-first century was not quite this archaic; in recent years it had reemerged as something more than just a historic curiosity. It was open for business again, though it catered to a less-lofty clientele—mostly families looking for a place to spend a few summer days.

After its doors had been shuttered for more than a decade, a husband and wife from Massachusetts had bought it at auction and reopened its first two floors in time for its centennial. And now, a few years later, Jim and Marty Wagner had gone to great lengths to restore its third floor in time for the new season. Unfortunately, with the sagging economy, most of the rooms on the renovated floor, as well as most of the lower ones, were yet to be booked as summer rapidly approached.

Jim and Marty were worried. Without the income they'd been expecting from a healthy season, they faced the real possibility of defaulting on their loan. For the devoted couple, who had "retired" from their original careers and bought the hotel as a twenty-fifth wedding anniversary present to themselves, this was a horrifying prospect.

It was against this backdrop of despair that a most unusual scene played out as noon approached on the second day after the mysterious accident at sea. It transpired just a few minutes before a Coast Guard spokesman at a regional command center in South Portland was to step behind a podium and tell the press corps on the "Sevigny beat" that the search for the missing man had yielded few leads, and was being suspended amid the grim acceptance that the lost man must have drowned.

But Jim and Marty Wagner knew none of this. They'd spent the morning not in front of the television in their modest first-floor suite, but in the lobby, where Jim was polishing the registration counter and Marty was cleaning the framed black-and-white photos lining the entrance. The first smattering of guests would be arriving in a matter of days, and they were making their final preparations.

As Marty sprayed a mist of blue cleanser onto a 1940s-era picture of the rotunda into which the fourth-floor stairway emptied, she was prompted to make an offhand remark to her husband, noting that it was a good thing they'd scaled back their original ambitions and had stopped short of renovating the fourth floor, since the additional expense would have surely bankrupted them.

"As a bonus," Jim agreed, "we can keep telling ghost stories." It was true. When young visitors asked what lay beyond the barrier blocking the stairwell beyond the third floor, the hotelkeepers delighted in spinning a fanciful yarn about the ghost of Eben Staples, to whom, they said, the entire fourth floor was deeded as a sort of peace offering.

"Remember that one little boy?" Marty replied, recalling with a smile a brave tyke who had embarked on a midnight ghost hunt, only to spook himself into a tizzy and wake half the hotel with shrieks for his mortified mother.

Just then, as if on cue, a noise arose from one of the upper floors.

"Don't tell me," Jim said.

"The squirrels?" Marty said. They'd been battling an infestation for two years. Upon further reflection, Marty didn't think the noise was congruent with the little suckers' capacity for disruption. "That sounded like a door," she said.

Before Jim could reply, the faint but unmistakable sound of someone descending the stairs drifted down into the lobby. The husband and wife exchanged a look but said nothing as they listened to the person's slow, measured gait.

Finally Marty said, "Did you call Roland?" Roland was a local handyman who tended to the Brunswick's plumbing and carpentry needs. Jim shook his head.

"Janet?" Marty said. For the past two years, Janet had helped Marty vacuum the rugs and make the beds while the guests sunned themselves. Again, Jim shook his head.

Thus, at a complete loss, Jim and Marty shrugged and waited in the lobby. They were not so alarmed as a couple might ordinarily be when detecting an intruder in their home, simply because the Brunswick, though it was their home, so frequently welcomed strangers into its rooms that over time it had come to feel, to them, more like a public place. Still, they usually remembered to lock the doors at night during the off-season, especially since an incident that had occurred two winters prior, when a homeless man had sneaked in and spent nearly a week on one of the upper floors before being discovered.

Marty, with her rag and bottle of cleanser, instinctively moved toward the counter, behind which Jim remained. In tandem, they fixed their eyes on the landing, midway between the first and second floors, where the stairway made a sharp turn before continuing. Finally, a pair of brown shoes came into view, then khaki pants, then the full specter of a distinguished gentleman, with neatly groomed salt-and-pepper hair and a similarly salted beard. He walked with a casual grace that befitted a guest who'd seemingly made himself quite at home. He appeared entirely at ease.

Both Jim and Marty found themselves reassured by the cool confidence the intruder exuded. He was such a stately-looking man, nodding affably to them in way of greeting; he appeared to be in no rush to explain himself, so they instinctively felt he was not a threat. The man continued down the stairs, then walked right up to the counter so he stood practically beside Marty. He smiled.

"What can we do for you?" Jim asked.

Before the man could reply, Marty found her voice and sputtered, "How did you get in?"

The man only shrugged like a child caught in a lie. "My name is Ferdinand Sevigny," he said. "I've spent the past two days as a guest on your fourth floor, and with apologies for not already doing so, I'd like to formalize my arrangement."

"You're the man who drowned," Jim said in a barely audible voice. Then he asked, "You've been *here*?"

"Indeed," Sevigny said, raising a hand to his beard and tugging on it slightly, though it was too close a beard for any serious tugging. "Only not drowned. *Nearly* drowned, *apparently* drowned." His accented voice lingered on each qualifying adjective in a way that reflected neither amusement nor regret concerning his state of affairs. The only aspect of his personage that seemed discordant with his calm demeanor, and hinted that he'd been through some recent ordeal, was an ugly wound on his forehead.

"But how have you managed . . . what have you been doing for meals?" Marty asked.

But Sevigny didn't answer her questions. Rather, he said, "I'd like to book your entire fourth floor. Make it for the entire summer, if you like; I'll pay whatever it costs."

"The fourth floor isn't open to guests," Marty said mechanically.

"It is now, my dear," Sevigny said, smiling. "It is now."

Part Two

Chapter Twenty

Rendezvous with a Troubled Mind

Three hours before setting sail, Ferdinand Sevigny sat on a park bench in Halifax Harbor, reviewing his notes. His final preparations required that he memorize part of a speech he would deliver before boarding the *Wind Dancer*. It was his custom to address the media prior to each adventure as a way of putting the big boys at *Guinness* on notice that another record was about to fall. Usually, he leaked hints about his capers a few days before he went public, to build suspense. Then he brought the particulars into focus right before setting out. In the present instance, rumors were already circulating that he would be attempting a voyage that would cement his legacy as a master seaman and inspire a generation of physically challenged youngsters to believe their disabilities could never prevent them from achieving their dreams. It was vague, but provocative, and had the sort of social message that would cause folks to stop and wonder just what in the world old Ferdie Sevigny was going to do next.

He would have to deliver the second half of the speech from memory, since the blindfold would prevent him from glancing down at his notes. But that would only be the first hurdle; shortly afterward, another routine chore would be made difficult by his lack of sight. Without binoculars, or even his naked eye, he'd have to arrive at the right point on the water to retrieve Marisol. Sitting on the bench, he smiled inwardly. Actually, he'd have some help with that one. Soon after, though, there would be matters of navigation, tending the sails, and performing the other duties of maintaining the ship. At least then, he supposed, he would have her to assist him, if she were in the mood. And yet, he was almost sure she would not be. Even so, he was confident he could manage the trip. After all, Pamela Habek and Scott Duncan, both of whom were legally blind, had crossed the Pacific in 2005. If they could do it, Sevigny figured, then he could too. But it would be nice to have a little help from Marisol if she were so inclined.

While the pretext for Ferdinand Sevigny's rumination on the cheery Canadian afternoon may have been the pageantry and execution of his latest stunt, beneath the surface of his thoughts something else was grating, churning, and slowly building momentum like a machine lurching into gear. As that engine began to rumble, it slowly drowned out his superficial concerns. Then, finally, Marisol came into view at the far end of the park.

He had made sure to arrive well before her and to make himself busy on the bench, so that by the time she approached he would have melded into the scenery as seamlessly as the fountain, the monuments, and the gulls picking through the trash cans. With his baseball cap pulled practically over his eyes, he made a scant impression on the locals who passed through the park, never suspecting that an international celebrity was sitting in their midst.

As for Marisol, she could feel his eyes upon her with every step she took. It was stifling to be watched in such a way, but to her, familiar. It was the reality of a life in which she enjoyed something akin to freedom but always within certain bounds. After passing a few other benches, some occupied, others not, she sat on the far end of Sevigny's and opened her journal. While she knew the intrigue added some pleasure for him, it had long ago grown tiresome for her. Before their conversation had even begun, she found herself struggling to disguise her annoyance.

After a quiet moment, during which they pretended not to notice one another, Sevigny said, "Rupert has the coordinates." He spoke quietly and without looking up, as if he were addressing the papers in his lap.

He did not see Marisol roll her eyes. They'd discussed this detail already, just as they'd exhausted the others he proceeded to rehash. She already knew that Rupert was aware of the rendezvous point. She already knew that she and Rupert would depart in a motorboat at seven that evening, and that they'd intercept the *Wind Dancer* sometime between ten and ten-thirty. She already knew that she would get a little wet when she climbed aboard, and that her personal items and food for the trip had been smuggled aboard the *Wind Dancer* the day before. And yet, Marisol smiled inwardly as his review continued.

Free, she kept telling herself. *Soon I will be free.*

He was lecturing in a voice she had once admired, one she had found endearing but had since come to perceive as the tone an adult uses with a child. It was the same voice he'd used to transfix her, and the people of her village. While once it had charmed her, now it stirred within her a desire to escape the life she'd been left to live in his shadow. She wondered if he had changed or if she had in the years since she'd left Little Tobago with him. Then, all at once, it ocurred to her that *she* had. He had not. He had stayed the same, but she had grown up. She was an adult, a woman, and she would no longer accept her role as Sevigny's dependent. She would no longer accept her role as his secret companion. She would no longer accept being told where to be, and where to go, and *how* to be, so as to best adapt herself to his schedule and his priorities. She would no longer accept being anything less than his equal. And to be Sevigny's equal, she knew, was next to impossible, for no one was that. After all, he was the Great Ferdinand Sevigny, whose very name opened doors and hearts across five continents.

"The only variable will be my location," he said, snapping Marisol out of her thoughts. "It may not be as precise as usual."

"Why not?" she asked.

"I've decided to keep the blindfold on," he declared.

It was something he'd been debating; maybe he would or maybe he wouldn't, he'd told her, as if sharing his uncertainty could make her care. She'd always assumed he would have some elaborate way to take it off after the *Guinness* people had done their inspection of him and the *Wind Dancer*, and after the *Wind Dancer* had ventured out of camera range. Now he'd surprised her. He was leaving it on. She was glad. It would make it that much easier for her to escape.

"I hope you don't expect me to steer," she said.

"*That* I can manage," he replied, his voice shifting into the saccharine tone she knew well. "But going so many days without seeing your eyes will be nearly impossible."

She looked at her wristwatch, then closed her journal and zipped it back into its leather case. She opened her purse and took out her lipstick and compact mirror, holding the mirror in one hand while she traced crimson on her lips with the other. "I'm going shopping," she announced. She almost stood up, but before she could, his next words froze her in place.

"Marisol," he said sharply. "There is something else. It concerns Rupert."

She didn't think he saw her flinch, but realized too late that he would feel the weight of her body as it sank back onto the bench.

Rupert was Sevigny's nephew. He had been her tutor after Sevigny had plucked her from Little Tobago. As his uncle's only relative—and, Rupert hoped, sole heir—Rupert intermittently traveled with them. He saw to Marisol's needs when Sevigny was away, and managed some of Sevigny's estates, ensuring they were stocked with the things Sevigny needed when he arrived. More than that, he handled the "professional" chores that Sevigny could not entrust to any other servant. Rupert was the one who helped coordinate Sevigny's capers, even though doing so required Rupert to bite his tongue while his uncle squandered the fortune he saw as rightfully his.

What Sevigny did not know, or what Marisol *hoped* he did not know, was that for the past four months Rupert had also been her lover. She had seduced him—at least, she thought she had—not out of love or lust, but because she'd identified him as a means to an end. Now, when her design was about to come to fruition, the sound of his name on Sevigny's lips sent a chill through her body.

"I wish to say a word about my nephew."

"Oh?"

"I don't trust him," Sevigny said. "And you shouldn't either."

"Rupert?" Marisol said, turning to face him for the first time.

"Yes, Rupert," he said, and he turned toward her with smoldering eyes. Marisol looked away.

"He has been stealing from me."

"Stealing?"

"For a while," Sevigny said. "And I've allowed it."

"Allowed it?" She was trying to figure out how much Sevigny knew.

"Yes," Sevigny said. "I expect he will soon disappear, but in case he doesn't, I've taken measures to protect myself."

"You have?"

"Yes," Sevigny said. Then, without warning, he rose from the bench and fully broke protocol. He stared directly down at her as she sat there, trembling. "I'll see you on the *Wind Dancer*," he said. Then he walked away.

Chapter Twenty-One

Sevigny's Second Act

Ferdinand Sevigny considered himself well into the second act of a life he'd come to understand as something akin to a three-act play. First, there had been his opening salvo, those early days when he was working his way up through the ranks of his father's company, on his way to becoming its president. That opening act had ended on the day he'd taken the Australian Independent Television Network public in 1996. At age thirty-five, he'd become just one face among many on a board that assembled periodically to "steer" the network in whichever direction the new CEO had already decided to take it.

His life had lost all meaning and purpose, and before he knew it he was nearly forty, still without the slightest idea of what to do next. By then, he had lost both parents, had participated, if only slightly, in a failed marriage, and had begun to sport a hint of gray in his beard. Within six months he managed to wash away the gray, enter into a second, though similarly ill-fated union, and regain a bit of his former clout at the network. But ultimately the problem of what to do with so much time and so little influence consumed him. On walkabout in the Great Victoria Desert, he had a revelation.

Thus began Sevigny's second act.

Over the next decade, he had chiseled out a spot for himself in the Australian and, before long, international public consciousness, by completing one "impossible" stunt after another. He began with simple hot-air balloon expeditions, which, in truth, anyone with the requisite means and a rudimentary understanding of wind patterns could have done. Next, he graduated to single-engine flights. Then he moved on to more physically strenuous feats, like his barefoot trek across the Great Victoria, his sojourn through the heart of Africa, and his weeklong encampment atop Everest.

In the past few years, he'd been methodically rewriting the nautical chapter of *Guinness World Records*, because, like those airborne marks he'd cherry-picked early in his "career," sailing was more a matter of means and know-how than physical prowess. Now, two years shy of his fiftieth birthday, he was going through the motions but finding less pleasure in his adventures. It was an ennui he knew well, because he'd felt it at the end of his first act, when he'd decided to relinquish his grip on the television network. Soon, he would have to begin what he supposed would be the third and final act of his remarkable life, although he didn't have the slightest idea what it should entail. But first, he had to put an exclamation point on the second.

In these moments, he thought of himself as a magician whose magic required that he first mesmerize his audience with snazzy effects and expansive promises. And so, on a breezy afternoon in Halifax, Ferdinand Sevigny climbed the steps of a makeshift stage midway down a wharf and tapped two fingers to a microphone. He surveyed the crowd. There was Max Winters from NBC, and over there, Mary Engle from CNN. Right up front was Bennett Harris from Fox News. There were lesser lights, too, including a familiar face from the CBC, and several print and web journalists he recognized. Each had him to thank for their latest vacation, and would have him to thank for the trip to Morocco when he made news again in eight weeks. He wanted to give them a good show.

Sevigny began by reviewing the course the *Wind Dancer* would follow, pointing out—on a large map pinned to a flipchart—the obstacles it would encounter as it crossed the Atlantic without any crew except for its "fearless captain." Then he smiled, and said, "Now I will allow myself to be blindfolded, and blindfolded I shall remain until you see me again in Casablanca sometime between the eighth and tenth of August. You'll find a more-detailed rendering of my course in your press packets, as well as some particulars concerning the lengths to which I'll go to guide the *Wind Dancer* without my sense of sight. I'll aim for a midafternoon landing local time, but, considering my challenge, I know you'll forgive me if I run a bit late."

He gestured over his shoulder to where the *Wind Dancer* bobbed in the harbor. "It will be dark and lonely," he said, raising a hand to his chest as he lowered his voice, "but the light I have within will preserve me." As he delivered this line, two men who had been waiting beside the stage climbed the steps, one holding a black hood, the other holding a device that looked like a handgun. Sevigny allowed the hood to be drawn over his head so that only one large opening remained for his nose and mouth. There was another opening at the top through which a tuft of his silver hair protruded. The bottom of the mask hung straight down, extending four inches below his chin.

"As you can see," Sevigny said, "I can eat, breathe, and even comb my hair." He ran a hand through his tuft so that it stood in a more pronounced way, and then paused so his audience could laugh before continuing. "Of course," he resumed, "I could cheat easily enough." He raised one hand and used it to lift the mask so that his right eye suddenly peered through the breathing hole. He winked, eliciting another snicker from the reporters and cameramen. Then he pulled the mask back into place so that both eyes were again concealed and his mouth and nose fit snugly in the cutout. "And that is why," he said, "my second assistant will create an unbreakable seal." Sevigny raised both hands and tugged on two previously overlooked drawstrings woven into the bottom of the bleak contraption. When he pulled these, the bottom tightened beneath his chin. "As you can see," he said, holding the strings with one hand, while attempting in vain to move the opening to his eyes with the other, "once he does, I will be unable to cheat."

The second assistant stepped forward. "We will need the most honest person among you," the assistant said.

A voice from the crowd offered an impromptu endorsement of Bennett Harris, from Fox, but this suggestion was quickly met with a murmur of derision.

"He said the *most* honest," Sevigny said, joining in the fun.

"Mary Engle!" another voice called out, and when this nomination was met with approval, Mary blushed and handed her notepad to a colleague.

"Mary," Sevigny said, when the veteran reporter was standing on the stage, "my associate is going to clamp these braided aluminum drawstrings and heat them with a soldering gun so they will melt into the metal fastener." Then he paused before saying, "You'd better step back, Mary; there are going to be sparks." And indeed there were, as Mary and the crowd watched the assistant perform the task Sevigny had described, molding the drawstrings and fastener into one amalgam beneath the eccentric adventurer's chin.

"Now, Mary," Sevigny said when this was done, "you might wonder—what's to stop me from cutting off this blindfold at sea and affixing a fresh one after I've crossed the ocean, before I've made port? Well, Mary, I'll tell you what's going to stop me—you!"

"Me?" Mary said.

"That's right," Sevigny replied. "Don't worry; I'm not going to force you to come along. You see, Mary, you're going to sign your name over every inch of this hood, and over the clasp itself, so that if I cut any part of this mask you'll be able to detect a breach in one of your signatures. Putting on a fresh mask would require that I forge your signature a hundred times."

"You want me to sign my name—a hundred times—on this hood," Mary groaned, as Sevigny bowed.

"Well, maybe not a hundred," Sevigny said from where his head rested on the podium. "But as many as you can."

And thus the press conference concluded—or appeared to conclude—with the type of flourish befitting a typical Sevigny launch. The journalist signed her name all over Sevigny's mask with a glittery purple marker that showed up nicely on the black hood. She signed it thirty-seven times, until Sevigny had *Mary Engle* written over every inch of his noggin. When she was done, and when the laughter had subsided, Sevigny said, as dramatically as he could, "My lone companions will be the sea, the sun, and Mary Engle."

The journalists broke into polite applause.

Sevigny was about to depart the stage with the help of an assistant, when a voice piped up. "Wait just a minute," it said. Sevigny froze. It was a voice everyone recognized, that of the most jaded reporter on the Sevigny trail: Bennett Harris. Through the years Harris, who prided himself on his searing "gotcha journalism," had defined himself as no friend of Sevigny's, but now, when Sevigny heard his voice, his eyes twinkled behind his mask, even if his mouth betrayed no hint of a smile.

"Can you confirm or deny, Mr. Sevigny," Harris said, in his condescending drawl, "that although you will be blindfolded, you've outfitted

the *Wind Dancer* with a state-of-the-art voice-activated satellite position-
ing system that will make navigating a breeze?"

Sevigny paused, and again willfully suppressed a smile. "Well, I
wouldn't call it a breeze," he replied. "For that, I'll still need the wind."
He paused again for appreciative snickers from the crowd. "It is true my
efforts will be aided by the new Windetron 2000, scheduled for release
next month by Motorola. The Windetron speaks forty-seven languages,
runs on solar power, and is capable of guiding vessels as large as two hundred feet long around underwater obstacles, ominous weather patterns,
and foreboding currents. And it does all that while fitting in the palm of
your hand."

Sevigny reached into his pocket and extracted the small device. He
held it up for all to see. "It's going to revolutionize the dry-shipping
industry," he said. "If you want to make sure your freight arrives on time,
why not back up your captain with this invaluable safeguard against all
those things that can go wrong at sea? Again, that's the Windetron
2000, available the first of August from Motorola."

The crowd chuckled again. Such endorsements were not uncommon
to Sevigny's act. Once, he'd subsisted exclusively on Smart-Harvest granola bars during a two-week balloon ride. Another time, he'd shilled for
Speedo during a treacherous swim. Once, he'd picked a backpack full of
green coffee beans for a Starbucks blend called "Sevigny's Roast" during a
rain-forest hike. Now he'd obviously signed an endorsement deal with
Motorola. And Harris, who had been "tipped off" ahead of time, had
played right into his hands.

"The *Wind Dancer* raises sail in an hour," Sevigny said with a laugh.
"I'll *see* you next in Casablanca."

Chapter Twenty-Two

Another Departure

A few hours later, Marisol and Rupert departed from Yarmouth Harbor in a sleek vessel Rupert had purchased, registered, and moored a month earlier, using an assumed name. The speedy craft would catch the *Wind Dancer* in no time.

As the boat sliced through the placid bay and the small Canadian village slowly disappeared beneath a crimson sky, Marisol stood at the stern and shivered. Inside, Rupert sat with one eye on a tacking screen and the other on a copy of *Cigar Aficionado*. He was reading about the stogie preferences of the world's fifty richest people, on which list, he had learned, his uncle had slipped all the way to forty-third. Sevigny was frittering away the family fortune, and it seemed everywhere Rupert turned he saw further evidence of his profligacy. When Marisol stepped into the cabin, Rupert spoke without looking up, in a tone that seemed discordant with the scowl on his face.

"Puerto Escondido is lovely this time of year," he said.

"It'll certainly be warmer than it is here," she replied, bringing her arms in tight.

"It's hotter than hell," Rupert said. "You'll feel right at home."

Marisol forced a smile and replied, "You'll wait until midnight?"

"Midnight," he repeated, tapping his wristwatch.

"If I flash twice, he's sleeping," she said. "Any more means he's awake."

"That would ruin everything," Rupert said. "Just wait until he's asleep. If I have to sit there an hour longer, I'll sit there."

"No—midnight," Marisol said. "He'll be asleep. If not, we call it off."

"Call it off?" Rupert barked, as if the suggestion were lunacy. "I have ten grand, plane tickets, passports." He gestured to the small carry-on bag at his feet.

"Listen—" Marisol said, uneasily.

"What?" Rupert sneered. "Did he say something?"

"No," Marisol lied. "It's just—you're sure Warren doesn't suspect anything?"

Warren Masters was Sevigny's friend and lawyer. Marisol had rightly guessed that Warren had been the one who had alerted Sevigny to Rupert's embezzlement. Now, she wondered if he'd also found out about the house in Escondido and told Sevigny about that as well.

"He's as blind as my uncle," Rupert scowled.

Marisol did not reply.

"Relax," he said. Then he lowered his eyes to the magazine. "Go write in your journal or something."

Marisol sat down a few feet from him. Her mind was soon far away.

She wasn't sure if she'd be able to follow through with it, but somehow, she had to. She could be free—free of Sevigny, free of his lecherous nephew. It had seemed so simple a month ago. Rupert would bring her to the *Wind Dancer* as planned and then speed off. She and Sevigny would spend one last night together. Meanwhile, instead of returning to port, Rupert would double back to where the *Wind Dancer* sat anchored for the night. At midnight, she would sneak from Sevigny's bed, scatter evidence of her presence on the deck, and quietly slip into the ocean. She would swim to Rupert's little boat. She would leave Sevigny asleep upon the sea. He would awake the next morning to find her things on deck, think she'd ventured out to pass a sleepless hour, and had somehow fallen overboard.

She and Rupert would be in the sky by the time Sevigny noticed her absence, flying from Halifax International to Mexico City. There, they would rent a car and drive to Puerto Escondido, where the money Rupert had squirreled away was waiting for them. She would take her share and inform Rupert that his fantasy—that they'd remain together—was just that: a fantasy. He could have the house. She'd take half the money and start a new life in a new place that sounded almost as beautiful as Little Tobago. Rupert would have no way of stopping her, and Sevigny would have no way of finding her.

Marisol did not know if Sevigny would finish his voyage or if he would radio for help and admit he'd smuggled a companion along with him on this trip. She did not relish the idea of him stumbling about the deck, calling her name, before eventually accepting that she was gone.

She had fewer pangs of conscience when it came to Rupert. She knew he was only helping her to cause his uncle pain. She was glad the bond between them would soon be broken. She only hoped Sevigny had indeed taken measures to protect himself, as he'd said, because it was true: Rupert could not be trusted.

Chapter Twenty-Three

Good-Night Kiss

After welcoming his young mistress aboard the *Wind Dancer* and discharging his nephew, Sevigny led Marisol from stern to bow, showing the ease with which he was already moving about the deck. Then he led her downstairs and told her to sit. He fetched a diet soda and a bowl of cherries and joined her in the little room.

Only then did he resent his blindness. He'd kept the ship on course, or close to it, by tacking into a southerly wind. He'd bumped his knee on the mast-mount, and at one point had struggled to locate a rigging line that had danced in the air for several minutes. But he'd done well enough. He was glad he'd decided not to cheat—to wear the blindfold from port to port.

Now, he could smell Marisol's perfume and hear her movements on the sofa across from him, but he could not see her. As they made small talk, he tried to form a mental picture, but found the exercise both distracting and upsetting. It seemed he had grown so accustomed to a look of disaffection on her face that he could now envision her no other way. He could not remember when this blank stare had replaced the wonder with which her dark features had greeted the world he'd opened to her. Try as he might, he could envision only a vacant gaze, flat mouth, and forlorn brow. Strangely, imagining her this way was far more jarring than actually seeing her in such a state had ever been.

"Are you happy, Marisol?" he asked.

The boat listed slightly.

"Of course," she answered. Then she sighed and asked, "What's it like, not being able to see?"

"It's strange," he said. "In a way I feel less encumbered. I feel like those people who float over the operating room while the surgeon tries to restart their heart, when they describe the operation afterward. They say, '*That* nurse handed him the scalpel, and then *that* assistant said I was gone. But then the monitor showed a blip, and I wasn't finished after all.' They recall the entire sequence, even though they were unconscious. They say it was like looking down on the room. To me, it's like I'm watching myself from above."

"You handled the stairs pretty well," she noted.

"It's more difficult going up," he replied.

"Oh," she said.

The boat listed again, and as if roused by the sensation, Sevigny steered the conversation into more substantive territory. "Rupert hasn't found out yet," Sevigny said, "but I have changed my will. He will be very displeased. He'll know by the time we reach Morocco."

Marisol said nothing.

He again regretted his blindness. "I have done this to protect myself," he continued. "Hopefully when he finds out, he will take his stolen money and go away. But if he doesn't, I want you to pay close attention to anything he says."

"Sevigny," she said, "he wouldn't tell me—"

"Marisol," he said sternly.

"When he speaks of you, it is kindly," she persisted. Then, reconsidering, she added, "It is only when the family secret comes up that he speaks bitterly. It has always tormented him."

"Marisol," he said more sharply. At that moment, Ferdinand Sevigny made a decision he'd scarcely known he would make when the night had begun. In his blindness, he had gained clarity. He saw all at once that there was only one thing to do.

"Marisol," he said, "go to the drawer on the nightstand."

He heard her rise and then the drawer slide open. He smelled her perfume again as she returned and lowered herself to the sofa.

"It's a jewelry box," she said.

"The clasp sticks," he said, "but it isn't locked. Push down and then lift."

He waited and listened, then heard her say, "Sevigny," with an air of astonishment that almost made him regret the decision he'd just made.

"It was going to be an engagement ring," he said, forcing an uncharacteristic smile. "I've been carrying it around with me for four months.

But I've realized something: Let's enjoy one last adventure together, and then I will take you home. I want you to keep it as a memento of our time together. Or, if you want, you can give it to your father to trade to the Brazilians who pass by the island."

"Sevigny," she whispered.

"It will fetch a lot," he said. "Perhaps enough to buy your mother's forgiveness."

"Sevigny," she said, standing.

"You were young when I took you," he continued. "I gave in to a side of human nature I shouldn't have. Maybe it was loneliness, maybe something worse . . ."

He heard her fall back onto the sofa.

"Tell me you're unhappy," he said.

"But—" she began.

"It's true," he insisted. "And I want to hear you say it."

There was a long delay, during which he heard her close the lid of the little wooden box. "I have not been happy," she said finally.

"I know," he replied. "Let's enjoy one last adventure, and then I'll bring you home."

Her heavy breathing gradually subsided, until she was only sighing.

"Come," he said. "Kiss me good-night."

Chapter Twenty-Four

Betrayal

What if the weight of my body rising from the bed should wake him? What if the stairs creak beneath my feet? What if his talking navigational aid comes alive at the approach of Rupert's boat or the scent of my desertion?

Marisol entertained these misgivings, and others, but before she knew it, she had slipped from bed, retrieved the bag she'd packed with items to scatter on deck, and taken three steps on the stairs. She paused on the fourth, waiting to hear Sevigny exhale. Then, she continued on her way.

On deck, she drew several short breaths of salty air. Then she tiptoed to the side bench where she often sat, and placed the items intended to suggest her presence. She took special care to arrange her iPod exactly where she might have placed it on the bench if she'd stood up abruptly, to bunch her sweatshirt how she might have done, to cushion her back, and to place each additional item in just the way she wished.

Then she did something she was loath to do, but understood was necessary. She took her journal, the one she'd been writing and drawing in for the past six months, and tossed it overboard. She did not want Sevigny to read her innermost thoughts. She'd been careful not to write anything too condemning of him, or Rupert, for fear that either would unzip the little case one day. But she had written enough, and when words had proven insufficient, she had expressed her feelings in sketches. She watched the leather book disappear in the water and then reemerge as the air zipped inside brought it back to the surface.

Next, she squinted into the fog and tried to locate Rupert's little boat. The sky was dark except for a hint of moon radiating through the clouds. In the fog and dim light, she could not spot her means of escape. She wondered whether Rupert, wherever he was, would see her signal. She wondered if she would see his. Removing the flashlight from her robe, she bid the *Wind Dancer* farewell, not knowing exactly where the next chapter of her life would take her, but hoping it would be a brighter place than the one she was leaving.

She held the light over her head, faced starboard, and flashed it. She waited, and then flashed it again. Without delay, she saw the return signal. The lights on the little boat were brighter than she'd imagined, and mounted up high. They were blue and red, and attached to the radio pole. She found it reassuring to think that should she stray off course in the water, such high lights would be easy to see.

She slipped out of her robe, stepped onto the ladder, and slipped into the churning ocean. But the instant she felt the frigid water against her skin, she thought she heard Sevigny's voice, calling her name. She submerged and propelled her body beneath the swells in the quietest, quickest way she knew to swim. After ten underwater strokes, she raised her head and opened her eyes, and although she could not locate Rupert's boat, she inhaled and then plunged immediately back under, scissoring her legs and drawing back her arms as forcefully as she could.

When Marisol surfaced a second time, she heard a voice calling her name; it wasn't her imagination. In that instant, she could not decide whether it was Sevigny's or Rupert's. Then, before she could submerge again, the blue and red lights of the speedboat flashed, and she realized it had to be Sevigny calling her. Rupert's boat was still too far away for such a clear voice to have emanated from its deck. In fact, the lights appeared farther from her now than when she'd first entered the cold water.

When she next broke the surface, Marisol did not dare linger. Sometimes she would see the glare of Rupert's lights, other times she would not. Always, they seemed farther away than when she'd last seen them. Finally, she heard the hum of the motor and realized the lights were growing closer. Rupert was coming to retrieve her. Sucking air and treading water, she turned to locate the *Wind Dancer*, which had disappeared into the fog. She had swum far but had still not gotten very close to the getaway boat. Now it was coming, though, and Sevigny, on the foggy deck, would hear it. She didn't care anymore. She was ice-cold and tired.

Marisol waved both hands so Rupert would see her. But as the flashes drew nearer and the engine louder, the boat showed no signs of slowing. It was coming closer. And closer. The engine roared. The water at the surface churned. And at the very last instant Marisol reacted. She took a halting breath and burrowed as quickly and desperately as she could. When the *whoosh* of the hull and whirl of the propeller ripped through the water where she'd just been bobbing, she was deep below the surface.

A moment later when she came up, gasping for air, Marisol realized Rupert's boat was cutting its engine, finally, but only as it pulled astride the *Wind Dancer*. Sevigny's ship had become visible again in the flashing pulses of blue and red. She started to swim back toward the two boats, but after only a few strokes, she realized she was caught, and had been all along, in the grip of a current. She had been swimming with it; that's why she had traveled so far from the *Wind Dancer*, only not so far as Rupert's boat, which must have been drifting too. She didn't know why Rupert had not stopped for her. She didn't know why he had not seen her. She shuddered to imagine what he had in store for his uncle as he boarded Sevigny's vessel.

"Sevigny," she called. "Sevigny!" She wanted to say more, to warn him, but she couldn't muster the breath; the water was so cold.

Maybe Rupert wanted to shame him, to mock him with the news of their scheme. Or maybe he wanted to hurt him physically. She wondered if Rupert were capable of that—or worse.

Then, she entertained an even more horrifying thought: She wondered if Rupert had lured her as far from the *Wind Dancer* as she could swim and left her to drown. She wondered if he'd steered directly at her not because he'd failed to see her, but because he'd meant to kill her. It occurred to her at that moment that she was going to die. As the current carried her away, she watched the outline of the two boats fade into one rough shadow and then, finally, disappear.

Chapter Twenty-Five

Wind Dancer

After calling Marisol's name a third time, Ferdinand Sevigny sat up in bed. He lamented his blindness, his wariness, and his paranoia. These latter two characteristics, he knew, were what had driven the wedge between him and Marisol in the first place. He forced himself to wait. He counted to ten while listening carefully for any sound of her. Perhaps she'd just wanted some fresh air. She'd needed a moment of private reflection to sort out the conversation they'd had before going to bed. That was all.

When he reached ten, Sevigny started over. This time, he counted to twenty. Then, unable to stifle his curiosity any longer, he reached out a hand for his Windetron 2000. Finding it on the nightstand, he pressed a button and waited for it to receive the satellite signal. Three seconds later, a female voice announced, "Latitude: 43.5 degrees. Longitude: 70.25 degrees. Ocean depth: 51 meters. Nearest land: Bluff Island, 0.8 kilometers northeast. Nearest shore: United States, Maine, 2.1 kilometers east. Nearest vessel: 140 meters, east."

At this final disclosure—another boat *that* near—Sevigny burst out of bed. He was on the stairs and halfway up when, in his blindness, he missed a step. He fell hard, hitting his head as he tumbled. He blacked out before regaining consciousness to the feel of blood trickling into his eyes beneath his mask. In this second waking moment, he pawed at his blindfold, tugging violently at the fastener Mary Engle had signed. But it was no use. If only he had some sharp tool to cut it and free his eyes.

There should not have been another boat so close, yet there was, in the dead of night. He'd fended off pirates in the Indian Ocean, and though he couldn't imagine this visitor being of the same malevolent ilk, the thought did enter his mind. More likely, some paparazzo had followed him, which was not altogether a bad thing, but would be if the bloke spotted Marisol on board. It would shatter the illusion that he was alone.

He rose to his feet, and, grasping the rail, felt his way up the stairs. Upon reaching the deck, he hoped he might see through her eyes whatever boat lurked so precariously near. But she did not answer, even as his calls grew louder. Finally, he heard the drum of the other boat's engine, which he recognized immediately as the outboard of a small craft. His mind worked frantically to process the information available to him. A paparazzo so late at night didn't make sense. A slumbering boat wasn't photogenic. Pirates seemed impossible off the coast of friendly New England. Marisol wasn't answering. The motor sounded just like the one he'd heard two hours before. A picture formed in Sevigny's mind just as the engine cut out.

"Rupert," he called. "That you?" His warm voice covered, only slightly, his alarm. He tugged hopelessly at the mask, tried to pry his fingers between it and his beard, and then felt his way to the captain's chair beneath which there was a cabinet that contained some small tools he liked to have handy. He groped for something sharp. "Marisol!" he called. "Marisol!"

"She can't hear you," Rupert's voice finally said.

"You," Sevigny said.

"Put down the scissors, Uncle," Rupert said. "They'll do you no good."

Sevigny held, in fact, a set of rigging pins, which he obediently let drop, one, and then the other, so that they made two tinny clanks against the deck.

"Where is Marisol?" Sevigny demanded.

"Marisol has betrayed you," Rupert said, laughing.

"Is that so?" Sevigny said. "And you?"

"Me?" Rupert laughed. "I've been betrayed by *you*—by this provision you've had Warren insert in your will. What do you call it, 'the catastrophe clause'? Or are you even more overt? 'The untrustworthy nephew clause'?"

Indeed, Sevigny had instructed his lawyer to modify his will so that should he die of anything but natural causes, Rupert would receive no part of his vast fortune. And even if he died naturally, Rupert would gain only a small fraction of the sum a billionaire's sole living relative would normally inherit.

"Where is Marisol?" Sevigny demanded.

"I told you—she has betrayed you," Rupert scoffed.

"Marisol!" Sevigny bellowed. "Say something so I know you're okay."

There was only the sound of waves lapping against the side of the yacht.

"You're making a big mistake," Sevigny said, and he reached out two flailing hands in an effort to grab the younger man. But he came up with air, lost his balance, and fell to the deck.

"Pathetic," Rupert chided. He stepped forward and kicked his uncle in the midsection.

The famous adventurer clutched his side in pain, but managed to lift himself to his hands and knees. "You're going to regret this," he snarled. He lunged blindly for Rupert's legs, but missed. "You won't get away with it," he said.

"I've already gotten away with it," Rupert teased, dancing around him, and stepping forward to deliver another swift kick to his uncle's stomach.

Sevigny coughed and wheezed for air. He spit. "My will's already been changed," he said softly.

"I know," Rupert said. "That's why I'm doing this."

"Rupert," Sevigny said, between gasps, "help me take this mask off. We'll talk about it like men, like two headstrong Sevigny males. Conflict, distrust—they're in our blood. Perhaps I acted hastily. Perhaps I should have come to you. But it was Warren; he turned us against each other. He told me you were embezzling. He told me you were working toward some secret aim. If I acted hastily, if I was wrong—"

Rupert kicked him again, only not as hard as the previous times. He laughed. "No, you were quite right," he said matter-of-factly. He smiled the smile of the matador in the moment after the bull has been disabled but before he's decided to finish it. "It's all true."

"Wasn't I kind to you?" Sevigny pleaded.

"Too kind," his nephew snarled. "You pitied me."

"Pitied you?"

"I stole from you," Rupert said. "And Marisol was more mine than yours—the whiny bitch."

"Rupert, what have you done?" Sevigny cried with horror. He struggled back onto his hands and knees. "Marisol!" he called. "Marisol!"

"It seems you'll die by a relative's hand after all, Uncle," Rupert said. "I believe that's what you call a self-fulfilling prophecy."

"You won't kill me," Sevigny said.

"I will," Rupert said. "And even if I don't inherit my grandfather's fortune, I'll still live comfortably. This is what you get for making me grovel for what was rightfully mine, or half mine, all along. You made me an errand boy, just so I might *earn* what should have been my father's in the first place. You pitied me, even as you were my oppressor. And now I have no pity for you." The young man unleashed another kick, the hardest yet, only this time his foot struck the older man squarely in the side of the head. The blow left Sevigny facedown on the deck, breathing in short gasps.

"Tell me before you die," Rupert said. "Tell me so the elephant in the room that has always lingered between us may die, too. What did my father do to deserve the early grave you and your father drove him to? And what did *that* have to do with me? Why was I destined to bear the sins—if there were any—of my father?"

It was true; the uncle and nephew had never spoken of the circumstances that had excluded Rupert's father, Sevigny's brother, from the old mogul's graces. And from the day Rupert was born, his father, Robinson, had steadfastly refused to discuss these matters with his son. Growing up, Rupert had known only that his father lived amid a crushing weight of self-loathing. It was not until Rupert's adolescence that he had come to understand that although he had a name known across a continent, he had no claim to any crown.

Years later, in his early adulthood, his uncle had reached out to him, but only after his father and grandfather had passed away. Uncle Ferdinand had expected him to be grateful. He had offered him a pittance of what might have been his to begin with, and in return expected him to worship at his feet. Now, Rupert was setting things right, taking back what had been stolen from him. But first he wanted to know why it had been taken in the first place.

"Tell me," Rupert demanded. "What did my father do?"

Sevigny glared at him from behind his mask but said nothing.

"Have it your way," Rupert said. "Take your secret to the bottom of the sea." And like the matador lifting the blade to the bull's throat, he reached down and grabbed Sevigny and hoisted him to his feet.

The older man staggered before arriving at an unsteady equilibrium. Then, despite his blindness, despite the wound on his forehead, despite the blows dealt to his body, he rose to his full height so that he stood, a proud man before his fuming assailant.

"Foolish boy," he said. "Foolish . . . angry . . . full of hate." He raised his fists and forearms in front of his chest—not in a defensive posture, but as if he had suddenly regained his sight and was about to strike his tormentor. And despite his utter vulnerability—for he *was* still blind—something almost tangible emanated from within Sevigny, something more than just his stature, more than just his words, and more than just the voice he used to speak those words. There was something else that gave Rupert pause: an indomitability of spirit that seemed so incongruous with Sevigny's present predicament, it made Rupert wonder, if only for an instant, whether there wasn't some part of the picture he was failing to see.

Then Rupert saw it, as the moon broke through the clouds. He saw the slightest shimmer in one of his uncle's fists and realized that Sevigny had found and brought with him when he'd risen one of the rigging pins he'd dropped on the deck a few moments before. Instinctively, Rupert recoiled, even though the man before him was blind, in pajamas, and badly wounded—even though the weapon he held was only four inches long. And in that instant when Rupert flinched, the great Sevigny, the fearless Sevigny—who'd skirted death, or at least sidled up beside it many times before—took three quick steps to the side until he felt the smack of the gunwale against his stomach, and dived headfirst into the sea.

By the time Rupert reached the railing, all he saw were rapidly dispersing ripples where his uncle had broken through. Then a rolling swell lifted the boat, and when it had passed, even the ripples had disappeared.

Chapter Twenty-Six

A Scoundrel's Consternation

Rupert had planned to swing the boom of the forward mast into his uncle's head to deliver the fatal wound. Perhaps the blow would have sent Sevigny overboard. If it hadn't, Rupert had planned to help him the rest of the way. If Sevigny's corpse washed ashore, he would be deemed the victim of an accident—the type that might befall a man so consumed with hubris as to set out on a sightless sea voyage. Or perhaps he would simply drift into whatever dark realm claims those souls lost at sea. It didn't matter. Rupert planned to be touching down in Mexico City by the time anyone realized Sevigny was missing from the *Wind Dancer*'s helm.

That was how things were supposed to happen. But his uncle had deviated from the script, and now Rupert was worried. On the one hand, he knew Sevigny was a capable swimmer. On the other, he knew he was injured and blindfolded. It seemed likely Sevigny would swim in circles until he drowned, which would be just as good as if Rupert *had* struck him with the boom. But Rupert worried about another possibility, too, however slight it seemed. He worried that Sevigny would somehow manage to reach shore and would return to haunt him.

Peering into the sea, Rupert touched the pistol on his belt. If he could only spot him, he could put a bullet in his head. But even in his rage, Rupert recognized that such an action would be imprudent. It was one thing to strike a young woman with the hull of a boat, knowing that no one would ever step forward to identify her body. It was another thing altogether to murder a celebrity and provoke a high-profile investigation. An errant mast boom said "accident," whereas a bullet said "murder."

Rupert stomped over to the *Wind Dancer*'s control box and flipped on the floodlights. There were seven bulbs mounted on the masts, angled to illuminate the deck and the water surrounding it. As they brightened, Rupert went from rail to rail, peering overboard.

"Uncle," he called, feigning a change of heart. "Uncle, where are you?" But even with the lights glowing brightly, there was no sign of Sevigny.

The current is strong, Rupert thought. *He's probably already floated into the fog.* "Uncle!" he cried. He retraced his steps. *Okay, chap, take a few deep breaths*, he told himself. *You can still come out of this okay. Even if he survives, he'll never find you in Mexico.*

It was true. Rupert had been meticulous in leaving no paper trail when he'd bought the house and made travel plans. He'd told no one but Marisol. He still had his passport—and Marisol's, for that matter—on the little boat. And he had a satchel of cash. He'd been denied the pleasure of finishing off Sevigny, but that was all. His own escape was still assured.

He pulled the lever to raise the anchor, and as the mechanical clank of the pulley wound the chain, he cursed his uncle and the darkness. Although his future was intact, he'd wanted more. He'd wanted a drop of blood for every time Sevigny had condescended to help him, for every time he had handed him a fraction of the sum that should have been his in the first place. He'd wanted restitution for every time Sevigny had forced him to humbly thank him, nod approvingly, or chuckle amiably.

When the anchor had come up, swinging and dripping with sea mud, Rupert began raising the sails. One at a time he sent them into the dark sky. There wasn't the slightest hint of a breeze, but the *Wind Dancer* would catch sail in the morning and drift to wherever the wind desired, leaving its captain far behind. Rupert smiled at the thought. It would have been better the other way—to deliver the final blow. He loosened the forward boom so that it might swing unpredictably and be deemed the instrument of his uncle's demise. Then he shut off the lights.

He turned toward the stern to where he'd tethered the smaller boat, and as he did, his rage overpowered his better judgment. *To hell with it*, he thought. He would climb aboard the little speeder and follow the current. If he found his uncle, he would beat him to death with an oar. It was more overt than a swinging boom, but would at least leave more room for inter-pretation than a bullet. With each step Rupert took along the deck, his resolve grew. He wanted to finish him. He *needed* to, for all those slights.

Then, as Rupert waded through the fog, his already-compromised caper became a full-fledged debacle. He noticed with a start that the smaller boat, his means of escape, had become detached. Its shadow bobbed on the waves, already a fair distance away.

No, he thought. *It isn't possible.*

He took up the rope he'd affixed to the *Wind Dancer*'s rail and began tugging at it frantically. He pulled and pulled, until he had brought the limp tether entirely aboard. He held its wet end dangling in his hands. And all at once, Rupert heard, or thought he heard, the other boat's motor turn. He could not be sure, but he thought he heard it against the sounds of the waves gently lifting the yacht, just before the smaller boat disappeared into the fog.

Chapter Twenty-Seven

Clearing the Deck

Rupert scoured the deck for Marisol's belongings and threw every last one overboard. If his uncle had indeed made it to the smaller boat, Rupert didn't think he'd radio for help, as doing so would compromise the reputation he so cherished. It would mean admitting he was vulnerable, just like everyone else. And more than that, it would mean confessing that he'd brought someone along on his latest "solo" adventure. In all likelihood, Sevigny would loop back with the little boat to reclaim his yacht. Then again, there was the chance that Sevigny's wounds would slow him down, or that his mask would prove more difficult to remove than Rupert imagined.

There was also the chance Sevigny would not return at all, and if that were the case, Rupert didn't want whoever boarded the yacht next to find evidence of a female passenger who'd only recently been aboard the *Wind Dancer*. He didn't want there to be any evidence to connect his uncle's ship to the female body floating in the current.

When he'd left Marisol in the water, he'd assumed Sevigny would soon be floating, too. He'd assumed the revelation that Sevigny had had company would posthumously expose him as the fraud he was. But if Sevigny survived, Rupert understood the need to protect his secret. If the authorities found the *Wind Dancer* and asked Sevigny what had happened, Rupert wanted to leave his uncle all the wiggle room he needed to craft a graceful explanation. He wanted to make it as easy as possible for his uncle to say he'd merely suffered a careless accident. Sevigny would want revenge—of that, Rupert was sure—but on his own terms. Sevigny would do everything in his power to avoid public humiliation, and by so doing he would ensure that Rupert never faced a murder charge for Marisol.

After throwing Marisol's iPod, robe, flashlight, and sweatshirt into the sea, Rupert went below and emptied the bathroom and pantry of anything that suggested a woman's presence. He carried these items up on deck and dumped them overboard. Then he returned to the set of drawers he'd covertly filled with Marisol's clothes just the day before in Halifax, when he'd still been acting as an agent of Sevigny's will. Rupert pulled the top drawer halfway out and with a broad sweep of his forearm, cleared the dresser's top of Marisol's barrettes, lotions, makeup, and necklaces. Among these items was a peculiar box Rupert had never seen before, with the initials M. S. engraved on its top.

Next, he completely removed the two lower drawers. Then, he pulled the brimming top one all the way out so that it sat upon the others. Finally, he hoisted all three and awkwardly maneuvered them up the stairs. He noticed the little box again, sitting just beneath his chin, and resolved to open it when he reached the deck. Rupert merely wanted to mock whatever trinket of his uncle's affection for the sad-eyed girl resided within.

It hadn't yet occurred to him that Marisol's last name began with a "P," not an "S," and that by pairing an "M" with an "S," the box hinted at an engagement ring. It hadn't occurred to him that despite the loss of the speedboat, and the satchel of cash and travel documents aboard it, such a ring might provide enough money in hock to fund his flight to Mexico. Rupert realized all this just a moment too late. He realized it only after he'd dumped the contents of all three drawers into the water and had spotted the little box bobbing amid Marisol's clothes. In his haste, he'd forgotten his curiosity about the box in the thirty seconds it had taken him to carry the drawers up the stairs. Now, it was drifting off into the night, destined to disappear into the deep waters off the coast, never to be seen again. He cursed his carelessness.

After purging the *Wind Dancer* of the other clues that Marisol had been aboard, Rupert unhitched one of the lifeboats and pulled the cord to inflate it. He jumped into the cold water and climbed aboard, hoping all the while that his uncle would be the next person to set foot on the *Wind Dancer*'s deck, hoping that Sevigny would double back and resume his trip, buying time for Rupert to get from Maine to Mexico. It would be more difficult without the papers and travel money, but at least his trail would be cold by the time Sevigny took it up to hunt for him.

On the other hand, if the authorities found the *Wind Dancer* first, Rupert didn't see any way they could connect him to what had happened on its deck, or to the woman whose body might or might not ever be found. He fixed the lifeboat's compass for west, flipped the switch on the little electric engine, and plodded ahead, with even more hatred in his heart than when the dark night had begun.

Chapter Twenty-Eight

Cold, Dark Penance

Marisol had known all along that her conspiring with Rupert would leave Sevigny emotionally wounded, but she'd never intended for him to suffer physical harm. Now, languishing in the cold water, she realized just how severely she'd underestimated Rupert. The last thing she'd heard as she'd drifted away was the splash of a body. She shivered at the thought of what Rupert might have done.

Rupert had been reconciled with and taken in by his uncle at about the same time Marisol had entered Sevigny's life. She'd observed a secret loathing in the younger man, but had never envisioned it culminating in murder. It had started, understandably enough—or so she'd thought, for it was in her own heart, too—as legitimate resentment toward the man who was their benefactor. But by degrees it had grown in Rupert into something that far exceeded her own inner turmoil.

"He's a child," Rupert would fume. "A child who's always gotten his way. A child, treated like a king—all because he has my grandfather's money." Marisol could agree with the first part. She could see how Sevigny's wealth had opened to him a world of opportunity. But she did not know if Rupert's gripe concerning the family legacy was also legitimate. She didn't need to know; that grudge was Rupert's, not hers.

Over time, the anger that had initially boiled to Rupert's surface in the form of snide insinuations metastasized into more virulent outbursts. "He's a tyrant," Rupert would smolder. "A tyrant who loves only himself—only the name he's built and the image he's constructed." Once Marisol had demonstrated some tolerance for Rupert's rancor, he had granted her greater access to its depths.

Somewhere along the arc of Rupert's decline, she had entered into a league with him, seeking relief from a life she'd entered too abruptly and at too young an age. Rupert had been her tutor, her concierge, her valet, her companion during long stretches when Sevigny was away. She had identified with him as a fellow wounded soul similarly dependent upon the imposing man, who *was* kind and generous, but could also be possessive, suspicious, and so accustomed to having his way that he was blind to others' happiness. *It was not Sevigny's fault*, Marisol thought. *It was just the way he was.*

Sevigny *had* been kind to her; he had bought her whatever she'd wanted. But he'd also kept her cloistered away. He'd demanded nothing of her, which in its way had been demeaning. In Rupert's case, his grudge always came back to the historic wrong that he believed had been done to his father. When he first told Marisol of the mystery that had hung over his existence for as long as he could remember, she had pitied him. She had encouraged him to ask Sevigny in some private moment for greater disclosure of the apparently scandalous details by which Rupert's short branch of the family tree had been sawed off from the trunk.

She had thought that if Rupert would only explain how consumed he was by curiosity and frustration, Sevigny would certainly agree to shed some light on the mystery, so that they might move past it together. But Rupert had practically flown into a rage when Marisol suggested this, telling her that she did not understand, that his father had taken his shame to his grave—that his grandfather, whom he'd tried to visit only once, in his old age, had left him standing outside the iron gates of his estate after sending a servant to inform him he was unwelcome.

Finally, Marisol had approached Sevigny herself, without the younger man's knowledge. She had asked him to explain the particulars of how the family had come to be estranged so long ago. But just as Rupert had suggested he would, Sevigny had refused to shine any light into that dark corner of the family's history. "That is a question," he'd told her, "that I would prefer you not ask again." As always with Sevigny, there had been no opportunity for debate.

Now, as Marisol floated in the cold, unforgiving sea and wondered for perhaps the final time about the murky convergence of genes and shared past that had united—and at the same time, divided—the two men with whom she'd shared the past six years, she reflected on how badly she'd misjudged Rupert. She had viewed him as something of a foil to his meticulously polished uncle, a crude but convenient ally whom she could mislead to facilitate her escape. Rupert's own disloyalty had seemed to justify that sort of exploitation. Now, ironically, he had repaid her in kind.

In this desperate, lonely moment, the realization of what she'd done—not so unwittingly—struck Marisol. She felt as though she deserved the fate that had been assigned to her. And in this hopeless state, she began to cry out, uttering Sevigny's name over and over again. She was under no illusion that he might hear her, or even if he did, that he would be in a position to help her. She cried his name mournfully, as if doing so might earn her some small amount of grace and mercy. She cried out to her own conscience, as her quivering limbs struggled to keep her head above the swells. "Sevigny!" she called. "Sevigny!" Numbness and hypothermia crept closer and closer. "Sevigny!" She flailed and sobbed and begged for forgiveness. "Sevigny!"

In the darkness and fog, Marisol scarcely imagined that the current had drawn her so close to land. She did not know that her salvation was already at hand, and in the water, swimming toward her with quiet resolve.

Chapter Twenty-Nine

Kindred Spirits

As Marisol's plaintive call lured Roger Simons into the water, Rupert was piloting the *Wind Dancer*'s lifeboat to shore two miles south. The ever-thickening fog had obscured the final portion of his journey, penetrated only by the bright lights tracing the contours of the Ferris wheel beside the Pier. Palace Playland wouldn't open for another week, but the rides had been tuned up and turned on just that day, and would remain illuminated until the chill winds of September blew. With no idea what they were, Rupert steered toward these massive glowing shapes.

After the breakers knocked him out of the lifeboat, he waded through waist-deep water with the inflatable vessel in tow, and then, after a wave sent it surging ahead, he followed it the rest of the way. He dragged the craft onto the sand, detached its small motor, and popped the plug to deflate it. Shivering, dripping, and trying to subdue the panic in his chest, he folded the boat into a small plastic mat, carried it into the dunes, and found a low spot between two rises. He dropped the mass and kicked a layer of sand over it. Then he kicked the ground more forcefully until he'd created a crater for the motor. He dropped it in and piled some sand on top.

Having thus concealed the means of his arrival, he turned his thoughts to finding a place to regroup and a way to sustain himself until he learned his uncle's fate. Word would spread quickly if people discovered that his blindfolded quest had ended in failure, or if he turned up injured. In the meantime, Rupert would have to raise some money. He would have to find a path to Mexico, to Escondido, where the house and 12 million pesos were waiting.

As a small breeze kicked up and began to disperse the fog, Rupert took comfort in the thought that it might soon carry his uncle away.

Sevigny would not stop to hunt for him; nor would he allow the loss of the girl to detain him. He would return to his boat and finish what he'd started. Only then would he come after his nephew, and by that time, Rupert thought, he would be far away.

In the shadows of the glowing amusement park, Rupert could make out the faint outline of a deserted plaza at the foot of the long wooden Pier. He was about to set out in search of shelter, when, suddenly, he felt the wind being sucked from his lungs. There was a dark figure walking on the beach. A man was coming toward him. *It's Sevigny*, Rupert thought. In that moment, Rupert knew genuine horror. After a few seconds, though, he realized the person coming toward him was too diminutive to be his barrel-chested uncle. Watching from the dune grass into which he'd instinctively dropped, Rupert saw a teenager drawing near. It was Billy Carter, he'd learn, who had come to curse the moon.

As the boy delivered his tirade, Rupert rightly or wrongly identified a kindred spirit. Accepting the opportunity the beach gods had tossed his way, he stood and addressed the quivering youth. When Rupert promised Billy escape in exchange for help and trust, Billy agreed. When Rupert asked for a secluded place, Billy said he would lead him to one. When Rupert asked for clothes and food, Billy said he could deliver both. And when Rupert asked if he could depend on Billy's silence, Billy swore it. In exchange, Rupert promised to deliver Billy from the town and the life he hated.

A few minutes later, the two were walking on the dark beach, with Rupert trailing only slightly behind as Billy led the way. Out of nervousness and curiosity, the boy asked questions. A lot of questions. After he'd asked a third time how Rupert had come to be stranded in the dunes, soaking wet in the dead of night, Rupert added one further stipulation to their agreement. "Listen," he said. "*I* ask the questions, not you."

"Sorry," Billy said. Then ten steps later the boy asked, "Are you a spy?"

"Something like that," Rupert grudgingly replied.

"I knew it. A *good* spy?"

"As opposed to what?"

"You sound like you're from Australia."

"As I said," Rupert barked, "no more questions."

They passed the sprawling houses along West Grand, then climbed the hill to where the buildings grew progressively smaller and shabbier. On the sidewalk outside a particularly run-down dwelling, Billy stopped. "This is where I live," he said.

"And I can stay here?" Rupert asked skeptically.

"No, but not far away," Billy replied. "There's a whole bunch of empties."

After a few steps more, the boy turned onto a side street that seemed even more desolate.

"This way?" Rupert asked.

"No," Billy said. "I want to show you something."

Rupert rolled his eyes, but followed. They passed three houses, then walked into darker territory still. When his eyes had adjusted, Rupert saw the outline of a car parked at the end of the wooded cul-de-sac. "What's this?" he demanded.

"He's not here," Billy said. "He's at my house."

"Your father's a cab driver?" Rupert asked.

"No," Billy said. "One of my mom's boyfriends."

"Boyfriends?" Rupert repeated.

"My mom has . . . drinks . . . with lots of guys," Billy explained. "They park here so no one sees them at my house."

"Oh," Rupert said.

"This is why I said those things on the beach," Billy explained. "This is why you have to help me."

"Be patient," Rupert said. "I already told you I will."

"Thanks," Billy said through a haze of tears. "Thank you."

"How old are you?" Rupert sneered.

"Fifteen," Billy said.

"Then quit crying," Rupert growled. "C'mon, you promised me some dry clothes."

Chapter Thirty

The Opportunist

After four hours of restless sleep in a dirty trailer, Rupert returned to the water's edge. His curiosity, he supposed, more than anything else, had summoned him there at dawn. He wanted to see if the *Wind Dancer* had washed ashore, or if the breeze had carried it away. As the sun glimmered on the horizon, Rupert observed only bobbing gulls and fishing boats leaving trails of current in their wake.

The beach was quiet as Rupert began to investigate further, responding to another concern that had arisen in the night. He wanted to know if Marisol's body had washed up. He hoped it hadn't, and supposed it never would, but still, the possibility gnawed at him. And so, he walked the tide line, passing by the Brunswick Hotel and between the wooden stilts of the Pier.

He was still a fair distance away when he spotted a woman scurrying into and out of the surf. He veered to the left so that by the time he walked past her, he was midway up in the dry sand. He pretended not to notice her as he made his way toward the closest path, the one that led through the dunes to the sprawling Copley Hotel. But he stole peeks over his shoulder and soon realized that the woman was sifting through Marisol's former belongings. He was shocked to learn they hadn't washed far out to sea, but not overly alarmed. There was no way anyone could connect those items to him.

Standing in the dunes, Rupert watched the woman wade into the sea to retrieve the flotsam. He watched her deliver certain items to her wagon. Even from a hundred feet away he could tell something was not quite right about her. Something about the way she moved and the jerky manner in which she tilted her head suggested she might be mentally challenged. Rupert stood transfixed. When she lifted something small and dark from the waves and began cradling it like a wounded dove, he knew she'd found the jewelry box he'd carelessly dumped overboard. He watched her hurry from the water and head back in the direction from which she'd come. He decided to follow her.

Ten minutes later, the woman stood on a patio beneath a towering building, rummaging in her pocket. From his vantage point behind one of the enormous concrete blocks that formed the building's foundation, Rupert assumed she was getting her key. She was about to open the outer door when Rupert emerged. The woman either heard his footsteps or saw some part of his reflection in the glass door because she started to turn to face him. Before she could, though, he smacked her face against the glass, grabbed the jewelry box, and left her there on the ground.

Rupert hurried away long before his victim regained consciousness. Earlier on his walk, he'd observed a luxurious beach house still boarded up from the winter. There was a FOR SALE sign in its yard. It would make a quiet hideout for a day or two, just until the dust settled. Returning to the trailer park was not an option. He did not want the boy to know where he slept.

When he thought about Billy and the special knowledge he possessed regarding the circumstances of his arrival, Rupert got an uneasy feeling. He could still see how the boy might be useful while he remained in Old Orchard Beach, but Rupert was already beginning to resent the threat he posed. He would have to take care of him before he left.

But he was getting ahead of himself. First, he needed to be sure Sevigny was far away; then he could make preparations to depart.

Chapter Thirty-One

Useful Information

While Roger Simons overslept in Scarborough, Ernie Sabo chatted with the new girl at Beach Bagels, and the first clam digger at the Saco mudflats radioed in a partially capsized boat, Rupert was pacing back and forth inside the winterized beach house south of the Pier. He'd broken in by jimmying the lock on a first-floor window. As the house beside it was also still boarded up, there'd been no one there to witness his crime. He knew the smart thing to do was to just lay low for a few days. Just a few hours later, though, he found himself returning to the beach, being drawn by the same spectacle that was attracting reporters and onlookers. His curiosity brought him to the very spot where he'd observed the woman picking items from the waves two hours earlier.

Hiding in plain view, wearing a Budweiser shirt the boy had scrounged for him the night before, he tried to put the fragmented pieces of information together into a cohesive whole. A fellow gawker reported that Ferdinand Sevigny had been lost at sea. A police officer's CB said the *Wind Dancer* had been found. A voice in the crowd proclaimed the grandstanding billionaire had finally fallen victim to his excessive ego.

Rupert allowed himself to wonder: *Was Sevigny really dead?* In his frenzied state, had his mind played a trick on him when he'd thought he'd heard the engine of the speeder growl? Was it possible the mooring rope connecting the two boats had merely slipped? He shivered with delight at the possibility that his uncle had indeed perished.

That afternoon, Rupert allowed himself a few hours of fitful sleep in the darkness of his temporary lair. Then he emerged again, under cover of darkness, when the sand was deserted once more. He had an appointment with the boy at which he hoped to gain more information. The cable television at his hideout had apparently been disconnected for the winter.

He'd been left to wonder all afternoon whether Sevigny was really dead. He hoped the boy would tell him he was.

There was a kayak in the house's garage, and Rupert dragged it onto the sand. Then he set out across the water. When he saw that the boy had indeed come alone, he made for shore and began to quiz him. But the dumb bloke knew nearly as little as Rupert did himself. Rupert took his provisions and left, but Billy began shouting at him, so Rupert had to return, thinking all the while that the little idiot was going to be even more of a liability than he'd imagined.

But Billy surprised him. He had overheard a police officer talking to his mother, and had learned that apparently the cop had found some evidence. What evidence? The boy didn't know, but it suggested foul play aboard the *Wind Dancer*. Rupert's mind raced, and his heart sank. Billy assured him that only this one officer knew, and he was keeping it a secret. It had become the boy's secret, too, and now, Rupert's.

He instructed Billy to tell him everything. Eventually, Billy revealed that there were actually two police officers who visited his mother: the ambitious older one who'd found the evidence—and practically never diddled his slut of a mother—and the other one, a family man who was leading a double life, doing base things with the hussy three mornings a week. Billy said that the older officer was heading to the island at first light, in search of glory.

Rupert began to see how he might nip in the bud the idea that his uncle's accident had been caused by anything but his own arrogance and recklessness. And so, he headed to Bluff Island.

Chapter Thirty-Two

An Unusual Request

A gentle rap on Billy's bedroom window recalled him from his dreams.

"Hey, bud, get out here," a voice whispered.

Billy opened his eyes to the predawn hours of Friday and realized it was the man from the beach, his friend and savior, whom he had at first suspected to be the missing man, Sevigny. When Billy had seen the actual Sevigny on television, he'd started to have doubts as to whether "his" Sevigny was, in fact, "the" Sevigny. Then, when they'd met for a second time on the dark beach during the night, it had become clear to Billy that they were different men. Billy wanted to ask exactly how his acquaintance was connected to Sevigny, but he didn't dare.

"Are we going *now?*" Billy asked, mistakenly thinking the man had come to deliver on his promise to take him away.

"No," the man scowled. "Come outside."

"You're all wet again," Billy mumbled.

"Get out here," the man said, and as Billy turned to lower himself through the window, he noticed a sliver of flashing light between his bedroom door and the door frame. He heard the familiar sound of the sleeper sofa groaning beneath two undulating bodies. Billy dropped onto the ground outside.

"I need to get into your room," the man said.

"Through the window?" Billy asked.

"Yes."

"Why?"

"Because I do."

Billy was confused. "How about later," he said, "when my mom's not home?"

"Now," the man demanded.

"My mom's awake," Billy said. "She's with someone."

"I know," the man said. "She's with one of the cops, and I want to listen."

"Listen?"

"To see if he talks about the shipwreck."

Billy knew both officers and their schedules. He knew that at the present hour his mother could only be with Officer Mason.

"You have them confused," he said. "This isn't the one who found the evidence."

"I'm not confused," the man said curtly. "Do you want me to help you, or not?"

Billy stepped aside and watched the man climb through the window.

"Wait there," the man whispered before Billy could follow him. Then he quietly closed the window, leaving Billy outside.

Chapter Thirty-Three

Ultimatum

Paul Mason loved his wife. He really did. He loved the way she asked about his day as they lingered over dinner each night. He loved that even though they both knew he was never going to make chief, he always saw in her eyes that he was number one, the glue that held the OOBPD together. When he recounted his skirmishes with miscreants, domestic abusers, drug dealers, and cats stuck in trees, Millie's eyes always reflected back at him a knight in shining armor.

And that was only one of the reasons he loved her. He also loved how she'd always put him and the kids first. There was the time, a few years ago, when she'd given up her papier-mâché class so she could drive Tammy to church league basketball on Thursday nights—which happened to be Paul's poker night. The paste had been making her fingers mealy, anyway, she'd said. No guilt trip. No bargaining. Nothing expected in return. He loved her for all the things like this that she'd ever done, and continued to do. He loved how she peeled the orange in his lunch bag each day, even though he was more than capable of peeling it himself, and even though he usually tossed it in the trash and got a donut from Beach Bagels instead. In the domestic roles they inhabited, Paul loved the way Millie kept the house spotless. He appreciated that she was always the one to get up and clean the mess when their yellow lab, Sassy, upchucked on the carpet.

Paul Mason loved all these things about his wife, and more. He cherished the life they'd built together. But after twenty-six years and two kids, there was not much excitement left for him when it came to those matters of the bedroom that had at one time been at the center of their relationship. At some point Millie's nooks and crannies had lost their mystery. He hadn't realized it at first, but this, as much as the gout, was the cause of his listlessness in their marriage bed. He'd accepted this change as part of middle age, and Millie had too. Their escapades beneath the sheets had gradually become reserved for special occasions—birthdays and anniversaries. They'd begun celebrating their affection instead by splitting a shrimp cocktail at the Steak & Rib on Friday nights, or by walking the beach together on Sunday mornings.

For more than two decades, Paul had remained faithful to his wife. But then, just two days after their twenty-fifth—one of those special occasions when a tryst had been called for, but had fizzled—in a moment of weakness, he had strayed. It was easier than he'd thought, and ever since he'd been living a secret life. He felt guilty about it, but quitting *her* was out of the question. He was hooked.

The hardest part had been those twenty excruciating minutes on the very first night, when he had sat in his cruiser outside Brandy Carter's house, debating whether he should, whether he'd even be able to. Finally, she had come out, apparently having noticed the car. She had leaned into the window and asked, "Is there a problem, Officer?"

"Umm, no, ma'am," Paul replied. "I was, umm, just pulling over to adjust my mirror, and I, umm, I must have—"

"Are you sure you weren't looking to adjust something else?" Brandy asked, coyly smiling and batting her heavily made-up eyelids.

"I'm sure," Paul said.

"Really?" Brandy said, and she raised her head above the car and leaned her body forward so that her breasts spilled right inside the window, so that Paul could see those creamy tops bobbing beneath her half-buttoned blouse in the glow of the porch light. He inhaled deeply, trying to calm himself, telling himself to think. *Was this what he really wanted?* But that only made his heart beat faster. He could smell her perfume.

When her face returned to the window, Brandy whispered, "It looks to me like you still need adjusting, hon."

Paul followed her eyes down to his lap, where, to his amazement, his resurgent manhood was making a tepee of his pants.

"Maybe I could come inside," he said meekly.

"Sure, for a drink," Brandy replied.

"Yeah," Paul said. "A drink."

"Park around the corner," Brandy instructed. Then she leaned in and kissed him on his left eye, which he blinked closed just in time. He'd never been kissed on the eye before. In a quarter-century of marriage, Millie had never kissed him like that, with a tongue that prodded into the crescent of his eye socket. It was soft and warm and made him tingle all over.

As he parked on the cul-de-sac nearby, Paul's heart pounded and his crotch pulsed at the thought of all those other things Brandy might do that his wife—who had never even allowed him to leave the lights on—wouldn't. He practically trotted to Brandy's door, which he found ajar, with a smiling gnome ornament hanging on the knob.

And thus, like an alcoholic who'd been sober for many years, suddenly reunited with a vice so insularly destructive that there existed no greater want in life than to immerse himself in it again and again, Paul Mason reclaimed his youth and masculinity beneath the sparkling disco ball in Brandy's living room. He became a slave to Brandy, who consumed his thoughts night and day. It was wrong, he knew. But it had been so long. Didn't he deserve it? And what was the harm, as long as Millie never found out? Now that he'd done it once, twice, three times, four . . . what difference did it make if he did it once or twice more, or a hundred times more? He'd already crossed the line and there was no way he could uncross it. That was how he rationalized the filthy, beautiful things he and Brandy Carter did together three mornings a week. It was raunchy sex, dirty sex. Love had nothing to do with it. He defiled her, and she loved it.

Now, after she'd brought a contented smile to his face on a Friday morning, Paul pulled up his pants, laid two twenties, a five, and five crumpled ones on the coffee table, and slunk out the back door of Brandy's house. This had become one of their times, thanks to a clever lie he'd thought up about an early-morning weight-lifting regimen he'd started as a New Year's resolution. Life was good and getting better. Summer was breaking; Paul could feel it in the morning air, see it in the hint of sun just beginning to light up the dark hillside as he walked to his cruiser with his body feeling sublimely satisfied and a fog of transcendence between his ears.

Paul walked up Atlantic and turned onto the little nub that petered into gravel and then dirt. Brandy's neighbors were still asleep. It was early. The sun's soft rays had not yet penetrated the wooded enclave.

Paul had already slid behind the wheel when he saw the note, pinned beneath one of the wipers. Only after he climbed out to investigate did he notice the cell phone on the hood. "Open phone and check out photos," the note read. "Face car and wait." Paul instinctively spun around, aware that someone was watching him from behind a veil of mountain laurel and beach pines.

"Who's there?" he demanded, speaking more loudly than he'd meant to. "Show yourself."

He was answered only by the quiet rustling of a sea breeze that permeated even this desolate part of town. He squinted into the dark foliage, turned left, then right, then left again, his heart aflutter. He saw no one, heard nothing.

He reread the note, and grudgingly reached for the phone. He clicked to the "Pictures" tab and opened it. The first photo showed them both fully clothed, groping one another. In the second they were naked. Brandy was on her hands and knees with her rear end held high, while he was lowering a hand to spank her. He was shocked not so much by the graphic nature of the photo or the depravity of the act in which he'd been captured as he was by the look on his own face. With a crazy grin and demonic glimmer in his eyes, he looked like a madman as he smacked her blushing buttocks.

Paul closed the phone. He tried to breathe but found it impossible to draw air. What struck him was the clarity of the pictures. His police skills told him they had not been taken through the living-room blinds, or through a window. They were clear and unobstructed. There was no glare. If he didn't know better, he would say they'd been taken from inside the house. Yes, judging from the vantage point, they'd been taken from the door beside the closet with the kinky toys. They'd been taken from the kid's room.

Paul's darkest thoughts fell to Bobby—or was it Benny? He expected that a teenager's voice would soon address him. He wasn't out of the woods yet, but he managed to draw some air into his lungs at the thought that it was just an angry teen trying to stick up for his mom, trying to scare him off, or maybe shake a few dollars out of him.

"Okay, who is it?" he said quietly. "What do you want?"

"Face the car," a detached voice replied from the foliage. It was not an adolescent's voice, but a man's, and Paul's stomach dropped as he turned away from the woods as instructed.

"I've made copies," the voice said. "Keep those as a reminder of what will show up in your wife's in-box, and Chief White's, and at the *Journal Tribune*, if you don't do as I say."

"Who are you?" Paul demanded. "What do you want?"

"Sabo is going to the island," the voice said. "Any minute now. You need to go, too. Look for an orange signal. Find the note. Bring it to shore and prove that the missing man drowned. Draw any other conclusions or ask any other questions, and everyone sees you spanking your whore."

"No," Paul practically bleated. He started to turn and almost began to inch a hand toward his gun, before checking both impulses. "What do you want?" he begged.

"I told you," the voice replied. "Deliver evidence that Sevigny had an accident. Break the case with your partner. Make sure Sabo doesn't carry on about foul play. Then go back to diddling your whore."

"You'd ruin me," Paul pleaded.

"Do as you've been told and this will all be just a bad dream," the voice said. "Go. Sabo is on his way."

"Just w-w-wait . . . one minute," Paul stuttered, and then, suddenly, he turned and charged into the woods, thrashing through the thickets and pushing aside the branches that snapped against his face. He heard footsteps crashing through the leaves, felt the frenzy. And then he felt the smack of a pine trunk against his forehead. By the time he regained his footing, his blackmailer had disappeared into the woods.

Through the whole of the encounter, neither the police officer nor his tormentor had noticed Billy Carter crouching in the bushes.

Chapter Thirty-Four

An Off-Day

Millie Mason was planting petunias when she looked up to see her husband's cruiser rumbling down the driveway. It was barely ten in the morning, and yet, here was Paul, pulling up beside the flower bed. After he had cut the engine and slowly opened the door, Millie began to greet him with a curious, "Paulie?" But before his name could escape her lips, she saw the blood on his shirt and the look on his face. "Paulie!" she cried. "What happened?"

Paul shook his head and staggered toward her, his knees weak, before wrapping her in a hug and hanging onto her as if his life depended upon it. By the time Millie could pull herself away, the tears were spilling down his cheeks.

"Paulie," she said, clutching him. "What's wrong? Are you okay?"

"No," he said, with incredulity at the very idea that he might be. "No." He burrowed his face in the nape of Millie's neck as they stood in the driveway, his wife practically supporting him.

Finally Millie said, "Come inside," and with their bodies still intertwined and the blood from Paul's uniform smearing fainter streaks of red on her blouse, she led him in through the front door. "It'll be okay," she said. "It'll be okay."

"No," he said. "It won't."

In the bathroom, Paul lurched heavily over the sink with his hands pressed against the countertop as Millie tugged at one sleeve and then the other, sliding the soiled garment off his body. It was splattered with a constellation of droplets. Millie had been fairly certain from the start that it was not Paul's blood. He'd come home plenty of times after accidents and rescues, having accumulated various fluids that were not his own. On the less-frequent occasions when his own blood had been shed, however—once by a knife-wielding teen, once by a shard of broken windshield, once by an assailant's boot—he had not come directly home, but had called from the hospital.

She was relieved nonetheless, as she undressed him, to see that his undershirt was just barely stained in the places where the blood had leaked through his uniform. Her husband's despondency remained cause for concern, however. As trying as the job could be, Paul usually kept his cool. She was not used to seeing him this way.

"Just breathe," she said. "Just breathe."

Paul stood with his hands spread on either side of the sink as she undid his belt and guided his pants to the floor.

"That's it," she said. "Breathe. I'll take you to the couch in a minute. We'll get you through this, whatever it is."

Millie was down on her knees lifting gently on Paul's right foot, when suddenly he fell to the floor, and pushing her aside, lunged toward the toilet and vomited.

Ten minutes later, after Millie had propped him on the couch with a couple of pillows and observed that his trembling had subsided, she tried to get him to talk.

"What was it, Paulie?" she asked, sitting on the coffee table, brushing back his bangs with a tender hand.

Paul slowly lifted his head and looked at her, and when he did, his eyes began to fill again. "I killed him," he said quietly.

"Who?" Millie said, standing up reflexively and practically shouting. "My God. Who?"

"I didn't want to," Paul said in a small voice.

"Who, Paulie?" Millie implored.

"I just wanted him to *stop*," Paul said.

"Who?" Millie cried. "My God." She crossed herself and then clenched her hands at her side. "Who, Paulie?"

Paul did not answer. He just let his chin drop onto his chest and winced as if he were in pain.

"Chief sent you home like this?" Millie asked, trying to remain calm.

"I radioed that there'd been an accident," Paul said, looking at her with an expression that made her feel as though she'd just struck him. "Millie—"

"What?" she asked frantically.

"He'll take my badge."

Paul turned away and buried his head in the upholstery.

"I'm calling Ernie," Millie said. "I'm calling his cell."

When Paul heard that, he let out an excruciating "No!"

But before Millie could bend down to console him, before she could ask if something had happened to his friend and partner, she saw them in the window. There were three cars, coming one after another down the driveway. Their sirens were off, but they had the blues and reds flashing.

"Paul," Millie said. "What did you do?"

Chapter Thirty-Five

A Guilty Mind

On the same morning that heralded the end of Paul and Millie Mason's marital bliss, Roger Simons awoke to realize that the mysterious woman he'd rescued only thirty-six hours earlier had left of her own accord. Sometime while he'd slept, she'd slipped away.

Initially, this revelation brought him relief, especially after a quick inspection of his wallet and other valuables assured him that she hadn't repaid his kindness with any foul turn. But as the sun rose and the players in a second day of breaking news began to crawl about the beach, Roger came face-to-face with his conscience. He stood on his deck, looking at the beach, and thought about the fact that he'd done something noble, in one of the rare instances life afforded when such an act was possible. But in the aftermath, once the immediate peril had passed, he'd undone much of the good. He'd found this young woman, this lost soul, washed up on a foreign shore with only a vague hope that her patron would come for her. And in her moment of need, all he'd been able to offer was some pocket money and a bus ticket out of town. She'd been vulnerable, desperate, lost, and he'd turned her away—or at least informed her of his intention to do so very soon.

As Roger stood looking at the sea, he observed two boats speeding toward the island, a mile or two offshore. The boats left trails of white as they headed for the spot where two vessels were already anchored astride the landmass. Farther down the coast, Roger saw the large Coast Guard cutter sitting in nearly the same place it had been the previous day. He observed a news chopper fluttering over the Pier, and another in flight, heading toward the island where the boats were congregating. Closer by, down on the sand, the news crews were in various stages of preparing and reporting. Roger wondered what new information would come to light today, and how it would shape his understanding of the strange woman he had known only briefly and suspected he would never see again.

Something must have washed up on the island, he thought. He wondered if it would put to rest the town's morbid speculation, whether it would allow the media circus to move on to the next celebrity overdose, kidnapped child, or ravaging fire. He wondered if it would allow the young woman, wherever she had gone, to find some peace. Roger Simons looked at the vibrant panorama spread before him and thought these thoughts, but before long his ruminations turned inward again. Yes, he felt guilty.

Roger turned his back to the sea and walked inside. It was strange; the news was occurring in real time just off his deck, but he needed the television to make sense of it. Turning it on, he was not surprised to see the words BREAKING NEWS scrolling across the bottom of the screen; however, he noticed immediately that instead of the sand and sea, a residential neighborhood was the backdrop of the live report.

"And here, just moments ago," a female reporter said in a grave voice, "Officer Paul Mason of the Old Orchard Beach Police Department was taken into custody, as the Sevigny mystery took a bizarre turn. According to a source with knowledge of the investigation, Officer Mason and another local officer traveled to Bluff Island, just offshore, to look for the missing man. Allegedly, a disagreement ensued that ended in a hail of bullets—" The reporter put a hand to her ear, tilted her head, and furrowed her brow as she listened to a producer speaking through her earpiece. The camera remained fixed on her face, waiting, and then waiting a moment longer, before its patience was rewarded when she refocused her gaze.

"We are just now receiving word," she said, "that Officer Ernest Sabo was the other officer. That's Ernest Sabo, longtime veteran of the Old Orchard Beach police force, who provided a live interview for this station only yesterday. We are receiving word that he has been killed. Of course, our thoughts and prayers go out to his family and friends in this small seaside community, which was just getting ready for its tourist season when it became the epicenter of this still-developing story."

Chapter Thirty-Six

Unexpected News

Two miles south, Rupert Sevigny watched the same report from the living room of his temporary hideout. He'd found a set of old rabbit ears in the basement and had hooked the antenna to the set just in time to learn that the frightened bastard had shot his partner. Rupert could hardly believe it. The other officer must have insisted, even in the face of the planted evidence, that foul play had been involved. And in a moment of panic, the dumb bastard had blown him away. *How wonderful.*

Rupert was sure that those investigating the new crime would discover the evidence and interpret it the correct way. Sevigny had been there. Sevigny had been injured. Sevigny had drowned. Rupert was actually starting to believe it himself. He had only *imagined* hearing the little speedboat's engine; he was almost sure of it now. It was only a matter of time before the authorities dredged his uncle's corpse from the bay.

Rupert did not worry about Mason coming clean and revealing he'd been blackmailed. He'd heard the quiver in his voice, seen the look in his eyes. The man would take his romps with the town pump to the electric chair if it came to that. Even if Mason surprised him, though, Rupert wasn't worried. Mason hadn't seen his face. Only the boy had—the boy who had tipped him off about the island and the other cop's suspicions, the boy who had provided the camera phone and opened his bedroom window—Billy, who had his own reasons for keeping quiet.

Rupert smiled. Things were breaking his way. Only the day before he'd fretted that they weren't. He'd been infuriated after reclaiming Marisol's diamond only to realize its inscription—Marisol Sevigny—made it valueless to him. Instead of funding his trip south as he'd hoped it would when he'd spied the half-witted woman ogling it, the only purpose it could serve now would be to incriminate him. Its diamond was too big and its engraving too overt for him to trust that any local fence would resist the urge to go running to the tabloids—or worse, the authorities.

Then Billy had delivered the bad news that Sabo had turned up evidence suggesting his uncle's "accident" had, in fact, been a crime. But now at last, Rupert could breathe. The cop was dead. Perhaps his uncle was, too. All he had to do was find his way to Mexico. Once he'd put a few thousand miles between himself and Maine and the festering story involving his uncle, maybe he would be able to hock the diamond after all. And oh yes, first he would have to take care of the boy.

Rupert watched the grainy television screen as the station cut from overhead shots of the island to the suspect's sunny green home, to a still photo of the two officers in better times, standing shoulder to shoulder. The smile on Rupert's face and the sick joy in his heart only continued to swell a short while later when the first reports began trickling in—that amid the ghastly crime scene on the island, evidence had been discovered that suggested, amazingly, that Ferdie Sevigny had been marooned there the day before.

"It appears the great explorer left a desperate note before attempting, in an injured state, to swim for his life," the reporter noted, before grimly adding, "Divers are redoubling their efforts to search the bay for his body."

Rupert cackled gleefully at every delicious twist the television delivered. And then, in an instant, his sweet dream turned into a bloodcurdling nightmare. One breaking story preempted another, as the station cut from its morbid speculation concerning his uncle's final hours in the cold water, to a news anchor sitting at a desk with a look of astonishment on his face.

"You're not going to believe this," the anchorman said, "but we're going to take you to Old Orchard Beach's Brunswick Hotel, where the FBI has assembled reporters in the past fifteen minutes to announce a major breakthrough in the Sevigny investigation. We are being told . . . that Ferdinand Sevigny has been found—alive—and is about to make a statement."

By the time the picture had switched to a podium in an elegant ballroom, Rupert's heart had nearly exploded. His jaw was clenched and his hands had begun to tremble. Stepping to the podium was his uncle, looking haggard but unvanquished. Sevigny stared into the camera with a glare that caused Rupert to instinctively flinch before he could return his eyes to the screen.

In an almost apologetic voice, the resurrected adventurer began to read from a piece of paper in his hands. "Hello," he said. "I am Ferdinand Sevigny. I am alive and well—or at least, on my way to being well. Two nights ago I suffered an accident at sea while attempting a voyage, blindfolded. This accident was exacerbated—no, *caused*—by my own recklessness. I tempted fate and nearly lost my life. In my blindfolded state, I fell from the deck of the *Wind Dancer* and drifted into a current that pulled me from my boat. Treading water, I managed to sever my blindfold with a pair of rigging pins that had been in my hands when I fell.

"I swam and swam until I reached an island. There, I left the few possessions the FBI has recovered today, and upon regaining my strength, I reentered the water in the black of night. I reached land just before sunrise Thursday. Wounded and delirious, I stumbled into the Brunswick Hotel. For more than a day, I was barely conscious, injured and exhausted. The hotelkeepers had no knowledge of my presence in one of their rooms until I approached them this morning, at which time they insisted we contact the authorities. We began the process that has resulted in my coming before you at this hour.

"I would like to offer my heartfelt apologies for the turmoil my failed adventure has caused this town. That is the true disaster. If my accident in some way led to the tragedy we are learning about this morning—involving the two police officers—I am deeply sorry."

Sevigny looked down and inhaled, then looked up again, visibly shaken. "For a long time," he continued, "I have been pursuing personal glory. I have not often stopped to consider how my actions have affected other people along the way. Hopefully, I will have an opportunity to do so now. I'd like to believe that I have not always left so wide a swath of destruction in my wake, but I fear I have. I cannot undo what is done; that is impossible. But words are hollow without action. If the good people of this town will have me, I plan to remain in Old Orchard Beach until I have made some small good of this awful situation. I do not yet know how I will do this, nor how I will be received. I ask only that the people of this town give me a chance. Thank you for coming, and for respecting my privacy as I recuperate."

With that, Ferdinand Sevigny walked from the podium with unusual humility in his gait. An FBI spokesman slid past him en route to the microphone. He explained that Sevigny had given an initial statement and would soon be providing investigators a more-thorough account of what had happened during the past thirty-six hours. The spokesman explained that the items on the island did indeed belong to the adventurer. However, the things that had washed ashore at Old Orchard Beach the day before had apparently come from some other vessel, because they did not match the description of items listed on the *Wind Dancer*'s customs manifest.

Rupert heard all of this but could barely process it. Sevigny was alive, which infuriated him. However, he had lied to protect his public image, which meant Rupert did not face any legal jeopardy. Nevertheless, Sevigny was close by, and would surely come for him, seeking revenge. *Unless I get to him first*, Rupert thought. Yes, it was the only way. Rupert had to finish him off before he could retire to his tropical paradise. Otherwise, he'd always wonder, always begin each day worrying that it would be the one that brought his uncle to his door.

Rupert smiled, suddenly glad to know his uncle was alive and nearby, glad to be proffered another chance to right the wrong that had been done to him and his father, glad to have another opportunity to shed Sevigny's blood.

Chapter Thirty-Seven

Packing Out

The only thing Billy hated more than when his mother was having "drinks" with strange men in the living room was when she was having drinks—as in *actual drinks*—all by herself. Usually, her binges were accompanied by uncharacteristic attention paid to her son. Experience had taught him not to trust these moments. His mother's interest in him always evaporated by the time she awoke, bleary-eyed and ill-tempered, the next morning.

Usually, Billy had no idea what caused her to reach for the big bottle atop the fridge and to hang the smiling gnome ornament on the door-knob even though she wasn't entertaining a guest. Billy had come to understand at some point during his childhood that the gnome usually meant she was with someone, and not currently available for new visitors. The gnome meant Billy should enter through his window, or not at all.

Today, Billy actually had a pretty good idea what had caused her to reach for the bottle and hang the grinning goblin on the knob before he got home from school. When he'd tuned his bedroom television to the same station he could hear in the living room, he'd learned that the two cops had been involved in an accident. One was dead, and the other under arrest. Some people were already calling it a murder. And that was why, Billy knew, his mother had reached for the bottle and hung up the gnome.

To Billy, this revelation was equally upsetting. He knew his mysterious friend had been involved in the murder. He'd watched with his own eyes as the man had told Mason to make sure Sabo didn't pursue the evidence Billy had brought to his attention just a few hours before. Now, Sabo was dead.

As Billy sorted through the revelations of the day, he began to pack. He emptied his laundry bag and began weeding through clothes on his bedroom floor. He had just started putting certain items back in the bag when he heard his bedroom door open.

His mother came stumbling in. "Billy," she said, as if she were surprised to find him in his room. "You're a good boy. Do you know that?"

Billy did not reply. He merely winced when she patted him on the shoulder. He hoped she was too drunk to notice what he was doing.

"You do your own wash," she said approvingly, noting the laundry in his hands. Then, after a pause, she added, "And you make your own dinner—" She noticed the half-filled bag on his bed. "Are you packing for an overnighter?" she asked.

"Yes," Billy said.

"Camping?" she asked, squinting as if she realized she should know the answer, but couldn't quite remember.

"Yes," Billy said.

"Oh, with Mr. Dono," she said, as if she'd suddenly remembered plans he'd told her about a few days ago. Mr. Dono was the leader of the Boy Scout troop to which Billy had belonged when he was in grammar school.

"Right," Billy said, continuing to pack.

"But Billy," she said, after a moment, "you don't go to meetings anymore."

"Yes, I do," Billy lied. "Every Tuesday."

She gave this some thought. "Oh, that's right," she said. "You go on Tuesday nights, don't you?"

"Yeah," Billy said. "Now you remember."

"And on Thursday and Saturday you have soccer," she said, as if proud to know the most basic details of her son's life.

"That's right," Billy said, even though he'd outgrown the youth soccer program two years before and hadn't been good enough to make the high school team.

"Billy," she said. Something about the way she said his name made him stop packing. "Billy," she said, "I want you to know . . . I want you to know—"

"What?"

"You're a good soccer player," she finally said. "You're always the best."

Billy sighed. "You never went to a single one of my games, Mom," he said quietly.

"Oh yes I did," she insisted. "You were always the best." She turned and stumbled from the room. "Billy?" she called back, after just a few steps.

"What?"

"Take the gnome off the door on your way out."

Billy heard the groan of the sleeper sofa beneath her weight, and the clink of the bottle against her glass. He wiped the tears from his eyes and tightened the drawstrings on his bag.

Chapter Thirty-Eight

Mr. Goodbar

Carrie and her two new friends were finishing their sixth round of margaritas by the time the house lights flickered on, then tapered back down to a dim glow, signifying that Mr. Goodbar would be closing soon.

"Three more Ruby Reds," Mandy said, before woozily sliding off her stool and staggering toward the bar.

"Like, I don't even *want* a boyfriend this summer," Sam said to Carrie. "I want to, you know, enjoy myself."

"Right," Carrie said. In the two hours they'd spent at the local watering hole, all Sam and Mandy had done was talk about guys they'd spurned, guys they'd dated, guys who were looking at them, and guys who weren't looking at them but should have been. At least a half-dozen times they'd asked Carrie, whom they regarded as an oracle of local knowledge, "So what's *his* story?" in reference to one of the drunken townies. Some of these men Carrie knew and could aptly characterize— "Owns a gas station, just got married," or, "A couple years older than me, was the starting quarterback his senior year"—while others she quickly sized up and pretended to know—"Just got out of jail, is on the sex-offender list"—partly to maintain the illusion of her omniscience but mostly for her own amusement.

These girls were a bit froufrou for her taste, but they were growing on her. At the end of a long week, and a longer day, it was nice to unwind. The surreal Friday that had marked the end of her first week at Beach Bagels had been a crazy and not very good one. As the sweet alcohol had saturated her brain and the bar's catalog of 1990s music had droned on, and as Mandy and Sam had chatted incessantly, Carrie's blurring thoughts waded through the past eighteen hours, trying to make sense of them.

There had been the excitement of making two new friends at the start of summer, then the horrifying shock of learning that the friendly cop, Officer Sabo, had been killed by the other friendly cop, Officer Mason. There had been the unexpected revelation that the drowned billionaire had not drowned after all, but had made it to shore and was staying down the street at the Brunswick. And now, a few minutes before closing time, Carrie was sitting at the local dive for the first time in her life. All night the place had hummed with speculation concerning the awful things that had happened in their town, or just off its shore. And yet the two girls at her table had spent the evening fixated on other matters entirely. The whole night had a surreal feel to it.

"I would totally *do* him," Mandy said, sloshing three pink drinks onto the table and tilting her head toward a slovenly middle-aged man at the end of the bar.

"You're such a slut," Sam said with obvious delight, turning her head to appraise the object of her friend's affection.

"Do you know what he's worth?" Mandy said.

"He's like fifty years old," Sam said, "And how do *you* know?"

"The bartender told me," Mandy reported. "That guy owns the Pier and all the shops." She looked to Carrie for confirmation.

"I think the bartender's having some fun with you," Carrie reported. "That guy's the school janitor. He's no millionaire."

"What an asshole," Mandy said, staring with mock disdain at the bartender but failing to catch his eye. She turned her attention to a man sitting at a table across the way. "*He's* kinda cute," she said. "What's his story?"

And so they sipped their final round and continued their banter as the crowd thinned out, including most of the men Carrie's two tablemates had identified as potential suitors. Whether her friends had been prospecting for the night, or for the summer, Carrie could not be sure, but when midnight came they were both walking out with her.

"Like I said, I don't want a boyfriend to mess up my summer, anyway," Sam said as they walked through the door.

"Don't worry," Mandy said. "Today we got our cottage, tomorrow we'll get jobs, and by, like, next weekend, we'll have guys."

"As if," Sam said. "That's the last thing I need."

Stepping into the Square, the three young women laughed. The air coming off the water was heavy, but the night was warm.

"Who's that?" Sam asked, gesturing to a thin, dark-complexioned woman standing impassively beneath a streetlight with her eyes fixed on the Brunswick Hotel.

"I don't know," Carrie admitted, failing to come up with a positive ID for the first time all night. The woman was so foreign-looking, so unlike the pale-skinned Canadians and hardscrabble locals, and with such a faraway gaze on her face, Carrie couldn't even think of anything to make up.

"She's a goddess," Mandy said, without a hint of jealousy in her voice. "But she has *no* fashion sense." The young woman was wearing baggy sweatpants and what appeared to be a man's flannel shirt. And yet she still made a striking impression.

"She's so beautiful," Sam said. "Let's ask where she's working for the summer."

"Maybe that's the *in* look in Canada—" Mandy speculated, as she followed Sam onto the cobblestones, with Carrie lagging another step behind. And so, they crossed the Square to introduce themselves to the exotic stranger.

Part Three

Chapter Thirty-Nine

Season of Renewal

On a warm June morning, summer came to Old Orchard Beach. School was out, the sun was shining, and by midmorning, cars were pouring off I-95 and funneling onto the extension the locals called "the Spur," which led to the narrower road that wended through town. Bearing license plates that announced origins in Massachusetts, New York, Quebec, and points beyond, they rolled past the middle school, fire barn, water tower, and police station, on their way to the motels and condos closer to shore.

And *pour* off the highway they did. The town's starring role in the most captivating cable news story of the past few days—the apparent death and surprising resurrection of Ferdie Sevigny—had put Old Orchard in the public consciousness just as people were making their summer vacation plans. The television coverage had piqued so much interest in the town that before noon on the first Monday, the townies were already reconsidering the dire predictions that had been circulating for weeks. The previously forecast dud of a summer now had all the makings of a blockbuster.

The relief was palpable on the hotelkeepers' faces, and in the easy banter between the T-shirt hawkers and pizza vendors who made their living in the Square. They depended on the two-month binge to sustain them for the next ten months, until the tourists would arrive again. Their relief shined through, even in the wake of the tragedy that had occurred in the aftermath of the Sevigny shipwreck. The townsfolk wondered how Paul Mason, one of their finest, could have killed his friend Ernie. They wondered why. And they worried that there might be another shoe still to drop that would bring further disgrace to their hard-working, tight-knit community.

Word on the street was that Paul wasn't talking to anyone—not to Chief White, not to Millie, not to his lawyer. It was like he'd lost his tongue. The latest rumor was that Ernie had been diddling Millie, and Paul had found out and flown into a rage. But it was just gossip—troubled minds trying to make sense of the unexplainable.

As for Ferdinand Sevigny, his continued presence in Old Orchard Beach had not only attracted tourists, but had also provoked its own array of gossip. Since his cryptic press conference, he'd scarcely been seen or heard. He'd only been spotted each day at noon, overlooking the beach, on the small balcony off the Brunswick's fourth floor. Some speculated his whole ordeal had been an elaborate hoax, a publicity stunt, the true intentions of which would soon be revealed. They said he was funding a hotel development project that would wipe out half the Square, or a new amusement park that would overshadow Palace Playland. Others suggested Sevigny had chosen the Brunswick as a quiet place to spend the summer, writing his memoirs. Still others maintained that the authorities were quietly detaining him in town in preparation for levying criminal charges against him related to the tumult his stunt had caused, or the murder it had somehow incited.

None of these hypotheses was correct, however.

Jim and Marty Wagner were the only two locals interacting with Sevigny on a daily basis. They brought him his meals and whatever else he requested while he awaited the arrival of his personal items. Jim and Marty weren't talking to anyone either. Even if they'd wanted to, they hadn't the time, so consumed were they by the wave of reservations that had flooded their phone lines as soon as Sevigny had announced he would be staying at the Brunswick indefinitely. By midmorning on Monday, Jim and Marty were already booked through the end of July.

Another townie who found herself even busier than usual was Sally Fiddler, who had undertaken a new pursuit. After performing her usual ritual at daybreak, Sally had taken to returning to the beach at midday to wander from blanket to blanket. It was creepy, the tourists said, how the strange woman would approach and study them, gazing, it seemed, with particular interest at their hands before moving on to the next party of sunbathers.

Farther up the beach, in Scarborough, Roger Simons had returned to his old routine, but without his usual conviction. He too had taken to walking the beach, looking for the mysterious woman he'd pulled from the sea. On this first day of tourist season, his feet carried him to the sand before the Brunswick, where he stopped and waited for Sevigny to emerge on his balcony. Roger wanted to see if Marisol would be standing by his side. But Sevigny, when he did step into the sun, did so alone, as the other celebrity seekers waiting on the wet sand told Roger he always did. Guilty though he was, Roger could think of no other way to locate the young woman, so he returned home to the minutiae of day-trading beneath the shade of his deck umbrella.

As for Marisol, she'd settled in comfortably with her new friends, Sam and Mandy, at their little cottage at Beach Villas. She hadn't found, or even looked for, a summer job, and didn't have any money. She called herself Marie, wore the girls' clothes and ate their food, and was in every way agreeable and exotic. Sam and Mandy made Marie part of their summer adventure, just like the waves on the beach and the bright lights in the Square, entertaining all the while the secret hope that they'd eventually arrive at some intimacy with her, although it was proving slower to establish than they would have liked.

Each morning when Sam and Mandy ventured to Beach Bagels for their iced cappuccinos, they updated Carrie on their progress with Marie. They detailed the latest dish she'd cooked or the latest insight they'd gleaned concerning her closely guarded past. They noted, for example, how during the course of a casual conversation she'd mentioned the year she lived in Paris. Yet whenever they pressed for more information concerning who she was or where she'd come from, Marie would only smile or frown or offer some other enigmatic expression.

Billy Carter was also spending the first week of summer in a sort of limbo. Over a series of hikes he'd transferred most of his essential belongings from his bedroom on Atlantic Avenue to the abandoned trailer that had once served as the hiding place of his mysterious co-conspirator. Billy had cleaned the living room and made up a mattress with clean sheets. Though the trailer lacked electricity and running water, he made do, using the woods as a latrine, and returning home each morning to shower while his mother slept. Then Billy would take a few dollars out of his mother's jar and go to the Square for lunch.

Otherwise, a busy opening-of-the-season week in the life of the town played out as usual. The lifeguards worked on their tans, the young Canadians manning the counters at the five pizza stands in the Square worked on their English, and the barkers at Palace Playland did their best to hawk their cotton candy and corn dogs. All of this was as it should be.

But there was one more thing that came to light as the first glorious week of summer unfurled. Chief White, who'd already lost, and lost forever, two of his best men, was swamped with calls—at least five a day—from tourists reporting they'd had valuables stolen from their blankets. At first the chief had chalked this up to just another symptom of the bad economy, which, thankfully, was not affecting Old Orchard's tourist season in any serious way. However, after the eighth call in two days, he realized he had a crime spree on his hands. He sent two of the rent-a-cops he'd hired for the summer to patrol the beach, but they spent most of their time competing with the lifeguards for the ladies' attention, and the calls kept coming.

On the fourth day, the chief had an officer post signs at all of the beach entrances, reading BEWARE: BLANKET THIEF. DO NOT LEAVE CASH/VALUABLES UNATTENDED. Despite this effort, he received three new calls that afternoon.

Chapter Forty

The Feckless Adventurer

Jim Wagner knew he had Ferdinand Sevigny to thank for his recent good fortune. The Sevigny press conference had sent images of the Brunswick's stately ballroom into homes across the country, and the deluge of reservations had begun that very afternoon. While some people had seen those pictures and thought simply that the hotel looked like a nice place to vacation, the idea that Sevigny was still on the premises was what prompted most of the calls. People wanted the chance to rub elbows with an international celebrity. The problem, however, was that Sevigny never left the fourth floor. And the more Jim interacted with him, delivering his meals and fetching his odds and ends, the more he sensed that some great weight was smothering his special guest. The hotelkeeper had worried that Sevigny might decide to curtail his stay and trigger a wave of cancellations, but now that his personal items had arrived, Jim felt reassured that his famous guest was planning to stay a nice long while.

"That's the last bag," Jim said, pausing to wipe his brow. He'd just climbed the stairs for the third time. "It's warm up here," Jim said as he lowered the final suitcase to the floor of the old Governor's Suite. "You sure you're comfortable?"

"Oh," Sevigny said, as if the question had caught him so entirely off guard that he had to think about it. "I open the window at night," he said finally. He was sitting in a rocking chair, facing the floor-to-ceiling window that overlooked the sea.

"You wouldn't believe the crowd that watched me unload your stuff," Jim said. "Any mention of your name and people start swarming."

Sevigny sighed, then added, "As if my luggage looked any different than theirs?"

Mistaking his guest's dour irony for an uptick in his mood, Jim plodded clumsily ahead, offering an agreeable, "You're the reason they're here."

"I see," Sevigny said. "And you'd like it if I made an occasional appearance in the lobby. It would be good for business?"

"Whatever suits you," Jim said, though he wanted to blurt out that yes, yes indeed, were Sevigny to mingle with the other guests at brunch or happy hour, he and Marty could probably book the Brunny straight through Columbus Day.

Sevigny replied only, "Hmm."

"All we care about is your comfort," Jim added, trying to stave off an awkward silence that set in anyway, as soon as he'd finished speaking. While Jim stood in the doorway beside the pile of bags, Sevigny stared solemnly out at the blue waves. Finally, Jim said, "It must be tough, always attracting a crowd."

"What's that?" Sevigny asked, without turning from the window, seeming as if he'd quite missed the point of whatever Jim was suggesting.

"I mean, being recognized wherever you go," Jim explained. "Sometimes you probably just need to—"

"That never bothered me," Sevigny said softly. "Only now, I don't see the point. I don't see the basis for the adulation."

"You shouldn't say such things," the hotelkeeper replied. "Haven't you seen them down on the beach? The crowd gets bigger every day."

"The crowd?" Sevigny asked.

"They wait for you to step outside," Jim explained. "You do it every day after lunch. They wait to see you on the balcony."

"They think I'll jump?" Sevigny asked.

"No!" the hotelkeeper cried. "Don't say such things. They just want to see you."

"I hadn't noticed," Sevigny said flatly. "I don't look down."

"I'm a waves man, myself," Jim said uncertainly. "I could stare at them for hours." Then he came right out with it. "Mr. Sevigny, is everything okay?"

"The bagel was fine," Sevigny replied, referring to the breakfast his host had delivered an hour earlier. "And the linens are always fresh. And you've observed my request that no reporters be allowed up."

"That's not what I meant," Jim said. "Is everything okay with *you*? You've been through a lot."

"My thoughts concern a woman," Sevigny said.

"Oh."

"There is nothing worse than regret," Sevigny continued. "It is the one emotion that can destroy any of us." He leaned back in his chair and stared intently at the waves dancing beyond the windowpane, while the hotelkeeper stood, trying to decide how much or how little to pry into his guest's malaise.

"Maybe we can talk again, if you'd like," Jim said. "And if there's anything you need in the meantime—"

"There is nothing I need," Sevigny said, definitively. But before the hotelkeeper could reach the door, his melancholy guest spoke again, without turning from the window. "There is one thing," he said. "I've been hearing noises at night, in the hall—not quite footsteps—in my bedroom, too."

"Oh, that," Jim said, forcing a laugh. "That's just Eben. He hanged himself on this floor a century ago." Jim meant to launch into the whole fanciful story of the fire and of how it had miraculously spared the Brunswick, thanks to Eben Staples's heroic actions, but before he could say another word, Sevigny offered an accepting "Oh," leaving Jim to understand that as far as his guest was concerned, the matter required no further explanation. Jim quietly closed the door and descended the stairs.

"So?" Marty prodded, when Jim had returned to the front desk.

"Well . . . ," Jim replied in a wavering voice.

"Any better?"

"Let's just say we'll be lucky if he doesn't hurl himself from the balcony one of these afternoons," Jim said gravely.

Chapter Forty-One

A Close Call

Billy passed the fountain, arcade, and carousel before slipping anonymously onto the sand. He tiptoed between the heavily oiled tourists until he reached the shade of the Pier, where he spotted his friend sitting in his chair, straddling the line where the early summer sun cast a long, thin shadow on the white sand. Billy caught his eye, but didn't smile, nod, or do anything else to acknowledge his acquaintance. He continued walking until he'd reemerged in the sunlight on the other side of the long wooden wharf. Then Billy removed his shirt and let it fall to the sand. He kicked off his sandals and walked toward the water.

There were people standing in the surf, riding the waves, floating on boogie boards, tossing Frisbees. Billy found an open spot and after twenty steps dove into a wave. Then he waded out farther and rode another one back toward shore. The pull of the ocean was powerful. It made Billy feel clean and alive. But he knew that when he lifted his head and came out of the white foam in knee-deep water, the man would be standing there. And he was. One man among thousands, one boy among tens of thousands, they exchanged a few brief words, remaining utterly unnoticed by the tourists, lifeguards, and two junior officers patrolling the massive beach.

"In front of the pink house," the man said. "Single woman, two kids. Blue umbrella. Stars-and-stripes blanket. Wallet's in the green cooler."

"Did they eat yet?" Billy asked.

"Just got back," the man said. "But the kids go in the water every ten minutes, and she walks down to watch."

"Got it," Billy said.

"Between the pirate ship and the Sandpiper," the man said. "Easy one. Bald guy in a Speedo. Old man, all by himself. Fanny pack's under his towel."

"Got it," Billy said.

Rupert proceeded to list off three or four other marks he'd identified during his morning reconnaissance. Now it was Billy's job to wait for the right moment when they'd strayed from their blankets—for a swim, or a drink, or to use the bathroom in the Square. He would walk up and casually sit down, looking, as his friend had instructed him to look, as if he had every right to be there, as if it were his blanket. He would empty the wallet or purse stashed in the beach bag or cooler. Then he would wander off.

And so, Billy got to work. He extracted twenty-seven dollars from the green cooler that belonged to the woman with the two kids. He found a measly six bucks in the man-purse that belonged to the old-timer sitting near Pirates' Patio. And he visited three other blankets, amassing a total of sixty-two dollars. Since the warning signs had begun appearing, he had been under orders to leave watches, rings, and cameras, and to take only cash. And in the rare instances when there was an exceedingly large sum—one purse he'd emptied on the second day had yielded two crisp hundred-dollar bills—he was to take only a portion. They were better off committing several small robberies each day, the man had explained, which were less apt to be reported. It would take longer to build their kitty of travel money this way, he'd told Billy, but it would carry less risk.

With just one blanket remaining and his bathing suit pockets full of crumpled bills, Billy was crouching over a handbag half-covered by a Hannah Montana boogie board when he experienced a fright. First he saw the shadow, which was not so unusual; people were always tiptoeing between blankets on their way toward or back from the water. But this shadow didn't pass; it remained where it was. He remembered what the man had said—to remain calm and project the illusion that he was doing nothing wrong. The man had said to pretend it was his mother's purse or his father's wallet. He had told Billy that if he were ever questioned, he should explain that his parents had sent him to the blanket for ice-cream money. If the accuser was not just some busybody, but the actual owner of the purse or wallet, then Billy was to say that his family had the same beach umbrella or cooler and that he'd gotten confused. Failing that, the man had told him to make a scene, to yell, "You're not my father!" or "Stop touching me!" to whomever tried to apprehend him. If that didn't work, he'd told Billy to run off and lose himself on the vast beach or in the crowded Square. But Billy hadn't yet had to employ any of these tactics.

Today, though, as someone hovered over him for an eternal few seconds, he feared the worst. Then, suddenly, a hand gripped his shoulder, sending his entire body into shock. As he shook free, he turned to see who was accosting him and was relieved to find not some Speedo-clad Canadian or tattoo-ridden biker dude, but the familiar face of the mentally handicapped woman he recognized from town. Her name was Sally, and he'd often noticed her wandering the Square or shopping at Zahares Market. Seeing her now, it occurred to Billy that she was the same woman the cop had been referring to a week earlier when he'd told Billy's mother about the evidence he'd found. The memory of Officer Sabo's final visit to his house, and the reality that his source was now standing before him, sent a chill down Billy's spine.

Rising to his feet, Billy noticed something: Sally's eyes weren't looking at his face, but at his hands, which he held fanned before him in a reflexive gesture of innocence. "I was just getting some ice-cream money," he said meekly. "It's my mother's—"

She didn't seem interested in what he was saying. Her eyes were still fixed on his fingers as she dejectedly began to swivel her head from side to side.

Billy lifted his hands practically in front of his face and watched as she raised her eyes. "What?" he said. "What?"

But Sally just shook her head and left him there.

Billy watched as she walked toward a man sitting a few spots away. He was lounging in a beach chair, holding a can of Budweiser. She surprised him, just as she'd surprised Billy. Perhaps he'd been dozing behind his sunglasses, because he lurched upright as she grabbed one of his hands and tried to inspect it. "What's your problem?" the man blurted out.

Before Billy knew what he was doing, he had traipsed across two blankets and a prone woman in a string bikini, arriving at Sally's side.

"Sorry," Billy said, just as the man was starting to realize his assailant was mentally challenged. "She doesn't talk much," Billy explained. "Sometimes she's too friendly." He reached for Sally's hand and took it in his own.

"I thought she was trying to take my ring," the man said sheepishly. "My wife woulda killed me."

"No problem," Billy said.

"Sorry," the man replied.

Billy led her away. He thought briefly about returning to the blanket where he'd been interrupted, but it seemed best not to push his luck. He led Sally up the beach toward the Square and told her not to startle people. He relinquished her hand, and observed that within twenty seconds she had approached another unsuspecting sunbather and had begun harassing her in the same way. *Oh well*, he thought. *I tried.*

Chapter Forty-Two

Under the Pier

That night, Billy met his friend under the Pier at the usual time to hand over the latest wad of bills. It had been a week already, and Billy was growing tired of waiting. He was shaken by the scare he'd had that afternoon. And so, as the pulse of music wafted down from the Square and the patter of footsteps on the planks above mingled with the lap of the waves, the trembling teen took a stand.

"Today was the last time," Billy said.

"I thought you wanted out of here," the man scoffed.

"I'm gonna get caught."

"Not if you're careful."

"How much more do we need?"

"For two tickets to Vancouver? It should take two more weeks. Maybe three."

"I can't."

"This will all be a memory, I promise."

"What if you're lying?"

"Lying?"

"You won't even tell me your name," Billy said.

"You don't need to know it," the man replied. "Don't you trust me?" Billy stared at him in the sliver of moonlight reflecting off the water.

"Call me Tom," the man said.

"You made that up. I'm not calling you that."

"What does it matter? A name is a name."

"But how do I know you'll take me with you?"

"You have to trust me."

"Why can't we rent a car and go?" Billy pleaded.

"Because we have to be patient," the man said, and he began to walk away.

"Who are you?" Billy bleated, just as his friend was dissolving into the shadows. Then the boy called out something else he thought might bring his friend back. "Sevigny!" he said.

The man resurfaced in the half-light. "What did you say?" he snarled.

"How do you know him?" Billy demanded. "How do you know Sevigny?"

"Know him?" the man asked as he walked back toward Billy.

"You're Australian; he's Australian," Billy explained. "And I've seen the way you look at him up on his balcony." Before the man could reply, Billy added, "You even look like him. Is he your father?"

The man slapped Billy hard across his face. The blow sent him stumbling into one of the barnacle-encrusted pylons supporting the weight of the planks and shops and clubs overhead. The music of the arcade droned cacophonously on, mixed with the crashing of the waves and the hum of the motorcycles looping the Square. The man stood glaring at the trembling boy, but then his face softened, and when he spoke again it was with uncharacteristic kindness.

"You really do want to leave?" he asked. "You *need* to go?"

"I hate it here," Billy sobbed.

"Maybe we can speed things up," the man said. "Come here." He extended an apologetic hand, which the adolescent tentatively took. "Give me a real shake," he said. Billy squeezed more firmly, until the man said, "That's it." The man squeezed back, but not enough to hurt him. "You can't ask any questions," he said, "but if you need to get out of here sooner, I know a way you can pocket some real money."

"How?" Billy asked.

Chapter Forty-Three

Girls' Night Out

On the tenth day of their cohabitation, Mandy and Sam decided it was time to make their roomie talk. They were tired of waiting for Marie to open up, insanely curious to learn more about her, and desperate for her to adore them in the way they adored her. As soon as Marie let down her guard, they just knew they would bond for life. She would be just like one of their Alpha Delta Pi sisters. Her secrets would be theirs and theirs would be hers, and the summer would be that much more "epic" as a result.

"Marie," Sam announced, approaching her as she sat writing in her journal. "We're going out, and we're not taking 'no' for an answer."

"I have to?" Marisol asked, scrunching up her nose.

"Yes," Sam confirmed. "We're getting you drunk, and you're gonna tell us your secrets. Mandy has a drinking dress all picked out for you."

"A drinking dress," Marisol said, laughing. "Is there such a thing?"

Two hours and five margaritas later, Marisol found herself swaying slightly to the beat at Mr. Goodbar amid the warmth and clamor of many happy people. She had held her own for the first two or three frosty glasses, continuing to play coy, but she had been unable to hold out much longer. The truth was that she wanted to talk. She liked the girls and understood what they wanted, but she hadn't had any female friends since adolescence. It was hard. Besides, her relationship with Sevigny was too complicated, too fraught with her own treachery, to even begin to explain. She didn't know how the two silly girls would react.

Before long, however, she found herself trying to express what she'd recently experienced. She tried to share the turmoil that in the past she'd only expressed in her journal. As she started to speak, she found the words easier to summon than she'd imagined. And though she stopped short of offering a full disclosure of who she was, where she'd come from, and how she'd recently faced and failed some great moral test, she was able to communicate more of it than she'd expected. Mandy and Sam nodded with sympathy as colorful glasses sparkled throughout the room, people chattered about their own triumphs and tragedies, and the house band played rhythmically on.

Marisol did not identify her lover by name, but she told the girls she'd been swept off her feet and taken away. She told them he'd been twice her age, and that he'd taken her all over the world. But in time she'd grown lonely and resentful. He'd told her where to be, and how to act, and she'd never had any real say in anything. She'd begun to feel like a kept woman, like she was just there for his pleasure. And in her sadness, she'd done something loathsome and absolute that had revealed a terrible truth about her character. She'd cheated on him and betrayed him. Only now was she trying to sort through everything she'd done and make sense of it. It was the first time in six years she'd been on her own. No, it was the first time *ever*. Before him, she had lived with her family. She had never been alone. Now, she wanted to start over. First she needed to right the wrong she'd done, but she didn't know how—or if—it was even possible.

"You need to let go," Sam said, when it seemed Marisol had finished. She laid a hand upon Marisol's on the table.

"You can do so much better than him," Mandy added. "He treated you like shit."

"I'd probably have cheated too," Sam said.

"No," Marisol said, feeling the need to defend Sevigny. "He's a good man. It was my fault."

"Your fault?" Sam scoffed, interrupting a sip. "He ignored you, didn't appreciate you, expected you to be his freaking eye candy."

Marisol was on the brink of tears.

"Marie?" Sam said.

"You don't understand," Marisol explained. "I always hurt the people I love. You'll see. I always do." Tears were rolling down her delicate cheeks.

Before she could completely unravel, Mandy suddenly blurted out, "I love you, Marie," and broke into tears herself. She spilled off her barstool and, catching Marisol off guard, smothered her in a warm, drunken embrace. Before Marisol knew what was happening, Sam had joined in the bonding moment. Although deeply affected by Marisol's pain, the two girls were delighted by their new closeness with her, and started laughing through their tears. In an instant Marisol was laughing too. They were all smiling and wiping their eyes as they returned to their respective seats a moment later.

"Okay, my turn," Sam said. "Want to hear about the guy I stalked last summer? Or about the professor whose marriage I ruined sophomore year?" And without waiting for Marisol to choose, Sam began to talk, while Mandy, who'd heard both stories at least a dozen times, went to fetch another round.

Chapter Forty-Four

Indoor Work

It rained for the next two days, leaving Billy no choice but to lay low at the trailer park. Then, just before the gloaming of the second soaker, the clouds disbanded to expose a pink horizon, and true to that promise, the next day's dawn brought sunshine to the soggy beach. The warm rays created a knee-high haze of steam as the sand baked in the sun. Soon the beach began sprouting umbrellas. It was time to go to work.

The man had told him to make plenty of noise. "Contrary to what you might think," he'd said, "you should make a racket. That way if they're home, they'll catch you before you do anything." In cases when someone returned after Billy was already inside, he was to feign confusion—he was a tourist who'd made an honest mistake. His family had rented a condo for the week, and they'd just checked in an hour ago. It was the right floor, the right room number, but it didn't look like the same unit into which he'd dragged his suitcase and Nintendo Wii before scurrying down to the beach. "Wait a minute," Billy had been instructed to say, "what building is this?" And *there* was the simple explanation for why a strange boy had wandered in on their lunch or on their unpacking: He'd thought he was in the fourth tall condo building, when he'd been in the fifth all along.

No matter how many times Billy rehearsed this routine in his head, he remained deeply skeptical that it would work—but maybe it wouldn't have to. It was such a nice day outside that no one seemed to be indoors. He'd already tried a dozen units, and had found two that were unlocked. Just as Billy's accomplice had predicted, a certain percentage of the tourists had either forgotten or not bothered to lock their doors. He'd knocked and then gone in, calling "Mom? Dad? Lunchtime?" And when no one had answered, he'd kept walking. He'd found two handbags and three wallets in all, and sure enough, they'd been bursting with cash—fun money brought from home, or crisp bills recently counted out at Saco & Biddeford Savings in exchange for Canadian loonies. Unlike on the beach, where he'd grazed, Billy stuffed entire billfolds' worth of currency into the fanny pack he now wore on his hip before carefully putting the purses and wallets back where he'd found them.

Now, Billy turned the unlocked knob of another door. But stepping inside, he didn't find the same breezy decor, the pictures of lighthouses and wreaths of seashells that he'd observed in the other units. The straight-backed polyester furniture he'd encountered in all the others was absent, too. In fact, as Billy's eyes adjusted—for the blinds were drawn—he couldn't tell if there was any furniture at all.

As the rough shapes became more defined, Billy slowly realized that the room contained mounds and mounds of what he could only quantify as "beach junk." In one corner sat a pile of lobster traps in various stages of disrepair. In another, he spotted a mass of tangled clamming nets. Next to the window was a chest-high stack of driftwood, spilling toward the center of the room. There were other piles too, but they were less uniform and more difficult to categorize. There were clothes, bottles, books, Frisbees, balls, towels, deflated inner tubes, plastic shovels, sand-castle molds, kites, and shiny fishing lures. And, sitting in the middle of it all, in a small rocking chair, was a woman. It was Sally Fiddler.

Her face came into focus just as Billy realized he was not alone. Immediately, he understood the pointlessness of launching into his confused-tourist act. Sally sat there, rocking slightly, fidgeting with something in her hands. She appeared unconcerned to see Billy in her apartment.

"It's you," Billy said. "Shouldn't you be on the beach?"

He searched the wall for a clock, but couldn't find one. Instead he saw a series of sketches. There were a half-dozen, each one affixed to the wallpaper with a piece of masking tape across the top. There was a towering sailboat. Dark clouds brooded in the background. Neat letters across the bottom read WIND DANCER. Another depicted a girl about Billy's age, standing by herself at the end of a long dock, looking as if she were about to cry. In the background was a town, high on a hill. Her eyes were fixed somewhere on the water. The caption read LITTLE TOBAGO. The next was of a beach house, but it didn't look like the cottages along Old Orchard and Pine Point. It had a thatched roof and was flanked by palm trees. There was a woman in front of it, smiling. At the bottom, the same neat letters read ESCAPE TO ESCONDIDO. There were three more drawings, all done in pencil and colored somewhat imprecisely in crayon.

"You made these," Billy said. "They're really something."

Sally smiled at the sound of his voice but did not look up. She was too engrossed with what was in her hands.

Billy stepped away from the wall and surveyed the room again, this time with fully adjusted eyes. Something was coming to him; he wasn't sure what it was, but he knew it was important.

"This is the stuff you pick up," he said. And as he spoke, he remembered. The cop had told Billy's mother that he'd hidden the evidence in the woman's apartment. Billy tried to remember if he'd said where. He wondered if it was still there, and what kind of a clue it might offer as to how his mysterious friend and Sevigny had arrived in town on the same foggy night.

"What do you have there?" Billy asked. He stepped forward to see what was consuming her attention. When she looked up at him with suspicion for the first time, he instinctively stopped. Her gaze soon softened, though, and she held it out for him to see. It was a tiny ring. She was trying to put it on but it wouldn't fit. She showed it to him, holding it with one hand and unsuccessfully attempting to slide it onto the pinkie finger of her other hand.

"That's a toe ring," Billy said. "The girls wear them." He pointed to his sandaled feet. "Pretty stupid if you ask me."

She looked at him.

"I'm telling you," Billy persisted. "There's a big sign on the Pier. They cost, like, twenty bucks. Girls my age wear them."

She lifted a foot and rested it on her knee, then reached for it with the ring, but this contortion proved too difficult in the rocking chair. She tried once again, but lurched forward just as her hand reached her foot.

"Give it to me," Billy said. "I'll do it."

And he did, sliding the ring onto one of her toes.

Sally held up her foot and admired it. She nodded.

"Good, huh?" Billy said. "It looks good."

She smiled, then held her foot higher still. She looked at Billy.

"What?" Billy said. "You want me to take it off?"

Billy twisted it off and returned it to her hands. Satisfied, Sally lifted herself from the chair, walked across the room, and dropped the ring into a plastic beach bucket. In the pail were a hundred rings, or maybe two hundred.

"Wow," Billy said. "You have a lot of rings."

She smiled.

"Actually, I came to ask you something," Billy said.

She furrowed her brow.

"I'm looking for something a friend left here," he said. "You remember Officer Sabo?"

If Sally knew the policeman was dead, her face didn't show it. She smiled at the name.

"He gave you something to hide," Billy said. "He told you not to show anyone."

Sally cast a reflexive glance at the pile of lobster traps.

"I need you to show me," Billy said, already walking over to the traps.

Chapter Forty-Five

The Liar and the Thief

Standing between the stilts of the Pier as the night sky lit up with color and the gawkers in the Square began to *ooh* and *ahh*, Billy realized that the man was on to him. Billy had just handed over the day's take and the man had counted it. It was nearly two hundred dollars, but the man was glaring at him. And Billy knew why.

"Where's the rest?" he finally asked.

"The rest?" Billy repeated.

"Do you think I'm stupid?" the man barked.

"No . . . I . . . I . . . I—" Billy stammered.

"You don't trust me?"

"I . . . I—"

"This makes three days in a row. You thought I was too stupid to notice?"

He took a step toward Billy and as the glare from the latest explosion flickered across his contorted face and the sound of it reverberated off the water and echoed beneath the long wharf, Billy realized he was about to be struck.

"You—" the man snarled.

All at once, Billy delivered a preemptive blow. He did it not with his fists or feet, but with a single word. It was not something he'd planned. It was a defense of last resort he'd been carrying around with him for the past few days, ever since he'd found the strange journal buried amid the debris in Sally's apartment. The word was a name. And with it, Billy stopped his would-be assailant's hand. He yelled it, even though his tormentor was just three feet away.

"Rupert!" Billy shouted. And Rupert froze. His hand fell to his side.

Billy's voice had trembled, but once he'd spoken and seen the effect of this word, he found himself suddenly able to unleash a stream of others.

"Don't ever hit me again, *Rupert*," he spouted, placing particular emphasis on the man's name. "I swear to God, *Rupert*, you'll be sorry if you do."

Rupert's face went blank. For a beat, the wrath it had reflected completely dissipated. In his dark features there was only confusion, even terror. Then, slowly, his eyes rediscovered some of their familiar malice, and his small mouth turned downward again. "Who told you?" he asked.

"I've known," Billy said, laughing an almost evil laugh.

"Who?" Rupert asked. He wasn't demanding, he was begging.

"I'll tell you who *didn't*," Billy replied. "How about that?"

"Who didn't?"

"It wasn't your uncle."

"My uncle?"

"No," Billy said. "You don't have to worry about that. It wasn't Uncle Ferdie." Sensing the new power he possessed, Billy dug the needle deeper. "I don't blame you for hating him, Rupert," he said. "If one of my relatives screwed me out of that much money, I'd hate him too."

"How—" Rupert began, but didn't finish. Billy could see that his mind was desperately trying to make sense of the situation, but finding little traction.

Billy laughed another mocking laugh. "I think I'll wait to tell you," he said. "And don't even think about laying a finger on me, because if you do, you'll be sorry. You have no idea how sorry. You know why, *Rupert*?"

"Why?" Rupert asked dourly. And Billy could see from the evil in Rupert's eyes that his own suggestion had turned his reluctant ally's thoughts dark—that indeed, it was occurring to Rupert that maybe there was a quick solution to his new "Billy problem."

"I told someone," Billy said, smiling. "If anything happens to me, and I mean *anything*, the police will be on you before you know what happened."

"You told someone?" Rupert asked, his face turning red.

"I told someone you're here, and who you are," Billy lied. "I told them all about you."

"No, you didn't," Rupert said.

"I did," Billy lied.

"Your mother?"

"Right," Billy scoffed. "I told my mother I'm planning to run away with some stranger who's making me steal stuff on the beach."

"Okay," Rupert said, and Billy could tell he was recalculating. "You win. So who told you about me?"

"I'll tell you when we're in Canada," Billy said. "Get me out of here and you'll have nothing to worry about. I won't tell your uncle or anyone else."

"Not yet," Rupert said. "There's something I need to take care of first."

"Then do it," Billy said.

Chapter Forty-Six

New Beginnings

"Marisol!" Roger exclaimed.

She'd walked the two miles from Old Orchard to Pine Point, traversed the sandy path to his cottage, and was about to knock on the door. She'd heard his voice, only now she couldn't find him. It sounded like he was all around her. "Marisol!" he cried again, beginning to laugh. She did a pirouette, but found herself surrounded only by patio furniture. "Up here," Roger finally said, and she lifted her eyes to find him sitting proudly on the roof.

"Roger," Marisol said. "What are you doing?"

"I've built an observation platform," Roger exclaimed, standing so that she could fully see him. "I just put in the telescope. Where have you been? You're okay?"

"I'm fine," Marisol said.

"I was worried about you," he said. "Where did you go?"

"A telescope. You're spying on people?" Marisol asked, squinting against the midday sun.

"People," he allowed, "and boats. And the island where the cop was killed. I've scanned the beach for *you*. Walked it a few times too."

A few minutes later they were sitting three feet above the dunes, sipping lemonade on Roger's deck. Each was intent on out-apologizing the other. After Roger expressed the sorrow he'd felt upon waking to discover Marisol had departed, she lamented, "I put you in a terrible position."

"I drove you away," he maintained, "when you needed help."

"I wasn't honest with you," she said.

Finally, Roger said, "I guess we're still butting heads."

They both laughed an uneasy laugh.

"I can't believe that was just eighteen days ago," Marisol said.

"I know," Roger agreed.

They chatted for nearly an hour. Their conversation at first focused on her current living arrangements, then drifted to the new independence she was enjoying. She spoke about the mixture of resentment and affection she felt for Sevigny, who remained unaware of her presence in Old Orchard Beach. She would reach out to him soon, she supposed, only she wasn't sure exactly how to go about it. Then she told Roger about her continued attempts to write a letter to her mother. She'd started it at least twenty times, but the right words never came.

When it was Roger's turn, he talked about the soul-searching he'd been doing. He explained the thirst for excitement he'd felt ever since the two nerve-wracking days when he'd been part of their clandestine encounter. He'd closed his laptop on the third day of summer, he said, and hadn't opened it since. He wanted to discover more in life, but didn't know where to look. He was taking the summer to figure it out. He'd never felt so alive, he confessed, as when he was pulling her from the sea.

"Maybe you can be a lifeguard," Marisol joked.

"Hmm, I hadn't thought of that," Roger said, apparently taking her suggestion seriously. Then he began to list off the other new activities he'd been making time for since abruptly curtailing his day-trading.

Eventually, their conversation veered back toward the two topics everyone in Old Orchard Beach and Scarborough seemed to be discussing. They wondered aloud why Paul Mason had killed his friend Ernie Sabo, and what the heck Ferdie Sevigny was still doing at the Brunswick.

Neither Roger nor Marisol could imagine what had caused the one cop to kill the other, and though Marisol seemed qualified to offer more than just a guess as to Sevigny's intent, she said she could not discern it. It was unlike Sevigny, she said, to keep such a low profile, and to stay sequestered in one place. She could not make sense of it. "Usually he gets itchy feet if he stays anywhere too long," she said. "He needs to keep moving."

"I can relate," Roger said. "Only I've stayed here three years."

"No," she said. "With him it's different. He *needs* to move, or he starts to make himself crazy. He gets depressed—especially if he's alone."

Roger didn't say anything. He sensed there was more, so he waited.

"I'm not going back to him," Marisol said, lifting her eyes. "I owe him an apology, but not my life. It's mine."

"That's good," Roger said. "I'm glad to hear it."

A short while later, after Marisol had promised to visit again, they shared a friendly embrace before she departed. As soon as she'd left, Roger wished he'd done something brave. He wished he'd swept her off her feet and carried her up the ladder and onto the roof. He wished he'd sat her down behind the telescope and showed her the seals on Bluff Island, the fishing rigs trolling the channel, the people on the Pier, even Sevigny on his balcony. He should have done *something*. Before the summer was over, he promised himself, he would.

For her part, Marisol was left more satisfied by their interaction. She'd cleared her conscience. Roger had rescued her. She'd thanked him for his bravery and discretion, apologized for putting him in a tight spot. She'd done the right thing. Now, she felt strong and independent, like she kept telling herself she really was.

On the walk back to Old Orchard, though, a most unexpected thing happened. She was halfway home when a boy came running off the dry sand, apparently making a beeline for the water. Marisol slowed her pace to avoid a collision. But then, he pulled up and addressed her.

"Is your name Marisol?" he asked.

"Yes," she answered, surprised. "Did Mandy send you? Or Sam?"

"A man did," the boy said. "He told me this is yours." The boy reached into his pocket and extracted a ring.

Marisol recognized it immediately as the diamond she'd last seen aboard the *Wind Dancer* on the night Sevigny had nearly proposed to her before she'd abandoned him. With the waves washing against her ankles, Marisol stood staring at the ring until finally the boy handed it to her.

"He knows you're here," the boy said. "He needs to see you."

"Sevigny?" Marisol said, astonished. "Sevigny gave you this?"

"He was just a man on the beach," the boy said. "He said he wants to meet you somewhere private. He's sorry for what happened."

"He knows I'm here?" Marisol asked, as much to herself as to the boy. "He wants to talk?"

"I'll take you to him tonight," Billy said. "But you have to come alone."

"Of course," Marisol said. "I will. I promise."

Chapter Forty-Seven

Date Night

"Girls, I'm home," Sam called, dropping her sweaty baseball cap on the table and tearing off her grease-smeared Rocco's Pizza shirt. She reeked of sweat, designer perfume, and pepperoni.

"In here," Mandy called from the back room.

Before Sam could pass through the tiny kitchen, Mandy stepped into the hallway. "Guess who's got a date?" Mandy asked in an excited whisper.

"He finally asked you out?" Sam said, mistakenly guessing that Mandy had made plans with the lifeguard who'd been hitting on her the past three days at Seaside Suits, while purportedly trying to find a gift for his "girlfriend."

"Umm, no," Mandy said. "I saw him today, with his girlfriend. Like, she actually exists."

"Bummer," Sam said. "So who? The guy from Carrie's shop?"

"Not me," Mandy said. "Marie."

"No way," Sam gasped.

"I know," Mandy sighed. "She doesn't even try. She went to the beach and came home all smiles. We've been hitting the clubs every night. What the heck, right? She's showering now."

"She *is* beautiful," Sam said.

"*So* beautiful," Mandy agreed. "Would you believe today she mentioned the time she visited the pyramids? I forget how it came up. Oh yeah, we were talking about the sand sculptures left over from the Fourth. One was a pyramid. Anyway, I'm picking out a dress for her. She leaves at eight. She's being very secretive."

Entering the bedroom, Sam found practically every item of clothing from their collective wardrobes strewn across Mandy's bed. "Wait 'til you see her," Mandy said. "She's glowing."

It was true. There was a new radiance in Marie's smile that afternoon. Even after she'd insisted to her friends—and more recently, to Roger—that she was a newly independent woman, able to fend for herself, the idea that Sevigny might forgive her had reawakened an emotion deep and unalterable within her. From the moment she'd learned he wanted to see her, she'd wanted to run to him, to tell him everything, to beg his forgiveness.

Two hours later, with a Valentino dress clinging to her lithe frame, Marisol met the same strange boy from the beach. She met him in the Square. Then she walked beside him as he took her not to the big hotel on the south side of the Pier, but up a long hill and away from town. As the twilight faded into a silky summer evening, he led her to a wasteland of abandoned trailer homes.

So, he still intends to keep me his secret, Marisol thought. *He won't meet me where he sleeps, which is perhaps just as well. Maybe I really am better off without him.* But with each step she took on the decaying asphalt, she could feel her heart breaking.

The boy guided her to a trailer that had windows illuminated by the flicker of candlelight. The boy swung open the door and Marisol saw him in the faint light.

"No," she cried, "not you!" She backpedaled right into Billy, who stood blocking the exit.

"Hear me out," Rupert said. "Then I'll let you go."

"No," she said. "Not you."

"Five minutes," Rupert said. "That's all I ask." His eyes shifted to Billy. "Get lost," he commanded.

Chapter Forty-Eight

Breakfast with a Twist

The next day an elegantly attired young woman walked confidently into the Brunswick Hotel. She paused at the reception desk and waited for Marty Wagner to finish upbraiding a young boy who'd been knocking on the side of the hermit crab tank in the lobby.

"May I help you, miss?" the hotelkeeper asked.

"Yes, please," Marisol said. "I'm here to see Ferdinand Sevigny."

"Oh," Marty said, frowning. "He doesn't accept visitors."

"I'm a friend," Marisol said. "If you'll only tell him I'm here, I'm sure he'll see me."

Marty's face expressed genuine sympathy and even reluctance to carry out her duty. It was clear she felt the young woman was fighting a losing battle. "You wouldn't believe how many people ask for him," she explained. "But we have instructions to admit no one."

"Could you give him a note then?" Marisol asked.

Again, Marty began the painful exercise of denying a request. "He really can't be bothered," she said.

"Just a note?" Marisol pleaded.

"This is all new to my husband and me," Marty said, "playing interference between a celebrity and reporters and well-wishers and people who come looking for handouts. It's all new, and it's not anything we asked for. Please understand."

"But—" Marisol began.

"Please understand," Marty repeated. She raised her hand and waved at someone, and suddenly a man appeared at Marisol's side. She'd scarcely noticed him when she'd entered the lobby. He'd been sitting at the bottom of the stairs. He was a security guard the hotel had hired at Sevigny's expense. "Come on, miss," he said, gently taking Marisol by the arm, "I'll walk you to the door."

Marisol heard Marty calling after her, "This is all new to us." And the next thing she knew, she was standing outside.

Twenty minutes later, Marisol walked into Beach Bagels. She waited for a lull in the customer flow and then approached the counter.

Marisol had met Carrie on her very first night in Old Orchard Beach, when Mandy and Sam had found her in the Square, and had seen her a few times since. She remembered her roommates mentioning that Carrie bore the daily responsibility of toasting a poppy-seed bagel, slathering it with strawberry cream cheese, wrapping it in tinfoil, and delivering it to the Brunswick, where the hotelkeepers presented it to the town's most distinguished guest. Mandy and Sam had bragged that Carrie made breakfast each morning for "the richest guy in the world." Marisol, who might have noted that a few sliced strawberries pressed into the cream cheese would have further delighted Sevigny, or that Sevigny was actually only one of the fifty richest men in the world, had only smiled.

Now, she stood awkwardly before Carrie.

"Marie," Carrie said. "Want a smoothie?"

"No, thanks," Marisol said quietly.

"What's wrong?" Carrie asked.

"I need your help," Marisol said.

The next morning, Ferdinand Sevigny opened his bagel to find a sliced strawberry pressed into the cream cheese. He also found two notes in the bag that had conveyed his breakfast. The first read:

Dear Mr. Sevigny,

I am the girl who prepares your bagel at the local coffee shop. A girl I know asked me to include a note to you this morning. She swears she knows you and that you'll be happy to hear from her. I hope this is true, but I also think she might be crazy. If this is the case, and you've never heard of her, I promise I won't mess with your breakfast again. Just please don't tell Mrs. Munson, because I could get fired. I kind of believe her, so I hope she isn't lying and that my note is unnecessary. Whew! I hope that makes sense. Enjoy your time in OOB!

Carrie

196

The other note read:

S—

I am sorry for everything. What Rupert said on the Wind Dancer *was true. I did betray you, but only because I desired a life more meaningful than the one I was living in your shadow. I never wanted any harm to come to you. I didn't know what he was planning. But it is too much to explain in a note. I will come to your hotel today to beg forgiveness. Maybe if you leave my name at the desk they will let me in. I tried yesterday but was turned away.*

Love,
Marisol

Chapter Forty-Nine

A Reason to Be

Marisol made an effort not to gloat. She simply announced her presence and smiled when Marty offered a meek apology. Despite her apparent poise, however, Marisol's heart was pounding as she followed the hotelkeeper to the bottom of the stairs to where the woman's husband was waiting to show her to Sevigny's floor.

"So you enlisted the girl from Beach Bagels?" Jim said, smiling at her. "Very clever."

"Carrie won't get in trouble?" Marisol said.

"Carrie?" the hotelkeeper said. "No. The big guy seemed happy to get your note. He said you're old friends."

"So you won't mention it to Carrie's boss?" Marisol persisted.

"Ginny Munson?" Jim replied. "No, I won't say anything."

"Thank you," Marisol said.

Before she knew it, she was stepping through a door and into the presence of her friend, benefactor, and lover. It had been three weeks since the incident at sea, but to Marisol it felt like a lifetime. So much had changed.

Sevigny stood just inside the balcony with his head slightly turned. There were tears on his cheeks. He waited until the hotelkeeper had retreated before speaking.

"Marisol," he said.

"I'm sorry," Marisol started to say, but before she could get the words out, she realized she was running toward him, throwing her arms around his neck, and burying her head in his chest. "I thought he'd killed you," she said. "I didn't want to believe it, but I heard a splash—"

"I thought he'd killed *you*," Sevigny said, whispering into her dark hair. "I thought you'd drowned."

"I almost did," Marisol said.

Sevigny held her tighter.

"Sevigny," she said, extracting herself to look into his eyes. "It was my fault."

"You needn't say any more," he replied. "I forgive you—for whatever you did."

"No," Marisol said, speaking in a firmer tone than she'd ever taken with him. "I need to say more. And I need you to listen. It will be hard, but listen . . . please."

They stood there, measuring one another, each noting how the other was the same but different from their time apart. Finally Marisol said, "I conspired against you. I want you to understand why. During these three weeks I have come to understand, and it's important that you do, too. There are no excuses, but I want you to understand."

Sevigny studied her as a distressed tourist might scrutinize a lost diamond, suddenly relocated on the sand. He studied the familiar angles of her face. "Okay," he said.

She spoke slowly at first, gradually picking up speed as she told him everything—about her loneliness and listlessness under his stewardship, about Rupert's rants, about her guilt concerning her flight from Little Tobago, about her conspiring with Rupert and their plans for escape, about the money Rupert had embezzled, the house in Mexico. Then she recounted in painstaking detail her final night aboard the *Wind Dancer*— how she'd laid awake, wondering if she'd be able to go through with it; how Rupert had tried to kill her with the boat, and how she'd watched helplessly as Sevigny had been thrown overboard—"Not quite, I *jumped*," he interrupted—how she'd floated and drifted as her hope for rescue dimmed, and how finally, good fortune had brought her close enough to shore for a man to rescue her.

"It was your name I called," she explained. "And he heard, and saved me." She told him how she'd parted from Roger, about her reluctance to leave the area while she still entertained the hope that Sevigny may have survived. She told him about the two college girls who had befriended her, and how she was living with them now, discovering a more-independent self.

At several points she fought back tears. She knew that if she broke down, Sevigny would wrap her in his arms and beg her to stop, so she was strong. She told him everything—well, almost everything. She didn't tell him she'd met Rupert two nights before.

When Marisol had finished, Sevigny said, "I forgive you. Perhaps I should say that I'm sorry, too. We could let our apologies carry equal weight. We were both to blame, perhaps I more than you. I wasn't honest with you, either. I knew Rupert was stealing. I'd even instructed Warren to let it continue. I'd hoped he would take his fill and then go away."

"You knew all along?" Marisol asked.

"That you were planning to go with him?" Sevigny asked.

Marisol nodded.

"No. But I wondered."

"You did?"

"I knew you were unhappy," he said. "Then, on the night of the attack, I knew for sure. After I had dived overboard and removed my blindfold, I climbed aboard Rupert's speedboat and left him there on the *Wind Dancer*. I found money, two plane tickets, the two passports on the boat. I realized that you'd intended to go. Only I knew you weren't on the *Wind Dancer*, and you weren't on the getaway boat. I looked for hours, but it was dark and foggy. Eventually, I abandoned the little boat and swam to shore. I thought he'd killed you."

"Sevigny—" she said, anguished by the thought of him imagining her dead, the same thought she'd intended to plant in his mind when that fateful night at sea had begun.

"At least all that is over now," he said.

"Yes," she agreed. "And Rupert is gone."

"Hopefully," Sevigny said.

"If you will have me," she said, "I'd like to come back to you. I don't know for how long. Then, I must return to my mother."

"Yes," he said. "That is long overdue."

"Sevigny," she said uneasily, "we can never go back to the way we were. When you found me, I was a child. I'm a woman now."

"Yes," Sevigny said. "I know."

"I need your trust," she said. "If I am to be *with* you, I must not be hidden like something shameful."

"I understand."

"But there is something else, too."

"What?"

"I need a reason to be."

"A reason to be," he repeated. "You mean, a purpose?"

"Yes," she said. "Being with you is not reason enough to exist."

"You need fulfillment," he said.

"Yes," she said.

Sevigny started to laugh, but it was a sad laugh that faded quickly. "Imagine," he said. "Sailing the high seas—blindfolded."

"I'm sorry?" Marisol replied, not quite understanding.

"We all need a reason to be," he said.

Chapter Fifty

Fair Warning

With Marisol back by his side, Ferdinand Sevigny rediscovered some of his old focus. He had a reason to remain in Old Orchard Beach. He wanted to make amends for the trouble he'd caused; only then would he depart.

The townies realized that Sevigny's arrival had somehow contributed to the fatal shooting involving the two police officers. Paul and Ernie must have been investigating Sevigny's disappearance when it happened, they figured. Why else would they have been on the very island, at the very spot, where Sevigny had briefly rested before miraculously swimming to shore? But that was all they knew. Most people didn't blame Sevigny for that. Privately, Sevigny feared that his family's complicity in the "Bluff Island Bloodbath," as the tabloid press had dubbed the shooting, ran deeper than the good people of Old Orchard Beach suspected.

Sevigny knew Rupert had played a hand in whatever had happened there, even if he could not divine exactly how, or why. He did not express this to Marisol; not at first. He only told her of his desire to do some good for the town. He was struck immediately by the interest she took in this endeavor. Just a few days into their reconciliation, he observed that she had taken the lead in the initiative. He could not determine whether he had implicitly ceded that authority to her, or if she had merely seized it. Nonetheless, he was seeing a side of her he had never seen before.

As they sat on the balcony one sunny afternoon, Sevigny found himself amazed by her philosophical approach as they debated how some small part of Sevigny's fortune might best be put to use in the community. At one point, she compared the town's needs to her own: Her life, she explained, could be divided into two halves. The first had consisted of her years on the island. Those were hard times, but mostly happy ones. When she was young, there had always been something to do. She'd only become unhappy when she'd run out of things to learn and ways in which to grow. The second half of her life, she said, comprised her six years as Sevigny's mistress. In this role, she had had too much free time. She'd been deprived of the daily pleasure of working toward a useful end, and this idleness had contributed to what she now recognized as a blue period, in which she'd slipped into depression and moral decay.

"But I brought you professors," Sevigny rebutted. "They taught you history, art, music—"

"Yes," she said. "You gave me knowledge, but you didn't give me the chance to use it. *That's* what I'm trying to say now, about Old Orchard Beach. Your goal shouldn't be simply to *give* something to these people; it should be to *empower* them."

"I see," he said.

As they brainstormed on the sunny balcony, the projects they imagined came to more closely reflect the principle Marisol had articulated. Their discussion was also informed by Marisol's street-level understanding of Old Orchard Beach, which was something Sevigny did not possess. She had spent three weeks mingling with the tourists and locals, and could note, for example, that residents like her friend Carrie felt an undercurrent of resentment toward outsiders. The townies, she explained, felt like they had nowhere to *be* in the summer when the tourists swarmed the town.

They both stared at the blue waves.

"Tell me more about these friends you've made," Sevigny said. He knew that she had been living with two college girls before they'd been reunited and that she'd called them on the phone a couple of times since, but he didn't know much about them.

Marisol told him about the cottage she'd shared with Mandy and Sam. She tried to explain how obsessed and unlucky they were with boys, and how funny they were, but she felt unable to do justice to their silliness. It was impossible to make Sevigny appreciate them in the way she did. But she tried. She told him about cooking together, listening to their problems, staying up late, watching TV, and eating pizza. "Actually," Marisol said, "I was hoping to visit them tonight to pick up a few things I left there—my journal, and a few other personal items they bought for me."

"Why don't you invite them over for dinner," Sevigny said. "Maybe tomorrow?"

"Yes," Marisol said, smiling. "So you can meet them."

"Only don't visit them in the meantime," Sevigny said. "I'll have Jim Wagner send someone to get your things."

"Why?" Marisol asked, and before Sevigny could reply, she decided to make a stand. "Sevigny," she said, "I'm an adult. I'll come and go as I please."

"You're right," he said quickly. "It's just—"

"What?"

"I know he's still close," Sevigny said, looking into her eyes.

"Who?"

"Rupert," he said.

"You *know*?"

Sevigny proceeded to tell her some more details of his story that he'd left out the first time. He explained that the police had found some of his belongings on Bluff Island; only Rupert could have planted them there. Rupert had been trying, he speculated, to make Sevigny's "incident" look like an accident, rather than an assault. Presumably, he said, Rupert had done so before he'd realized Sevigny had survived. Sevigny didn't know how Rupert had contributed to the murder of the police officer, or even why, but he was sure he'd somehow been involved.

"Do the authorities know?" Marisol asked uneasily. "Are they looking for Rupert?"

Sevigny looked at her for a long while before he finally said, "No." Then he went on to explain that he'd played along with the investigators. He'd validated Rupert's phony evidence. He'd let the police believe he really *had* visited the island in the dead of night. He'd done so to keep the family's dirty laundry out of the news.

"Would you believe," he continued, "there was even a note from me, commending my beloved nephew? It looked so much like my own writing that it almost fooled *me*."

"He has a talent for that," Marisol said.

"For what?" Sevigny asked. "Forgery?"

"He used to leave me notes from 'you,' " she said. "Only they weren't things you would write. I always knew. It was a game he played."

The new light in Marisol's eyes, to which Sevigny had recently grown accustomed, yielded to a pained expression.

"We needn't say more," Sevigny said abruptly, intending to save Marisol the embarrassment of rehashing her past intimacy with Rupert.

But Marisol surprised him. "You really think he's nearby?" she asked.

"Yes," Sevigny said. "He has enough money, and the house in Mexico. He should leave, but he won't. He wants to harm me first, to kill me. He won't leave until he's tried."

"How do you know?"

"I saw it that night on the *Wind Dancer*," he said.

"You *saw* it?"

"I *felt* it."

When Marisol realized he was studying her, she looked away.

"Go to your friends," he said, smiling. "Just remember, he may wish you harm."

"Yes," she said. "We'd both better be careful."

Chapter Fifty-One

Stargazing

Billy was surprised to observe Rupert's usual spot beneath the Pier occupied by a sunburned woman in an ill-fitting two-piece. Scanning the beach, Billy soon picked out his dour ally standing on the wet sand amid a crowd of tourists. To a person, they had their eyes fixed on the Brunswick's upper balcony. There sat Ferdinand Sevigny, accompanied for the first time all summer by a lady friend.

Billy recognized her immediately as the same striking woman to whom he'd given the ring, and whom he'd led to the desolate trailer park. Now, she was on the hotel's high deck, draped in a white sarong, leaning against the railing and gesturing with both hands as she conversed with the displaced billionaire. Billy couldn't decide if they were arguing or not. To the beachgoers below, who had made Sevigny-gazing a part of their daily ritual since summer started, this new twist was a delight.

It was not until Rupert placed a cold hand on Billy's shoulder and said "You've done well" that Billy realized Rupert was pleased, too.

"I couldn't get the lady with the SpongeBob umbrella," Billy said. He'd taken a break from the condos to work the beach again for a while. Rupert had said it was best to keep the authorities guessing.

"That's okay," Rupert replied. Then, speaking more to the man and woman on the balcony than to Billy, he said, "Fool you once, shame on me. Fool you twice, and you *are* a fool, old man." He smiled a wrathful smile.

"She's going to help us?" Billy asked.

"Don't play dumb," Rupert said, shaking his head but still speaking amicably. "I know she's the one who told you."

"Told me what?"

"About me," Rupert said. "Even if you both deny it."

It was only then that Billy realized the strange woman must be the author of the journal he'd found in Sally's apartment. *So, Rupert thinks she's the one who told me about him, and the details of his life*, Billy thought, remembering how he had surprised Rupert with this information that night, under the Pier. Rupert thought *she'd* initiated contact with *him* through Billy, and only then had Rupert sent Billy to her with the magnificent ring. Billy was confused about how all of these pieces fit together. He would have to revisit the journal and read it more carefully this time.

"She's beautiful," Billy heard a woman's voice say from somewhere behind him.

"*So* beautiful," another female voice agreed.

Two miles up the beach in Scarborough, Roger Simons sat on his roof, staring through the lens of his Celestron telescope. When he'd seen Marisol a few days earlier, she'd seemed at peace. She'd said she was a new woman, capable of fending for herself and emerging fully from the shadow of the domineering man who'd dictated her every move for six years. Roger had believed her.

Now, he saw through the telescope that she was back at his side. Staring through the lens, Roger observed her excited gestures. From two miles away, he read into her body language a narrative that simply was not present, one that confirmed his own anti-Sevigny bias and fed his burgeoning fantasy that the mermaid he'd rescued once before might once again be saved by his hand.

Yes, she'd been drawn back into a life that was not for her. She'd told Roger herself that with or without Sevigny, she had felt her life was meaningless. Yet somehow, when she'd come to visit him, it seemed that she'd found her footing.

Now she'd fallen back into Sevigny's trap. She was reverting back to the same sad-eyed girl he'd dredged from the sea. *No*, Roger thought. *I've saved her once. I'll do it again.*

Chapter Fifty-Two

Just Deserts

Contrary to what Roger had observed, or thought he'd observed, Marisol more than held her own during her first week back with Sevigny. It was difficult, but they were both working to redefine their relationship. As she'd desired, Marisol had gone to visit Sam and Mandy just a few hours after they'd looked up at her on the balcony. And as Sevigny had suggested, she'd invited them, and Carrie too, to the Brunswick for dinner.

The distinguished gentleman sat with the four young women around an elegant table in the room adjacent to the Governor's Suite. The chamber was serving as Sevigny's formal dining room for the first time, after having functioned as Marisol's makeshift office during the previous few days. Another table, pushed against the wall, stood as testament to the work Marisol had been doing. It was cluttered with town maps, Chamber of Commerce brochures, copies of Old Orchard Beach's last few annual reports, a directory of zoning regulations, and other materials Marisol had gathered during a trip to Town Hall. By introducing herself as an associate of Ferdinand Sevigny's, she'd been granted access to whatever she might find useful in ascertaining, as she'd put it, "the town's state of affairs and current needs."

Upon the room's central table, the Brunswick's most resplendent china glistened on linen placemats shaped like oyster shells, and extravagant crystal glasses stood brimming with pink champagne. After introductions and a bit of small talk, Marisol offered her friends a slightly more complete explanation of her past. When she'd called them a few nights earlier to say she wouldn't be coming home, she'd said only that she would be spending the night with a friend who'd just arrived at the Brunswick. When she'd visited them later, she'd confessed that the friend was actually Sevigny, but only smiled demurely when they'd tried to tease more details out of her concerning her relationship with him.

Now she told them her real name was Marisol, identified herself as Sevigny's friend, and said that she'd been observing the town "from the streets" during the past three weeks. With cheeks radiant from the summer sun, Marisol spoke and Mandy and Sam listened, quickly moving beyond their simplistic understanding of "Marie" as an exotic stranger, bewildered in an unknown world.

There was something else about her that they'd either failed to notice before, or that she'd carefully concealed from them, and that was her confidence and sophistication. Carrie and even Sevigny—who'd thought he knew her so well—also noticed this quality, as Marisol spoke over a plate of fricasseed lamb.

Marisol explained that she would be spending the rest of the summer developing a plan through which Sevigny would improve the lives of local residents as a way to repay the town for the tumult his arrival had caused. It would have many components, she said. She and Sevigny had already decided to make a grant to renovate the town library. They were also thinking about transforming the vast parking lot a block from the Square into a public park for residents and tourists alike to enjoy. Then, she detailed an idea to restore the abandoned ballpark behind the police station. The field had once served as home to Old Orchard Beach's very own minor league baseball team. The bush leaguers weren't coming back, but she and Sevigny were looking into renovating the facility for the town's recreation department. Next, Marisol outlined an idea to build a community center on the site of an abandoned trailer park on the outskirts of town. The facility would exist exclusively for year-round residents, she said.

They had other ideas, too, and while they wouldn't be able to bring them all to fruition, they were hoping to identify the three or four most important ones by summer's end. Then they would work with the town council to help realize Old Orchard Beach's potential as a four-season seaside community, not just a summer tourist destination.

As the dinner plates were cleared, Marisol moved on to the second aspect of the good works she and Sevigny hoped to do for the town, and this was where, she said, she needed the girls' help. More than just enhancing the town's physical face, she and Sevigny really wanted to help the townspeople in a more personal way. "We want to help those who are struggling, so they may make their own success," she explained.

"This part was my idea," Sevigny interrupted, citing a lobsterman the town manager had brought to Marisol's attention. Sevigny explained that the man had been stricken ill and had fallen behind on his boat payments. Although he was healthy now, he was about to lose his boat. "When he gets his next statement," Sevigny said, "he'll see that an anonymous donor has brought his balance back to where it would have been if he'd never missed a payment."

Marisol turned to Mandy, Sam, and Carrie and said, "We're hoping you will help us do a survey. You could go from neighborhood to neighborhood, interviewing people, saying you're gathering information for a possible community center, but also learning who needs help, and what kind."

"We'll pay you handsomely," Sevigny interjected.

"No," Marisol said. "We should pay them what they've been making in the Square. They aren't the ones who really need our help."

Sevigny looked sheepishly at the three young women and turned up his hands.

"Bye-bye, Rocco's," Sam said, smiling. "I was eating too much pizza anyway."

Mandy quickly agreed to participate in the magnanimous endeavor as well. After a brief hesitation, Carrie did too. She couldn't quit on Mrs. Munson, she said, but she'd find time to help in the afternoons.

Later, after the serious business had been put aside, the guests chatted on a more personal level. At one point, when Marisol had retired briefly to the Governor's Suite and Sam and Carrie had struck up a conversation with Jim and Marty, who'd come to lay the table for dessert, Sevigny found himself alone with Mandy by the window. Smiling, he told her how happy he was that Marisol had made such good friends. Mandy smiled and gave him a wink. "I know you two are more than just *friends*," she whispered, fishing for any insight into Marisol's relationship with Sevigny.

Sevigny only smiled.

"I can tell by the way you look at her," Mandy whispered. "And I could tell by how excited she got on the night of your big date. And by how upset she was when things didn't go well."

Sevigny looked thoughtfully at Mandy as she stood by the window. But before he had the chance to speak, Marisol reentered the room, carrying not the notebook that had been her excuse for stepping out, but a cake in the shape of a giant sand dollar. It drew *oohs* and *ahhs* as she lowered it to the table. Written across the top were the words SEVIGNY, THE MOGUL, but this was crossed out. Beneath were the words SEVIGNY, THE ADVENTURER, but this too had a line through it. Finally, across the bottom were the words SEVIGNY, THE HUMANITARIAN.

"It's your favorite," Marisol said. "Devil's food."

"Delightful," Sevigny said, without the slightest hint of a smile on his face.

Chapter Fifty-Three

Unofficial Visits

During the final two weeks of July, Sevigny steadfastly adhered to his promise to give Marisol her space. While he remained sequestered on the fourth floor of the Brunswick, she came and went as she pleased before returning each night to sleep by his side. Even between the sheets, Sevigny saw a new, more assertive side of Marisol. Where once she had been submissive, now she took on more of a leading role. And where once she had been eager merely to please him, now she wouldn't rest until Sevigny had fully satisfied her needs and wants as well. During the days, she joined her friends in administering the survey she'd drawn up, visited Town Hall to meet with the municipal officers, and ran whatever other errands were necessary to assess the town's needs. Marisol also began going out in the evening. From the start, she had taken the liberty of visiting her friends for drinks or dinner whenever she desired, but then her nocturnal sojourns took a different turn. Sevigny could tell by the way she dressed, and by the elusive manner in which she comported herself.

He tried not to show his alarm; he knew he needed to trust her. In the past, his suspicions had contributed to the ruin of countless relationships, and had played a part in his initial failure with Marisol. He'd been too controlling of her; he realized that now. He didn't want to repeat the same mistakes he'd made prior to their reconciliation. He wanted this time to be different. But he was worried.

Now it was nearly nine o'clock on another summer night and Marisol was emerging from the study to announce she was going out again. She had on a pair of blue jeans and a bulky shirt, which struck Sevigny as an outfit far more casual than the tasteful summer outfits she'd brought with her from Sam and Mandy's apartment upon rejoining him. He also noted that her hair was not done up, and that her face was wiped clean of makeup. It seemed as if she'd gone out of her way to make herself look plain, even though for her, such an undertaking was impossible.

"I shouldn't be too long," she said. She walked across the room to where he sat by the window, holding a book. She kissed him on the cheek.

"Meeting the girls?" he asked.

"No," she said.

"A late-night cigarette run?" Sevigny joshed. He knew how much she detested even the hint of smoke.

She smiled. "Just seeing to some of your interests," she said. She started to go, but then, as if unwilling to appear too eager, she turned back toward him.

"At this hour?" he asked. He knew he was crossing a line. Marisol had already divulged as much as she cared to. Yet she had said she was meeting someone on his behalf, and if it was his business she was attending to, didn't he have a right to know more?

"It's complicated," Marisol said. Then, with greater conviction in her step, she turned and strode across the room, pausing only for an instant to blow him a kiss at the door before she disappeared.

An hour later when Sevigny heard her coming back up the stairs, he was in bed. When the door swished open, he closed his eyes. He kept them that way as she undressed. But long after she'd fallen asleep beside him, he lay awake, staring at the ceiling fan in the soft moonlight that reflected off the water.

The next morning, she seemed unusually quiet. Or was it just his imagination? He could not be sure. As they sat on the balcony, eating their bagels, he thought he saw from the corner of his eye that she had raised a hand to wipe at the beginnings of a tear. But when he turned to look at her, something else caught his eye.

"Marisol," he exclaimed. "You're wearing your ring."

"Yes," she said, looking down at the massive diamond. "But on my right hand, so who knows what it means? We'll have to see."

"I thought it had been lost," he said. "I thought you'd lost it at sea, or that *he* had taken it."

"No," Marisol said. "It was on my hand when I slipped into the water and when the man rescued me."

Sevigny did not speak.

"I only waited to wear it," she said.

Sevigny stared out at the ocean. At dawn, the sun had crested, bright and brilliant, but in the two hours since, a haze had risen to obscure it.

"I thought . . . ," Sevigny began, but Marisol cut him short.

"Must we relive that night?" she asked. "What matters is, I'm wearing it now."

"Yes," Sevigny said, nodding. "Yes, of course."

Part Four

Chapter Fifty-Four

Threats and Insinuations

A shark sighting cleared swimmers from the waters of Old Orchard Beach during the first week of August, but only for a few days. The ominous fin also bumped, but only temporarily, the latest headlines concerning Paul Mason's crime to below the fold of the *Journal Tribune*'s front page. Mason still refused to say a word about the shooting or what had driven him to it, and his court-appointed attorney was indicating that Mason wanted to cop a plea, even though it would unquestionably result in a life sentence. According to the local chatter, even his wife Millie, who visited Paul daily at the York County pen in Alfred, still had no idea why Paul had killed his friend.

As for Marisol and Sevigny, they continued to diagnose the town's needs, with hopes of presenting a plan to the town council by the end of summer. High above the beach they worked, even as Marisol's secrecy and Sevigny's growing suspicion began to undermine their rediscovered intimacy.

Billy Carter, meanwhile, spent the first days of August trying to decipher the identity of the woman living with Sevigny, and how her plight might be entangled with his own. After presenting the woman with the ring, leading her to Rupert, seeing her on the balcony of the Brunswick, and then realizing she was the author of the journal he'd found, Billy returned to Sally's to pore through the cryptic book more carefully. It was lengthy, and the writing was difficult to read.

Initially the journal had allowed Billy to deduce that Sevigny had not been alone aboard the *Wind Dancer*. Rupert and the book's unnamed author had apparently accompanied him. The writer had reflected on Rupert's relationship with Sevigny in a passage in which she discussed the mysterious source of Rupert's malaise. Under the Pier, Billy had used this knowledge to impress upon his unlikely ally that he was no longer a boy to be bullied, but a young man to be respected and even feared. Billy had said Rupert's name to his face, to let him know he would no longer be abused.

Rereading the journal now, Billy paid special attention to the passages in which the author expressed her own unhappiness and yearning for escape. The writing was abstract and difficult to follow; she always stopped short of specifics. And while she referenced Rupert and Sevigny by name, she refrained from offering too much of an opinion about either man. This confused Billy. He could not know that in the weeks leading up to her escape, Marisol had feared either man opening her book and reading too closely into her intentions.

Returning to the journal did enable Billy to learn that the woman felt just as trapped in her life as Billy felt in his. At first he imagined that she'd been promised deliverance to the same house in Vancouver that Rupert continued to dangle in front of him as the eventual reward for his labor. But then, rereading the leather-bound book inside his annexed trailer, Billy found a passage he'd overlooked previously. It was buried amid a several-page reminiscence of a village called Little Tobago. Suddenly, the writing changed from the past to future tense, and described a place in Mexico called Puerto Escondido. The author did not say how she planned to get there. She only likened it to the island village she knew well. She described how the warm water would glisten at first light and how the palms would rustle. She was close. She was almost there. "And *he* will have no power over me there," she wrote. "He won't even be able to tell Sevigny where I am." Billy deduced that Rupert was *he*.

He turned the page, eager to learn more from this glimpse into the woman's otherwise closely guarded future. But then he realized the next page was missing. It had been excised so carefully by some sharp object run along the binding that Billy had failed to notice its absence before. Now, flipping through the journal with a keener eye, he discovered several other pages missing, too. And all at once he remembered the pictures hanging in Sally's apartment. He remembered how finely they'd been drawn and how roughly they'd been colored in. He remembered the one that had depicted a tropical scene with palm trees and blue waves and a happy woman. It had not looked like Vancouver or any other place

in Canada. It had looked warm. Billy remembered that there had been a name across its bottom. Had it been Escondido? *Yes*, he thought. She had planned to arrive one day soon in Mexico. She had been aboard the *Wind Dancer*. Rupert had, too.

But something had gone terribly wrong.

A few days later when the shark threat had passed, Billy returned to the beach, as did Rupert. On the first morning back, Rupert arrived at his usual spot to find that someone had dragged a toe in the sand to form several bold letters. COP KILLER, they read. RUPERT IS A LIAR.

Before Rupert could wipe clean the accusation with the sweep of his foot, he looked up to see Billy standing at the water's edge. The boy was glaring at him.

"Cop killer?" Rupert sneered a few seconds later, standing beside Billy in knee-deep water. "What does that mean?"

"It means I followed you," Billy announced. "I heard you threaten him."

"Who?" Rupert asked, trying to play dumb, but his face was already turning red. "Why are you telling me this now?"

"I could have turned you in," Billy said.

"And—?"

"I didn't." Billy looked at Rupert with smoldering eyes. "Why did you lie to me?"

"I lied?"

"There's no house in Vancouver," Billy said definitively. "It's in Mexico."

Rupert suddenly smiled, having apparently regained a bit of his composure, though Billy had no idea why. "So, you've been talking to Marisol," he said.

"No, I haven't," Billy said.

"What do you want?" Rupert asked.

"What I've always wanted," Billy replied.

"I already told you—you're coming with me."

"To Mexico?"

"To wherever."

How do I know you're not lying?"

"You don't."

"What if I call the police?"

Rupert laughed. "You'll spend the next decade in jail," he said. "You let me in your room. You were an accessory before *and* after the crime."

"I didn't know what you were going to do," Billy protested.

"And I didn't know Mason would kill him," Rupert whispered. "Do you think a jury will care?"

Billy didn't say anything.

"I love it," Rupert said, almost chuckling. "You're hurrying me to go, and she's begging for more time. And you're talking to each other, apparently. Go ahead; call the police. Say you helped blackmail one of their officers. Don't forget about your twenty counts of breaking and entering, and the beach bags you looted. You might as well provide a full confession."

"Maybe I will," Billy answered, but the quaver in his voice said otherwise.

Billy followed Rupert from the shallow water onto the wet sand where two boys his age were passing a football back and forth. He followed Rupert to one side so they would not interrupt the game.

"Get to work," Rupert said. "And the next time you write a message in the sand, I'll make you wish you *had* called the police."

Chapter Fifty-Five

A Hero's Observations

On the ninth of August, Roger Simons decided he couldn't wait any longer. An hour before midday, he rode a wave of caffeine and adrenaline down to the beach. He had not fully savored the moment the first time. He had hardly even realized he was doing something important. Now, he embraced the quiet pleasure of walking past so many blissfully unaware people, confident in the knowledge that he was about to do something that would be monumental and life-changing. He would save his damsel in distress for a second time, and in so doing, claim her heart. That was the fantasy into which Roger's altruism had morphed.

Half an hour later, he found his request to see Marisol greeted by skepticism at the Brunswick's reception desk. Nonetheless, the woman took his name and directed him to sit beside a burly security guard while she phoned upstairs to see if he should be admitted. "Oh, she'll see me," Roger announced, before sitting down. And sure enough, a moment later the woman informed him that Marisol would be right down.

Before he knew it, she was there on the stairs, wearing a yellow dress with a matching rose tucked above her ear. He hardly recognized her. With her radiant smile and calm poise, she looked very different from the scared girl who'd hidden in his living room back in June, and even from the blossoming woman who'd sipped lemonade on his deck in July.

"Marisol," he said uncertainly.

She greeted him with an embrace and then, when they separated, said, "Come, meet Sevigny." She motioned for him to follow her up the stairs.

Could it be? Roger wondered. *Could she really be happy with Sevigny?* Halfway up the stairs, he gently seized one of her wrists. Drawing her close on the landing, he asked, "Is this what you want?"

"Roger," she said, "what do you mean?"

"This—" he said, gesturing with the sweep of a hand at the hotel above and below and all around her. Then he put into words what he really meant. "Are you happy with *him?*"

Marisol hesitated. Roger saw introspection in her eyes, and observed none of the helplessness he'd seen when he'd first met her, and yet, in those dark pupils he detected some remaining trace of conflict. "It's different now," she said, finally. "He is. I am. I'm not sure if it's happiness, but it's closer." She returned his desperate gaze with kindness in her eyes. "I'm okay, Roger," she said. "Really."

"If you ever feel trapped," he said, struggling to keep his eyes fixed on hers, feeling the need to look away, but resisting, "just remember I'm right up the beach." By the time he'd finished, his voice was barely audible and he'd dropped his chin to his chest so that he was looking at the floor.

"I'll remember," she said kindly. "I promise."

Roger followed her up the final flight. He should have been happy for her, he thought, yet he felt let-down and terribly embarrassed. He wanted to run down those stairs and out into the sun, losing himself in the crowd on the beach. He cursed himself for coming.

But Marisol quickly dispelled the awkwardness. Opening the door, she announced, "Here he is—my hero. This is Roger, the one who rescued me!"

Roger stepped into the room to find Ferdinand Sevigny rising from a chair to greet him. In a few quick steps the famous adventurer had crossed the room and grasped Roger's hand. "Thank you," he said. "You're a brave man. Thank you."

Roger didn't know what to say. He just stood there, waiting for Sevigny to release his hand.

"Sit," Marisol directed. "They'll be up with some iced tea in a minute."

For the next half-hour, the unlikely trio spoke in generalities about the rapidly passing summer, the robust tourist season, and the community projects Marisol and Sevigny were planning to propose to the town. Then the talk turned to the night Roger had pulled Marisol from the sea.

Sevigny became more animated. Although he'd already heard Marisol's version of the harrowing night, he was eager to hear Roger's. He asked how Roger could have possibly heard Marisol from inside his house. He seemed flattered to hear Roger say that it had been the sound of Marisol calling his name—"Sevigny, Sevigny!"—that had summoned Roger from his dreams, even though Marisol had already told him this detail. He asked how long it had taken Roger to reach Marisol, how far he supposed he'd had to swim, how he'd located her in the fog, how he'd conveyed her to shore, how he'd learned of her connection to him, what they'd done the next day, and so on. As Roger answered, Sevigny met his every utterance with fascination, nodding readily, and saying, "I see, I see."

Sevigny's appreciation for Roger's bravery and discretion shined through to such an extent that Roger felt very satisfied with their interaction by the time an hour had passed. "Well, I should start walking before the tide turns," he finally said. A moment later, he shook Sevigny's hand, shared another embrace with Marisol, and then smiled agreeably when Sevigny offered to walk him to the stairs.

In the hall, the older man took his hand again. "I'm so glad you came, so very glad," he said.

"Me too," Roger replied. "I was a little worried about her."

"I know," Sevigny said, pulling at his beard.

"It's nice to see her so . . . happy," Roger said. Then he added, almost as an afterthought, "And that's quite a ring she's wearing." He had noticed it midway through the visit and had supposed it to be an engagement ring. Neither Sevigny nor Marisol had mentioned anything about it, though, and it had been on her *right* hand, so he wasn't sure. He hoped that by mentioning it he might cajole a bit more information from Sevigny and extinguish whatever embers of his fleeting Marisol fantasy might remain.

"I gave it to her a while ago," Sevigny said. He offered no more. But then, as Roger began to descend, Sevigny called after him. "Wait," he said. "You mean she wasn't wearing it when you rescued her?"

Roger turned and shook his head. "Just her panties," he said quietly. He thought about this memory for a second, before adding, "I'm pretty sure I would have noticed it. I've never seen a rock like that."

"I see," Sevigny said, furrowing his brow. "I see."

Chapter Fifty-Six

The Interrogation

After writing the message in the sand, and being left to wonder whether doing so had been a huge mistake, Billy awoke a few nights later to the glare of a flashlight being shined directly in his eyes. The crickets that had lulled him to sleep an hour earlier were quiet now. All he could hear was the pounding in his chest. He was on his mattress in his deserted trailer at Ocean Yard, trembling with the abject terror that seizes someone woken in such a manner.

"Who's there?" he asked frantically. "Who's there?" But there was no response. Gradually he detected a noise, a flickering, flipping sound coming from just beside his bed, and he became aware that someone was sitting beside him.

"Your eyes will adjust," Rupert's voice finally said. And Billy realized that the light had been taken off him. It was still in the room, but was no longer pointed in his face.

"I'm reading a most interesting diary," Rupert said. "I found it on your nightstand. I believe it belonged to a friend of mine." His voice was measured, but without a hint of sympathy.

Billy could make out only the blurry shape of the man beside him. He felt as if he were trapped in a nightmare. His eyes and voice were useless. His mind was racing, his heart pounding, pounding, pounding. He was paralyzed with fright.

"You've boxed me into quite the corner," Rupert said dryly. "You were right. I had no intention of bringing you to Mexico. But then you learned my name. So leaving you became a risk. I thought briefly about actually bringing you, but missing kids have a way of winding up on the evening news. A kidnapped boy. A manhunt. I'd have been caught before I even sniffed the border. Once you found out my actual destination, though, I knew I couldn't leave you here. You'd tell the authorities where to look. You'd tell them I blackmailed the cop, and my chickens would come home to roost."

Billy was slowly regaining control of his senses. He managed to sit up on the mattress with his knees pulled against his chest beneath the sheet. His vision was returning, and he was pretty sure his voice would be there when he needed it. His heart was still thudding away. He could see that Rupert was wearing thin gloves even though it was August. On his face was grim determination.

"You've become a liability," Rupert said, almost sadly. "You've left me no choice."

"You . . . you can't," Billy stuttered. "You can't."

"Oh, right. Because you've shared your secrets with someone," Rupert said, mockingly. "Do you think I believe that? No, you haven't told anyone. You haven't even been talking to Marisol. You learned about me through her diary. I could kill you and no one would know. No one would miss you. No one would connect the dots between you and me and the two cops."

"But people have seen us together," Billy objected.

"Who? Strangers on the beach?" Rupert scoffed. "There's a different lot of them every week. Besides, we've been careful."

"But . . . but—" Billy said, looking searchingly into Rupert's dark eyes. He saw that some great harm was about to be done him and felt powerless to stop it. Then, all at once, the grimace subsided on his tormentor's face.

"I'd like to take you with me, Billy—I really would," Rupert said in a softening voice. "You remind me of myself when I was your age. Angry, alone, scared."

"Then take me," Billy begged.

"But it would draw attention," Rupert reasoned. "Like I said, a kidnapped boy." He paused thoughtfully. "Unless . . . ," he said.

"Unless what?"

"Unless we did something to throw them off our tracks."

"We could," Billy said immediately. "I could write a note. I could say I'm running away. I could leave it for my mom to find. I could say I'm going to Canada, even though we'd be on our way to Mexico. They'd look in the wrong place. They won't think it's a kidnapping. They'll think I ran away."

"That . . . might work," Rupert said, nodding at first, as though he were pleased with Billy's suggestion, but then frowning. "But wait," he said. "There's still the evidence here in town that would link me to Sevigny's accident. You know, the evidence Sabo found." He looked at Billy. "Unless *this* was it?" He raised Marisol's journal.

"No," Billy said. "There's more."

"What?" Rupert asked.

"The hood," Billy said. "The hood he was wearing. It had blood in it. And there are pictures."

"Pictures?"

"From the journal," Billy said. "Pictures of Mexico."

"Where?"

"I know where they are," Billy said. "I can get them."

"And you'll write the note?" Rupert asked.

"I swear."

"Why don't you write it now," Rupert suggested. "That way I can help. And I'll hold on to it; that way the timing will be right."

"Okay," Billy said. He took the pen and notepad from Rupert's gloved hands. He did not stop to wonder why his would-be assassin had broken in, toting stationery. He was just relieved to have changed Rupert's mind.

Rupert proceeded to dictate a note just like the one Billy had described. When Billy was finished writing, Rupert told him to sign his name at the bottom like he would sign a check. When this instruction was met by a befuddled look, he told Billy to sign it like he'd sign any other note to his mother, only this time, he should sign his last name too, which, though it seemed unnecessary, Billy did. When the exercise had been completed and the note tucked safely in Rupert's pocket, Rupert promised Billy it would be just a few more days before they departed. Then he told Billy to get some sleep.

Outside, Rupert took a satisfied breath of night air and suppressed the urge to cackle. The terrified lad suspected nothing. He even believed that writing the note had been his idea.

Chapter Fifty-Seven

Trust

Sevigny concealed the festering doubt that was growing within him from Marisol, the two hotelkeepers, and the three girls who sometimes came to visit. An intense spiritual battle was playing out within his soul, pitting his promise to trust Marisol against his inherent skepticism of others. On an intellectual level, he recognized that his reluctance to fully trust people had at times preserved him in life. More often, though, that same tendency had led him astray. It had always been a part of him; for as long as he could remember, he'd found it impossible to take things on faith, to extend the benefit of the doubt, to assume others' intentions were purely benevolent. He'd always wanted to know more. He'd always *needed* to, just to be sure his own interests were protected. Now, he wanted to be content. He wanted to love Marisol the way she said she needed to be loved. But his unquiet mind kept asking questions that it could not answer. And as these questions mounted, they threatened the new relationship he and Marisol were building.

Sevigny's suspicion had first reared its head on the night Marisol's friends had come to dinner, when Mandy had mentioned Marisol's "date." According to Mandy, Marisol had gotten all done up and had been quite excited to meet a beau, yet she'd come home in tears, leaving her friends guessing at the reason. Just a short while later, Marisol had arrived at his door.

Whom had she met that night? Sevigny wondered. *And why?* What had so upset her, and why had she come to beg his forgiveness so soon afterward?

Sevigny had not wanted to even entertain the thought that Marisol had met Rupert, and, in fact, had not allowed his mind to stray in that dark direction—at least, initially. Perhaps she'd met some young man from town, and things had not gone well. Was that so wrong? Did that bother him? Did that compromise the authenticity of her renewed interest in him? He didn't think so, and he hadn't minded living with the uncertainty of that one mysterious escapade.

But then, in mid-July, Marisol had started embarking on evening adventures, and she had evaded his prompts for more information. He hadn't wanted to smother her, to control her, or even attempt to. He'd let those awkward moments pass. But he needed to know where she was going, and with whom. And why did she always seem to have a tortured conscience the next day—or was that just a figment of his imagination?

Next had been Roger's visit and his disclosure concerning the ring Sevigny had given Marisol. When the ring had disappeared, Sevigny hadn't worried about it; it was a small loss in a greater tragedy that had only narrowly been averted. But then, the very morning after one of Marisol's nocturnal excursions, the ring had reappeared on her finger (albeit, on her right hand), brandished as proof of her devotion. She'd had it all along, she'd told him, but had chosen not to wear it until just then.

Only Sevigny knew better. He'd met her hero, who'd told him she'd been practically naked when he'd carried her from the sea. She'd worn no ring. Roger Simons had no reason to lie; did Marisol? Sevigny didn't know. And if she hadn't had the ring for all that time, who had? When had it been returned to her—and why?

Sevigny knew that posing any of these questions to Marisol would strain their new relationship. His distrust would remind her of a part of him that he was incapable of suppressing. But each day he became more and more ensnared in a web of doubt. He couldn't help it; he felt as though he were inching closer and closer to a line he'd promised not to cross but eventually, inevitably, would.

There was another thing bothering Ferdinand Sevigny, and that was the ghost that Jim and Marty Wagner often joked about. It had begun to haunt him. It seemed intent on making his nights as sleepless as possible. He did not fear the ghost, but rather regarded it with curiosity. He smirked at the rattle of the bedroom doorknob, the flight of a magazine from table to floor, the unfurling of the blinds. But night after night, these paranormal occurrences prevented him from drifting into the kind of sleep his mind required. The ghost was definitely trying to tell him something, only he didn't know what. He suspected he never would.

It seemed incapable of speaking any more artfully than in cryptic demonstrations.

During the daylight hours, Sevigny sat groggily before the massive window, gazing at the sea, wondering where the *Wind Dancer* should take him next, and with whom, once its repairs were completed. The ghost did not visit him then. He never mentioned the visitations to Marisol, who would have thought him crazy. In the daytime, it did sometimes occur to him that he might be losing his mind, but then Jim and Marty would tacitly reassure him of his sanity whenever they joked about Eben Staples, who'd hanged himself in the room where he and Marisol were currently sleeping.

Now, on this hazy August night, darkness was encroaching, bringing with it another dreamless night, another round of jousting with unanswerable questions, and, in all likelihood, more supernatural shenanigans. Sitting by the window, Sevigny looked up to find Marisol standing by his side, dressed casually, looking as if she'd just seen a ghost herself.

"I'm going out," she said.

He furrowed his brow.

"You have to trust me," she said.

"I do," he said. "And will continue to . . ."

After her footsteps had carried her away, Sevigny turned from his reflection in the glass. He faced the door. "I will," he said quietly, "even if it is the end of me."

Just then, a vase containing five purple dahlias began to wobble on the coffee table. It did not fall, or tip. It merely wobbled, slowly, gently, until some water had sloshed onto the surface of the table. Sevigny stood up, took three quick steps, and abruptly seized the ceramic omen. He steadied it and then sopped up the water with a handkerchief.

"Ha," he said, with some of his old bravado. "You'll have to do more than that to chase off Ferdie Sevigny."

Chapter Fifty-Eight

The Family Secret

Marisol spent the next morning in her study, ostensibly fine-tuning the proposal she and Sevigny intended to present to the town council by summer's end. In truth, her thoughts were elsewhere. She knew it was impossible to delay any longer. She only hoped she would find the right words, and that Sevigny would not make it more difficult than it needed to be.

He was sitting by the window, flipping through a copy of *Newsweek*, when she finally approached him. "Sevigny," she said, "I need to speak with you. It's not a pleasant topic, but I need some answers. And I need you to not ask why I need to know."

Sevigny closed his magazine and turned to face her as she pulled up a chair.

"Will you promise?" she asked.

"I don't know what I'm agreeing to," he protested.

"Just promise you'll answer, and not ask why," she said. There was pain on her face but no room for compromise.

"Okay," he said. "I promise."

"I need the answer to something I asked long ago," she said. She looked away before quickly returning her eyes to his face. "What caused the rift between your father and your brother, Robinson?" she asked. "What happened that allowed you to remain at your father's side while Rupert's father was disowned?"

"That is a question—" Sevigny began, mechanically, just as he had when he'd evaded the query once before. But this time he checked himself. "That is a question," he restated, "that remains a cause of great shame for my family."

"Your family?" Marisol said quietly. "But it's only you and Rupert now; you're the only two Sevignys left. And he doesn't even know why."

"Well," Sevigny said, "it remains a cause of shame for me."

"Tell me," she said.

"My father . . ."

"Tell me," she pleaded.

"My brother Robinson . . . ," Sevigny began again. "From an early age there was something odd about him. No, more than odd. There was something *off*. My father saw it first, but eventually my mother did, too. And I saw it, even though I was just a boy.

"One of my earliest memories is of an 'accident' Robinson had with a cat that belonged to one of our neighbors. It would climb the fence and we would play with it. Then one day, something happened. I was too young to understand; I only knew my parents were displeased, the animal was gone, and Robinson was being punished. I was seven or eight, he was two years younger. Later, there was another accident. This time, with a little girl, a playmate of ours, whose father worked for our father. Robinson did something to her, or said something . . . I don't think I ever knew which, but I remember how my father screamed. After that, she didn't play with us. And not long afterward, Robinson went away to a special school."

Sevigny paused, staring for a long moment out the window before he resumed.

"We saw him on holidays and long weekends when he would come home. After a while it was almost like he wasn't my brother anymore. He was just another little boy who sometimes came to visit. My parents were careful never to leave us alone together; there was always a nanny or some other adult. I remember how he hated me. I had a train set—it had taken months to build—and I remember he stomped all over it before my mother could stop him. He was nine or ten. I didn't see him again for a long time after that."

Sevigny paused again; Marisol was about to encourage him to go on but didn't want to interrupt his remembrances.

"Then, when he was fourteen or fifteen, he came home," Sevigny said, "and I remember my parents making a big to-do about it. We were supposed to be a happy family again. But by then I had my own friends. I was driving, finishing prep school, and we didn't have much in common. I remember he kept to himself. My parents tried to include him, tried to make me include him in whatever I was doing, but eventually they gave up. Then I went to university, and I was the one who only came home for holidays. I was the one who started losing track of the family's day-to-day life.

"When I was twenty-two or twenty-three, I remember Robinson got into bigger trouble. As far as my parents were concerned, he was no longer a Sevigny. That was it. They wrote him off. I didn't know what he'd done until my mother lay dying years later. It was one of the last times I saw her, and I asked if I should call my brother. I didn't even know where he was living or how to reach him, but I knew she didn't have much time.

"She said no, and *that* time when I asked, she told me what had happened. He'd gotten a girl pregnant, she said. Not a woman, a girl. She was twelve, my mother said. Mind you, he was in his twenties by then. My father paid the girl's mother to hush things up . . . her mother was one of our maids, or cooks. My mother told me my father did something to Robinson to make sure he'd never do anything like that again—I didn't ask what. But my father was a hard man. I can only imagine what he did to his child-molester of a son."

Sevigny grimaced.

"And the baby?" Marisol asked.

"Rupert."

"Your brother raised him?"

"That's another story," Sevigny said. "The girl—Rupert's mother—was supposed to get rid of the baby; that was the deal her mother made when she took my father's bribe. For whatever reason she decided to carry the baby to term, only her body was too small, and when Rupert was born, she died. Rupert's maternal grandmother raised him for a while. Then, she either ran off or disappeared, I don't know which. She left Rupert with Robinson, and apparently he brought him up—as unsettling as that may sound.

"You have to understand: I only knew that there had been a big blowup while I was away, and that my parents were suddenly estranged from my brother. It was years before I even knew I had a nephew, let alone where he was living, and with whom. By then my brother was dead."

Marisol raised her eyebrows. "That explains why Rupert is—" she began.

And left to finish her thought, Sevigny added, "The way he is."

She forced a bleak smile. "Thank you for telling me," she said. "I can see why you haven't wanted to talk about it."

"And you can see that it doesn't change anything."

"You mean between you and Rupert?"

"I mean anything."

"Yes, I see," Marisol said. She looked at him tenderly. "I'm sorry your family went through that," she added.

"I know," Sevigny said, wiping away tears.

She hugged him.

From that point on there could be no further doubt in Sevigny's mind that Marisol was indeed meeting Rupert. He did not want this knowledge, but it had been thrust upon him. More than anything, he worried for her safety. Secondarily, he wondered if she would betray him a second time, or if she already had. He didn't worry too much about this latter possibility, however; he'd worried enough about it already.

He didn't realize it until just that moment, when she embraced him, but at some point he had decided to refuse himself the right to accuse her. He was not sure why. He did not know if that was what trust was, or love, but he knew that from this point on, he would not break the promise he'd made. Wherever she was leading, he would follow, and only then would he know for certain that he'd done all he could to resist the demon within him that had sabotaged his past relationships.

Chapter Fifty-Nine

A Look of Fear

As Marisol and Sevigny sat talking about the Sevigny family's dark history beside the big window overlooking the sea, Billy Carter walked past the Brunswick on the beach below. After Billy had delivered the bloody hood and crudely colored drawings from Sally's apartment, Rupert told him to pack his things and be ready. He told him that whatever Billy pilfered on his last day would be his to keep. It could be Billy's "spending money," he'd said, for the trip to Mexico. They would leave an hour before dawn the next day. He would pick up Billy at Ocean Yard in a "borrowed" car.

But that was still half a day away. First, Billy had work to do. He still didn't like doing it, but it was almost over. And at least today's take would be his own, not Rupert's.

Walking on the flat sand of low tide, Billy observed a new sign hanging from the underside of the Pier. There had been one like it at the edge of the dunes on the footpath, too. Looking up the beach, he could see several more, extending all the way into Scarborough. Printed on blue paper and laminated, they read BEWARE: BLANKET/CONDO THIEF. LOCK ALL APARTMENT DOORS. GUARD VALUABLES ON BEACH.

Billy tried not to look at the signs as he walked along the water's edge. He tried to focus on the people on the dry sand, just to his left, on their bags, coolers, and purses. Rupert had explained he would be busy finalizing arrangements. Billy would have to go it alone. "Do whatever you want," he'd said. "Just don't get caught."

Billy had no intention of getting caught. He was so close to what he'd always desired. There was no sense ruining it now. Blankets were quicker than condos, but more risky. He kept walking. He'd hit two or three bags, maybe past the Royal Anchor where the sand wasn't as densely packed with people. He walked and walked, and before he knew it, he had passed the Anchor, the pink house, and all six condos. He was stepping into Scarborough where the sand of "his" beach joined Pine Point Beach. Somewhere along the way, he'd stopped looking at the blankets. Without Rupert close by, somewhere, anywhere, it seemed he'd lost his will. Maybe he'd hit a couple of blankets on the walk home, or maybe he wouldn't. How much spending money did he really need?

Billy walked as far as he could. Then he stood on one of the large flat stones at the foot of the jetty. Two lobster boats were chugging through the channel. A boy his age was casting for bluefish off the rocks. Across the gulf, the distant silhouette of a beach umbrella rose against a field of yellow-green dune grass. The shadow of a woman lay beneath it on the narrow strip of sand. *So that was it*, Billy thought. He'd walked the whole beach. He turned to head home, no longer entertaining thoughts of plunder. It just wasn't something he wanted to do. Not on this day.

Heading back toward Old Orchard beneath the warm afternoon sun, Billy allowed his eyes to stray up to the dry sand. For the first time all summer he saw the happy panorama for what it was. He saw the tourists and townies as the people they were, not as potential marks. There was a curly-haired toddler streaking toward the surf, wearing a puffy diaper, a plastic shovel in his hand. He shrieked with joy as his mother pursued him. There was an elderly couple, each wearing blue jeans, long sleeves, and sneakers as they walked together on the flat sand. Billy wondered if it was the hundredth time they'd walked at low tide together, or the thousandth. There was a boy a few years older than him, lifting a giggling girl off her feet with muscular arms and staggering toward the water as she pretended to fight back. He dumped her with a splash and she screamed, even though the water was only up to her knees. Billy thought he should have carried her farther. But they were happy.

Turning from the happy pair, Billy saw a familiar face up ahead at the water's edge, and, having felt a part of him reawaken at the sight of so many smiling people, his heart flooded with unexpected emotion. It was Sally, the woman he'd been seeing all summer, his silent friend. He worried that she might suspect his treachery. Would she see it in his eyes? Would she know that he was the one who'd let himself into her apartment and stolen her pictures?

As Billy drew closer, he realized she didn't see him. It would have been easy to just walk by, but he didn't want to. He stopped and waited for her to turn his way.

"Hello," he said.

She started to smile, but then, all at once, her body clenched.

No, Billy thought. *She can't know. It's impossible. She was on the beach the whole time.* "It's only me," he said. Then he realized she wasn't looking at him—she was looking past him, up the beach. She shook her head and stepped back, and then back again, right into a big-bellied man carrying a fishing pole.

"Sorry," Billy said to the man, who had already resumed his trek.

"It's just me," Billy said again. She'd backed into the shallow water, stunned and cornered against the surf.

"The man," she said meekly.

Billy was shocked. She hadn't spoken a word to him all summer. He'd figured it was something she wasn't able to do, but she'd spoken, in a thin, uncertain voice.

"The man?" Billy repeated.

"Behind you," she said.

Billy turned and observed men and women and children walking the tide line. They were the same happy people who'd filled the beach all summer, but he'd only today opened his eyes to actually *see* them.

"—from under the Pier," she added.

Billy wondered if she meant Rupert. Had she seen the two of them together?

"What about him?" Billy asked.

"He took my ring," Sally said. "He's the one."

"What ring?" Billy asked.

"Shiny," Sally said. "My shiny ring. He pushed me. He didn't think I saw him, but I did."

"That's what you've been looking for," Billy said, remembering the diamond Rupert had given him to lure Marisol to the trailer park.

"He hurt me," Sally said. Her eyes were still fixed beyond Billy's right shoulder as he stood facing her in the shallow water. Slowly she began to raise a hand. Billy thought she was going to touch his face, but that wasn't it. She was pointing.

"There," she said, "there he is."

Billy swiveled his head again, but saw only herds of passing tourists on the wet sand. Above, the brightly attired sunbathers on the dry sand appeared similarly indistinguishable.

"Don't worry," Billy began, and he meant to say more, but before he could, she took three splashing steps to his side and began to run. Billy watched her dart along the shore and then turn up into the blankets, which she stepped between and over in flight. She did not look back.

Now it was Billy's turn to stand there, stunned, in the surf. Rupert had hurt Sally. Maybe she'd spotted him somewhere in the crowd, or maybe she had just imagined it; regardless, the very thought of him had terrified her. Billy scanned the beach, trying to determine if Rupert really was there in the crowd, but there was no sign of him.

Chapter Sixty

Billy's Farewell

As the sun set on the August day, Rupert slunk back to his latest cheap motel room. He'd been careful to keep moving all summer, and to leave as slight an impression as possible on each new place he slept. Fortunately, discount lodging was plentiful a few blocks north of the Pier, and the steady stream of money Billy had provided more than paid his way.

Now, after making sure the boy had stayed out of trouble on his final day, Rupert retrieved a letter from his room at the Friendship Motor Inn and carried it to a mailbox on East Grand. The envelope was addressed to the Old Orchard Beach chief of police, upon whose desk Rupert intended it to land the next day. It was Billy's letter—only not the one the trembling boy had written to his mother. It was a new one that Rupert had penned in the boy's hand.

Using Billy's draft as his guide, Rupert had mastered the sloppy M's and slanted T's that characterized his handwriting to produce a note that better fit his needs. Billy's note had stated merely that he was running away from home, hitching a ride with some tourists to Montreal. Rupert's letter said much more.

Dear Chief White,

My mom was screwing both cops from the shooting. Some great cops—and some great mother! I didn't have much choice, but you did. And that's why I'm writing. I want you to know what those pigs did to my life. You hired them, so you're partly to blame.

Anyway, I stole Nick Balbone's phone from school. I used it to take pictures of them with her. I was hoping they would pay me to make the pictures go away. Sabo refused. But Mason told me not to show anyone. He said he would get Sabo to play ball. The next day he killed him.

At first I thought it was my fault, but the more I thought about it, I blamed Mason. Let him rot in jail. But it was Sevigny's fault too. If that jerk hadn't come to OOB, my plan would have worked. Your cops wouldn't have gone to the island. Mason wouldn't have had a chance to do it. I would have gotten the money for a new Wii.

Your cops messed it up, and so did Sevigny. He's gonna get what he deserves. As for me, by the time you read this I'll be long gone. Don't bother looking, because you'll never find me.

Billy Carter

Chapter Sixty-One

A Hero's Obligations

Roger was just drifting off to sleep when he was awakened by a vigorous rap on the door. Too groggy to be alarmed, he stumbled out of bed and into the kitchen to find Marisol standing on the other side of the slider. It was strange; just when he'd thought he'd enjoyed a pleasant last encounter with her—granted, not the one he'd been fantasizing about all summer—here she was again. And in the dead of night.

"Roger, open up," she pleaded.

He slid the door aside.

"Marisol—" he began, but she didn't allow him to finish.

"I need your help," she interrupted.

"*My* help?" Roger said, slipping instinctively into his default position of caution. "What about Sevigny?" But then, seeing the desperation on her face, he realized that fate was presenting him with another chance to play hero for her. It was something he'd longed for ever since he'd failed to properly fill the role once before. "Sure," he said. "Whatever you need."

"It may be dangerous," she said.

"That's fine," Roger answered.

"Really. It *will* be dangerous."

"I'll do it, whatever it is," Roger said.

"I need you to drive me somewhere."

"You've got it."

"And you must promise never to tell Sevigny."

"I promise," he said.

Chapter Sixty-Two

Confession

By now, it was nearly midnight. The Brunswick's lobby was empty, except for the overnight concierge, who was fighting sleep, and Bo, the security guard, who was working on a crossword puzzle. Marisol walked past both men on her way to the stairs. Two minutes later, she pushed open the door to the Governor's Suite and walked briskly into the bedroom. She found Sevigny lying facedown in the middle of the big bed. It was the first time in at least a week that he'd fallen into the kind of sleep he needed, but Marisol didn't know that. She'd grown gradually aware that her comings and goings were distressing him, but hadn't yet grasped the full extent of his suffering.

"Sevigny," she said, "wake up." She placed a hand on his shoulder and gently shook him. "Wake up," she implored.

The great man—the proud and bold adventurer who'd spent the entire summer sequestered in the ancient hotel—groggily lifted his head.

"Wake up," she insisted. "It can't wait."

Sevigny squinted against the soft light trickling in from the living room. Marisol gave him a minute, but just a minute.

"Sevigny," she said, when his brow had furrowed. "Are you awake?"

"I'm awake," he announced, shaking his head and sitting up more fully against the headboard.

"Just listen," Marisol said. She was sitting at the foot of the bed, facing him. "Listen, and remember that I have your best interests at heart."

"Tell me," Sevigny demanded. "What is it?"

"Rupert is near," she announced, speaking rapidly so that he couldn't interrupt her. "He has been moving from motel to motel, and I've been visiting him. At first I thought he was you. He sent a boy with the ring."

She held up her hand to indicate Sevigny's diamond. "The boy said someone I knew wanted to talk, so I thought it was you."

"What boy?" Sevigny interjected.

"I don't know," Marisol answered. "A boy from the beach."

Sevigny raised a dubious eyebrow.

"The boy took me to Rupert, who insisted I already knew he was here
in town. Sevigny, I thought he was crazy. He accused me of giving the boy
information about him. He said he'd sent the ring to signal a truce. He
said he hadn't known I was near, or even alive, but then the boy had
started saying things to Rupert that only I would have known. Then,
Rupert spotted me on the beach one day. He begged me to stop talking to
the boy; he swore he'd looked for me in the water that night. He said *you*
had tried to kill *him*. He said we could still run away to Mexico."

"That's what I was hoping he'd do," Sevigny said. "Just leave the
area—but on his own."

"He needed money," Marisol said. "The first time we met, he told me
to get close to you and steal enough money for our travel expenses, so we
could leave together. I told him I wouldn't do it, that I didn't want to go
anywhere with him. I was strong, Sevigny, but he wouldn't take 'no' for
an answer. Like you, I thought it would be best if he just went away, so I
finally agreed to help."

Marisol's voice had gradually steadied and her face, which had been
anxiety-ridden at first, now appeared as serene as it had been during the
first few days of their reconciliation. Sevigny, for his part, sat momentarily stunned by the information Marisol was sharing.

Marisol continued: "During that first meeting, he asked me to gain
your trust. He said, 'Spend three nights with him and then come back
and see me again.' I did go back to see him, but not for the reason he
thought. I'd betrayed you once, and you'd forgiven me. I wanted to protect you. I wanted to prove you could trust me again. So I went back to
see him the second time and told him about the charity work we were
planning. I told him about the checking account, and said I would skim
some money from the account if it would get him out of town and out of
your life. He said he needed five thousand dollars.

"A week later, I met him for a third time. I wrote a fake check, Sevigny.
I wrote a check to myself and cashed it. I stole five thousand dollars from

you and handed it to Rupert. By then you had told me you'd known about Rupert's initial plan. Warren had told you about Escondido and the money waiting there. You'd told me you were hoping he would just go away.

"I was going to try and make that happen. I thought he'd take the money and disappear. I told him I wasn't going with him—that I never expected to see him again. I planned to tell you everything as soon as he was gone. I thought you'd finally get out and enjoy the summer. I thought we'd spend August on the beach together."

Sevigny made no effort to interrupt but sat there sadly, nodding.

"There was just one problem," Marisol continued. "He took the money, but he didn't go. He told me he couldn't leave. He said as long as the family injustice was allowed to stand, he would know no peace. He told me he had to face you. He needed answers from you, and then he would leave. So I said I would ask you about his father, and that I was sure you'd tell me the truth. Only he wouldn't believe me. He said I had to arrange a meeting between the two of you.

"I refused. I said I would be back with the answer to his lifelong mystery. And so, I asked and you told me. I went to him tonight. I was cautious. I brought Roger and had him stand just outside Rupert's motel room. I showed Rupert that Roger was there, through the window. I thought that I would tell Rupert the story of his father's banishment and that he would finally leave us alone. I thought maybe one day soon I would be able to tell you how close he'd been to us all summer, or maybe I would just let you forget he'd ever existed.

"I told Rupert tonight that I'd learned the truth about his father and mother, and I started to tell him. But would you believe, Sevigny, he didn't want to know? It was the secret that had driven him crazy for his whole life, and when I started to tell him the story, he told me to shut up. He said, 'None of that makes any difference now. We have money and the house in Mexico.' "

Finally, Sevigny interrupted. "He wants *you*, because he knows that would cause me pain," he said. "That's why he won't just leave."

"No," Marisol said. "He wants something even worse. He wants me to lead you into a trap. He says he won't go until he speaks with you. Sevigny, I'm sure he means you harm. I told him I wouldn't help him, and I backed toward the door and opened it, and stood where Roger could see me. Rupert just stood there, glaring. He told me he would have his justice with or without my help. When I asked what he meant by that, he said only, 'You'll see.'

"I stepped back inside and asked what he wanted me to do. He said, 'There's a security guard at the bottom of the stairs at Sevigny's hotel. I can't get past him. You need to bring Sevigny to me. Get him out on the beach. Tell him you want to go for a walk under the stars. Tell him he's been inside too long.' I said I would try, Sevigny. I only said that because I thought it would be better if you knew what he was planning and where he would be.

"And that's how I left it. He expects me to lead you outside tonight. He'll be waiting. He said I should flash the balcony light before we head downstairs. Sevigny, I only agreed because I wanted to see what you thought—whether it was best to call the police and have them waiting, or to . . . I don't know. I thought *you* would know what to do."

Marisol exhaled a long breath and looked into Sevigny's understanding eyes. "You must believe me," she said. "I've only been trying to protect you."

Sevigny squinted. "You came directly here after meeting him?" he asked.

"Yes," Marisol said. "Roger dropped me off and I came right upstairs."

"And you're supposed to flash the light if you can convince me to walk on the beach?"

"That's right."

Sevigny scratched the side of his face as he thought about this. "You've tried," he said, "to fix something that can't be mended."

"What now?" Marisol asked.

"Nothing," Sevigny said. "Bo's guarding the stairs. Let's go to sleep. Let him wait out there all night."

"That's it?"

"Either he'll swallow his anger or he won't."

"And if he won't?"

"Then I'll deal with him."

"We do nothing?" Marisol said, perplexed.

"Not long ago," Sevigny explained, "I would have stepped onto the balcony and yelled, 'I'll be right down, you son of a bitch,' but that would have only made things worse."

"Maybe," Marisol said, uncertainly.

Sevigny looked at her, smiling slightly. "Marisol," he said finally, "I've looked death in the eye before. I know it will come for me someday, but it won't come by my nephew's hand. Not tonight. Not ever."

Chapter Sixty-Three

Cruel Night

Billy lay in the small bedroom that had constituted his home for the better part of fifteen years. Since the night he'd awoken to find Rupert beside his mattress at the trailer park, he had been sleeping at home. But this was the final time. In six hours he would walk to Ocean Yard and Rupert would pick him up and they would steer whatever car Rupert had "borrowed" onto I-95. They would ditch it at the Amtrak station in Boston, and their real journey would be under way.

But it was strange. With salvation so close, Billy found his resolve faltering. Staring at the ceiling, he thought about the town that had held him captive for so long, and about the man who was about to deliver him from it. He did not trust Rupert. The man had struck him, threatened him, taught him to steal, and, in all likelihood, had been shadowing him on the beach for some nefarious purpose that very afternoon. Nonetheless, Billy could not resign himself to another three or four or five years of the only life he'd ever known. He could not stomach the thought of even one more night, hiding in the darkness, bearing witness to the things his mother did.

Another thing was bothering Billy as he lay there, the minutes ticking away until dawn. Sally, his friend on the beach, had finally spoken, and he hadn't liked what she'd said. Her words had shaken him. They had been simple, but he'd felt their sting. He did not doubt what she'd said: Rupert had hit her. He'd taken something from her. And that infuriated Billy. It was one thing for Rupert to hit *him*, to intimidate *him*. It was another thing altogether for him to hurt someone like Sally. The fear in her eyes in that instant when she'd spotted Rupert had allowed Billy, finally, to understand the depths of Rupert's malice.

And yet Billy had chosen to join him. He'd taken things from her apartment without her knowing. Rupert had stolen her ring, and Billy had stolen her drawings. Billy didn't like the way that made him feel.

For the first time all summer, Billy began to wonder if it might be best to call off the entire thing. School would be starting in two weeks. Maybe tenth grade would be better than ninth. There would be chances to do new things. There would be new kids who'd moved in over the summer. Maybe it wouldn't be so bad. Just because he *could* run away didn't mean he *had* to.

Billy heard the front door stick as it always did on humid nights. Then he heard it burst open. His mother spilled inside, giggling, tossing her keys on the table. A male voice said, "You're so effing funny." There was laughter, soft words, and a moment later Billy heard the mechanical groan of the sleeper sofa as the mattress accepted the weight of their bodies. "You're a naughty one," the man said.

Billy rose from his bed, grabbed his backpack off the floor, and thrust it violently out the open window. Jamming his feet into his sneakers, he lowered himself into the night.

Chapter Sixty-Four

A Perfect Night

A sea breeze kicked up in the hour after midnight. As it did, the air grew heavier and thicker until the beach finally disappeared. Wading through the moisture, Rupert was reminded of the night he'd dragged the *Wind Dancer*'s little lifeboat ashore. Now he was finishing what he'd started. It seemed fitting that the beach should again be ensconced in preternatural fog.

After a hundred paces, he veered away from the dunes and onto the flat sand of low tide. He stopped, turned to face the invisible beach, and smiled. It was a perfect night for what he had in mind. Unseen waves spilled onto the wet sand at his back while sheets of moisture drifted lazily past on a southerly breeze. Rupert turned and walked a bit farther, then stopped and waited. Staring at the spot where Sevigny's unseen balcony hovered somewhere in the clouds, he waited for the blur of light Marisol would send into the night, or, perhaps, would not. He waited until the appointed hour had passed, and then smiled a wicked smile.

He looked down at his belt and felt the cold metal of the weapon against his skin. He thought it would have been nice the other way, too, if she'd played along, but this way would do. It might even be better. This way he knew he wasn't walking into a trap. And in the aftermath, flight would be easier. He'd already picked out the car. It had been sitting in front of the Red Squirrel Lodge all week, its owners moving it in and out whenever a new guest arrived. The keys had been tucked above the driver-side sun visor all week, so that even if the curly-haired guy and his wife were down on the beach, the new arrivals could get their vehicles into the driveway. Amid the clamor and spectacle, the sirens and smoke, a missing Nissan would go practically unnoticed. Yes, it was just as well.

Like the boy, the whiny bitch had served her purpose. She'd come through with the money, and now she was no longer needed.

Rupert trudged up the slope and climbed the little ledge that separated the sand of the beach from the dunes. He found the gas can he'd placed there an hour earlier, and he headed for the old barn, the stable, attached to the main building. The relic was barely visible. In the fog he could just make out its shadow, but he had studied it in the daylight. He knew it had not been restored with the rest of the old hotel. Its exposed planks told him that. They were discolored from years of salt and neglect. Its wide double doors, too, were ravaged by dry rot, and were "locked" only with a plank wedged into two notches in the frame. Even to his untrained eye it had looked like a fire hazard the first time he'd spotted it. He wondered how it had ever passed code.

He knew that the hotel's sprawling deck, which faced the ocean and wrapped around the east wing, would also burn. It was long and narrow and offered the only access to two of the Brunswick's three doors. If Sevigny were lucky, he'd be one of the fleet-footed guests to stagger out the lone remaining exit, the one facing West Grand, before its awning and the lattice above would succumb to the flames as well.

But even if Sevigny *were* lucky, Rupert would be waiting for him. He would put a bullet in his uncle's heart in the midst of the chaos, the frenzied rush to safety. And he'd put one in Marisol's too. Then, he would disappear into the smoke and fog.

Chapter Sixty-Five

The Soundest Sleep

A century ago, there had been a hitching post just outside the stable, to which Eben would tether his gentle friends so they could nibble the dune grass. Now, what was left of the post lay buried deep in sand. There had been a pen, too, but it had stood a quarter-mile away, at the foot of the hill. Sometimes, Eben would walk the horses two at a time, down West Grand, then onto Heath Street, before swinging open the gate and guiding them through. On busy nights, when Mr. Drake admitted more guests than the stable could accommodate, Eben would be in constant motion, shuttling between the hotel and pen as guests arrived and departed.

But in an era long past, the corral had become Memorial Park, then a paved lot that fetched as much as twenty dollars a spot on summer Sundays. It was no place for horses. The beach wasn't either. While once Eben had exercised them, galloping from the hotel to the jetty at Pine Point in twelve minutes at low tide, now horses were barred from the beach from May through September. The twenty-six stalls where Eben had brushed and stroked and tended to them were all that remained. Even here, the salt air had gradually overpowered their scent.

The stable doors had swung open a year before, when the latest owner had hauled some glassware outside that she'd discovered on the third floor. It had been right before the carpenters came. She'd piled the crates in the center, beside some antiques that had belonged to Mr. Drake. She'd looked up into the cobwebs and a curious expression had come over her face. She'd shivered—the same way she reacted whenever she ventured up to the fourth floor. Then she'd turned and left.

Now, the plank across the doors was sliding away again. The doors were creaking on their rusted hinges, and a man was entering with fire in his eyes, and soul.

A saddle, tattered and brittle, which had hung for decades on a nail, crashed to the floorboards just as the man began dousing the foremost boxes with gasoline. But the man did not notice. Nor did he appear alarmed when both doors swung shut, leaving him momentarily trapped in the darkness. He just felt his way forward, cursed when he bumped his knee against a mounting stool, and pushed the doors ajar. With his feet he piled sand against the bottom boards so the breeze would not move the doors again. Then he found the offending stool, placed it under one arm, found another in a front stall, and carried the two until he reached the back wall. He dropped them. Next, he retrieved two more stools, along with an old trough, and when he'd made a big-enough pile, he hoisted the red plastic jug and poured. A distinct metal clank—the sound of two horseshoes falling, one on top of the other—reverberated from somewhere in the front of the stable. But as the man lit the match, he did not hear. After that, the crackle of burning wood drowned out any sound that might have deterred him. Eben Staples was powerless to stop him.

In the main building, meanwhile, the man slept. The Governor's Suite had been Mr. Drake's room for the hotel's first eleven summers, but afterwards, Drake had ordered his furniture removed and the room barricaded. He'd proclaimed that no one should venture beyond the partition. Drake's chambermaids and valets had assumed the old man was suffering pangs of guilt for the way he'd treated Eben, but they'd been only partly right. There was something else, something Drake was too embarrassed to confess even to his wife, who stayed year-round at their house on Saco Avenue. It was confusing and embarrassing, but Drake had come to believe it: Eben had never left. Drake had felt his presence every time he'd walked into the room, no matter which way he turned the bed, or how steadfastly he refused to lift his eyes to where Eben's body had dangled from the crossbeam.

Eventually, Drake's time passed. Another owner moved in. The fourth floor reopened. Visitors came and went. Some said they saw things; others said they heard things. Most saw only the moonlight trickling through the windows, heard only the waves lapping against the pylons of the Pier. New decades brought new owners, new guests, periods of activity and slumber. Then darkness fell and lasted for a long time before the hotel had reopened once again, a year ago. The guests began to inch closer. The first floor, then the second, then even the third began to hum with life. Then all at once, the man had come. Before the fourth floor had been made ready, he'd come in the dark of night.

There was something about him that had worried Eben right from the start. The shorter his stay, the better, something had told him. Something about him had said "danger." Eben had tried to convince him to go. In time the man had come closer to looking Eben in the eye than anyone had in years. But still, the man hadn't budged. A woman had moved in, too, a woman who also carried the scent of peril. But she had proven deaf to Eben's language. The danger had remained.

Now, they slept. Just when the threat was greatest, they slept like babes. And no matter how Eben cried, they would not stir. He ruffled drapes, blew papers to the floor, but still they slept. He snapped a window blind, but the man only rolled over, and the woman only yawned and reached for his arm to draw it back over her. And Eben, who had saved his stable and Drake's hotel once before, could only watch.

Chapter Sixty-Six

Fortune's Fickle Smile

Billy stomped down the hill, across West Grand, down the little driveway, and onto the footpath. It wasn't fair. It had been his chance to leave it all behind—the shame and the misery. He'd been so close. But now he'd come face-to-face with his conscience. It stood there staring at him. It wouldn't let him forget what the man had done to his friend. It wouldn't let him forget what he, himself, had done to her, and to all of the other happy people who'd wanted nothing more than to enjoy the sun and sea but instead had been violated by his hand.

Billy tore his backpack from his shoulder and hurled it onto the sand without breaking stride. Why had he even bothered to bring it?

Walking in the fog it all seemed clear. Clear, but terrible and unfair. Of course he would not go with him, the devious man who'd preyed on his and the police officer's weaknesses, who'd sent him to the prettiest woman on the beach with a treasure stolen from the most innocent. He would not go. And his life would continue as it had always been.

Billy walked the shore, cursing the familiar rivulets that chilled his ankles. This fog too, he knew. And in that moment, he allowed himself the pleasure of hating it, as well. It was the blinding kind of fog, the kind that sometimes petered into mist, and other times gave way to hard rain. Billy tried to decide which it would be tonight. The wetness on his face said it would intensify into rain, but usually when he walked the beach at night, if he walked far enough and felt badly enough, the sky cleared so that the moon shined on him. He kicked the water, begrudging the little swells their timeless consistency.

He'd been in this same state of mind when the summer had begun. Nothing had changed. He'd been as angry then as now. He'd escaped it only for a while, only in the delusion of a stranger's promise. In June, he'd spent worried nights fearing that he would fail Rupert in some way. Now, in late August, Billy was the one who had to break the arrangement. It occurred to him that maybe *he* had changed, even if nothing else had. But this thought brought him no pleasure. He kept walking on the foggy beach, and when he'd traversed another hundred feet or so, he decided there would be no moon tonight.

He continued only so far as the chain of boulders visible on the sand at low tide before the Brunswick. The barnacle-encrusted rocks, which rose chest-high to form a slender protrusion into the sea, were favorites of the tourist kids who scoured them for mussels and starfish. To Billy, they were just another landmark in the insufferable paradise that was his small world. When he reached them, he headed up the slope toward the dunes.

Reclining on his elbows a moment later, he continued the same train of thought that had brought him to the water's edge. Feeling the cool of the sand against his back, he wasn't so much angry as defeated. Kicking the waves, he'd realized what he now supposed he'd known all along. He would not go. He could not go. Then what *would* he do? He did not expect the sand to furnish an answer, or the hiding moon, or the coarse grass.

But they didn't need to; after a summer of misguided longing from which he'd at last awoken, fortune was ready to smile on Billy Carter. As he lay there, the salt air drew him toward the long, still-treacherous road to salvation. It did so with something as simple and as complicated as a puff of smoke on a tired breeze.

Slowly but steadily, the heavy air took up and began to carry the hint of fire. The campgrounds were on the other side of the hill, but even on gusty nights Billy had never known the scent of their fires' embers to drift as far as the beach. This wasn't a windy night, and this smell was different. It was burning gasoline.

Billy rose and struggled to get his bearings. He began walking, apprehensively at first, into the dunes. But soon he was trotting over the clumps of grass, inhaling deeply, and gaining on the source. Through the thick air, he made out a leap of flame, and only then did he realize it was more than fog his eyes were struggling against. It was smoke, growing denser and denser with every step he took. He saw that the little building attached to the Brunswick was burning.

"Fire," he called out timorously, then "Fire!" more assertively. "Fire, fire!" Cupping his hands around his mouth, he cried, "Wake up!"

In a flash, a new flame flared on the porch, and that was when Billy saw him. He saw his darting outline in a plume of smoke and recognized him immediately.

"It's him," Billy said faintly, then "Rupert!" a bit more loudly, before realizing that the name carried no special weight to anyone but himself. "He's setting it," Billy yelled. "It's him. He's lighting the fire!"

There were three distinct conflagrations now that combined to create a flickering effect as each one flared. "Fire!" Billy cried, hopping in the sand. "Fire! Get out! Get out!"

Then there was another flash closer by. At first Billy thought it was another fire, but it was one of the first-floor windows being illuminated by a light inside. Another light came on, and another.

Billy brimmed with relief as he watched the windows light up, forgetting for a moment the man who'd been his lone hope all summer. By the time he turned back to search for Rupert, it was too late. He felt the pain of something cold and hard against his face and then, all at once, it seemed, he was kneeling in the dunes with a mouthful of blood and sand. Through eyes stinging with sweat and tears, he watched Rupert scurry into the dunes.

"Help!" Billy yelled, "Help!"

The first guests were already spilling onto the sand. The porch beneath the stairwell was burning, but there was still a path to safety.

"He's getting away!" Billy screamed as they stumbled out.

But the people either didn't understand or just didn't care to pursue a man who had in the dead of night endeavored to burn them alive. There was an elderly man and his wife, a young couple, each holding a child, a woman wearing nothing but underwear and a towel around her top.

"He's getting away," Billy shouted. "He started the fire!"

As the first siren blared at the station a mile away, Billy took flight. When no one else would follow, he pursued Rupert into the dunes, shouting all the while, "Help! It's him! Stop him!" And then Billy was soaked, saturated to the bone, and he realized that the heavens had at some point opened and begun pummeling the beach with rain.

By the time Billy reached the far side of the grass, Rupert was only twenty feet ahead of him. With bare feet that struggled to find traction on the slippery sidewalk, Billy stayed on his trail, streaking past Big Licks and Rocco's, and into the Square.

"Stop him!" Billy shouted. "Help! Stop him!" And then, all at once, Billy caught up to Rupert in the middle of the cobblestones, beside the fountain. He realized too late that Rupert had turned to strike him again. Billy saw the closed fist accelerating toward his face and then, in a flash, found himself down on the ground. To his surprise, he realized he had not been struck, only jostled. Suddenly he saw that several of the guests from the hotel had followed him through the dunes, onto the sidewalk, and into the Square. When Rupert had turned to assault him, one of them had surged forward and tackled him, knocking Billy to the ground in the process. Now the other man held Rupert against the ground, grinding his knee into Rupert's back.

The rain poured down as the sirens drew nearer. Someone said, "The boy did it. He followed him!"

"Hold him," another voice called, referring to Rupert, who was squirming beneath the man who'd tackled him.

"The boy saved us," another voice said.

"Hey, he's got a gun!" someone cried.

"I've got it!" said the man holding Rupert, who had grabbed the gun from the waistband of Rupert's pants.

"Hold him, hold him," someone implored. "They're coming. See the lights?"

"How's the boy?" someone else asked.

"He's all bloody."

"He's a hero," another woman said.

By the time Billy had staggered to his feet, his face dripping blood, there were a dozen people around him, the tourists whom he'd always detested. One stepped forward and held him against his dizziness and the driving rain. Another reached out a hand and gripped his shoulder. Billy realized there were more onlookers forming a larger circle just outside the inner group of brave souls who had first followed him into the Square. Roused by the commotion, the second wave had emerged from the motels and cottages nearby. The woman holding Billy pulled him close against her body. In French, she said something soft and soothing.

Billy felt the sudden urge to confess, to announce that he was the blanket thief, and to point to the man writhing beneath the other and relieve himself of the weight he carried. But before he could, Chief White's cruiser came skidding onto the wet cobblestones and nearly barreled into the outer circle of onlookers before finally screeching to a halt.

Then, a voice from the inner circle called out loudly enough for all to hear, "Hey, the man who's got him—it's the famous guy." And another voice rejoined, "It *is*. It's Ferdinand Sevigny that has him pinned!"

Chapter Sixty-Seven

Daybreak

The downpour continued long enough to dampen the flames and deter the local firebugs from lingering too long where they might have gotten in the way of the firefighters. Of course, the Brunswick's owners braved the torrent to watch the men and women of the Old Orchard Beach Fire Department fight the fire, but only after ferrying their guests to the Palace Playland arcade, which had been opened up to provide them shelter.

As Jim and Marty watched the streams of water douse the flames, they came to understand that their losses would be significant but not catastrophic. The wraparound porch was gone and the first-floor shingles were singed beyond repair. The vintage windows on the first and second floors were uniformly shattered, but the powerful streams of water that had destroyed them had succeeded in preserving the hotel's structural integrity. The beach entrance lay in soaking black ruin. So, too, had the quaint stable been reduced to ash, save for the occasional glow of a horse-shoe protruding from the wreckage. The blockbuster season was over, but Jim and Marty's "baby" would live to see another summer.

Meanwhile, Billy Carter sat at the police station, looking out the window of an interrogation room. The sun was lighting up a new day, and as it did, the high school across the parking lot was emerging from the shadows. In the glare of the late summer morning, its bricks looked redder than usual, the grass of its grounds, greener, the asphalt of its driveway, darker. Everything about it looked crisp and clean. Even the two basketball hoops at the far end of the lot, which for as long as Billy could remember had tilted forward, seemed to stand straighter. Looking through the barred window, Billy wondered if he'd ever get the chance to shoot hoops there again.

After nearly an hour, the door swung open. "Sorry for the wait," an officer said. He put a can of Coke in front of Billy and sat down across from him. "The bastard ain't talking," he said. "Won't even produce a name. I'm gonna take your statement, then you can probably go home. We sent someone for your mom."

"Okay," Billy said uneasily. He had expected to be in trouble by the time the officer returned. He was sure that Rupert would have ratted him out for robbing the blankets and condos, and that maybe he'd even implicate Billy in the fire.

"You did a brave thing," the officer said. "Start with your presence on the beach. What you were doing there? How did you notice the fire? What did you see at the Brunny?"

"I need to start before that," Billy said.

"Okay," the officer said.

"I was the blanket thief," Billy announced sadly, looking down at the unopened soda can on the table before him. "I did it . . . for *him*." Billy could feel the officer staring at him, but did not look up.

"Wait a minute," the officer said. "You're talking about the suspect?"

"His name is Rupert Sevigny," Billy declared. "The rich guy's nephew."

Before Billy had finished speaking, the officer had leapt from his chair, opened the door, and begun calling for the chief.

Billy told them everything. He started with the night he'd found Rupert on the beach. He told them about the two policemen who visited his mom, and the morning Rupert had taken the photos and threatened Mason. He told them about the money he'd stolen for Rupert, about meeting him under the Pier, planning to run away, and sleeping at Ocean Yard. He confessed that he'd stolen evidence from Sally's apartment. He told them how trapped and lonely he felt at home. He'd thought it would be hard, but once he started talking, it all came spilling out. It felt good.

Chief White had turned bright red the minute he learned that the suspect in the other room was related to the international celebrity who'd been summering in his town, who had emerged unexpectedly as one of the heroes in the morning's drama, and who sat, still waiting in another interrogation room, to give his own eyewitness account. As Billy talked, the chief's face gradually returned to its normal hue—until Billy got to the part about the two officers and their sleepovers with his mother. Then his face flared again. When Billy explained that Rupert had blackmailed Officer Mason on the same morning Mason had killed Officer Sabo, the chief looked as if someone were running a dagger through his gut.

When Billy was done, he turned to the chief and other officers and asked, "Am I going to jail?" But no one answered. They just got up, starting with the chief, and filed out of the room. The door was only closed for a few seconds, though, before it reopened.

Chief White stood with one leg in the room and one out in the hall. "How old are you?" he asked.

"Fifteen," Billy said.

"You won't go to jail," he said, and then quietly closed the door.

The chief stomped down the hall to another interrogation room where the second witness, Ferdinand Sevigny, sat waiting. Like Billy, Sevigny had been ignored for the past hour while the chief and his men had interrogated Rupert. That had been a mistake. Both witnesses were more familiar with the suspect than the chief had realized. Now, it was more than just arson the chief was investigating. The boy's confession had brought him closer to solving the mystery that had tormented him all summer. The rich Australian was involved in the tragedy on the island after all—or at least his nephew was. And the chief wasn't about to wait a minute longer to find out exactly how.

Fortunately for Sevigny, before Chief White could even threaten to slap an obstruction of justice charge on him, he started talking. Like Billy, Sevigny had decided to cleanse his conscience. As the chief entered the room, Sevigny blurted, "He's my nephew. And I believe he was involved with the slaying on the island."

Sevigny proceeded to explain that he'd never been on the island where his belongings and the fabricated note had been found. Though he had no proof Rupert had been there, either, he said he suspected it. He said Rupert had tried to kill him aboard the *Wind Dancer*. Sevigny believed Rupert was trying to cover up that crime when he'd planted the evidence on the island. Sevigny wasn't sure what had brought the officers to that place, but now he was sure Rupert had somehow played a hand in them being there.

"I know it," Sevigny said, "but I have no proof. And I didn't want to make a baseless claim." He smiled sadly and looked at the chief. "No, that's not it," he said. "I wanted to keep my dirty laundry out of the press. I played along with what the investigators had cobbled together. My selfishness made me hide the truth."

"You're gonna do the right thing now, though," the chief said. He wasn't asking. "You're gonna help us put him away."

"Yes," Sevigny said.

"Even if you need to testify."

"Yes."

"And you're gonna apologize to the good people you've dragged into this goddamned soap opera."

"Yes."

"Starting with the terrified kid in the next room . . . and Jim and Marty down at the Brunny . . . and—"

"Chief," Sevigny said, "I'm going to do much more than that."

Chapter Sixty-Eight

Setting Sail

Summer ended two weeks later. The calendar may have said there were three weeks remaining, but schools were opening across the country. The tourists were heading home. To the shopkeepers and merchants who made their living in the Square, the sea and sun had cooperated all season, providing one day of clean surf and blue sky after another. It seemed only fitting that Labor Day would be the same. And it was. The locals enjoyed one final payday before the beach and town became deserted once again.

According to plan, the *Wind Dancer* set sail on this day, too, departing from the boatyard where it had been repaired. Its captain stood at the helm even more erectly and confidently than he had when his strange journey began. His lover stood serenely by his side. The ship's course was set for Little Tobago. There, Marisol hoped for nothing more than to find her parents and siblings in good health. Sevigny hoped she would find forgiveness. The girl he'd taken away would return a woman—a woman who now assured him that come what may, they were doing the right thing. Even if her people could not relinquish the past, she said, the future was a new canvas. Yes, her family would be upset, but shouldn't they be? She would stay as long as it took, she said, to forge a lasting reconciliation. After that, she said, she did not know where the wind would take them. And neither did he.

"Just think," Marisol said, surveying the coast. "It was probably somewhere along here that I almost drowned. It seems like forever ago, and like yesterday."

A minute later, Sevigny said, "That's it," pointing to the tallest building on the waterfront south of the Pier. "Look," he said. "Jim's got the framing up on the stable."

"I still don't understand why he's rebuilding it," Marisol said. "They don't use it."

"Just because," Sevigny said, smiling a secret smile.

Between the ancient hotel and the water's edge, the beach lay like a kaleidoscope of happy color. From the swells a half-mile out, no part of the sand was visible, only great swaths of blue and red, green and yellow, pink and purple. Their eyes took in the colorful blankets, umbrellas, and swim trunks, and assembled the most prominent among them into rough patterns. There was a strip of red beside the Pier, an island of orange near the Brunswick. There were people, tiny as ants, swarming on the sand, dotting the white waves with dark heads.

"I promised I would," Marisol said, when she caught Sevigny eyeing her curiously as she waved toward the beach, where her friends had said they'd be watching. "I know they can't see me."

Only the *Wind Dancer*'s sails were visible from the sand as the great yacht traced the full length of the expansive beach. It seemed to glide slowly over the dark water, and yet, in hardly any time at all, it was veering out toward the slender horizon.

Mandy and Sam, who would be leaving themselves the next morning, both had tears in their eyes as they stood on the beach and waved. Carrie, who had observed their gushing emotion with amusement all summer, was surprised to find her own eyes misting over.

"We never even took her to the mall," Mandy lamented.

"It's okay," Carrie said, reaching out an arm to the more distraught of her two friends. "She'll be back."

It was true. Sevigny and Marisol had promised to return to monitor the progress of the projects they'd presented to the town before departing. More immediately, they would be returning as witnesses when the "Rogue Sevigny," as the *Journal Tribune* had dubbed Rupert, stood trial for arson and attempted murder. There was also a chance Rupert would face blackmail and malicious mischief charges for his role in the Ernie Sabo murder. The girls had promised to leave school and rendezvous at a cheap motel during whatever weekend dates coincided with Marisol's return. And they had vowed to return the next summer for a vacation together.

As for Paul Mason, the revelation that he'd killed his friend to hide his infidelity had extinguished any public sympathy remaining for him.

And yet, as the Labor Day sun rose high in the sky, his wife Millie was heading to the county penitentiary for the extended holiday visiting hours. Ten days earlier, on the night the news had broken of a perilous link between Brandy Carter, Paul, Ernie, and the suspect in the Brunswick fire, Millie had been beset by denial, anger, self-reproach, and humiliation. But the next morning she'd packed two peeled oranges and two cans of Moxie and had set out to see her husband. She was going to him now, even as the ship that had brought so much sadness into her life made a final sweep along the shore.

Jim Wagner was among the locals scanning the horizon to bid the *Wind Dancer* farewell, although he nearly missed it. Jim's off-season had started earlier than he would have liked. He was working on repairs to the hotel while his wife took a well-deserved vacation to visit her family in Massachusetts. When the tall white sails finally came into view, he and his carpenter friend Roland stopped banging nails. Jim lifted a hand to shade his eyes.

"He may not have been Duke Ellington," Jim said, "but he drew the biggest crowd of my time. Filled the place, then damn near burned it down." He pinched a nail and, without waiting for a reply from Roland, gave it a whack.

Meanwhile, up the beach in Scarborough, Roger Simons was also hammering away, working on the screened-in porch he'd started building atop his deck a few days earlier. Since helping Marisol one final time, he'd been working nonstop on the cottage. He wasn't sure if he would put it up for sale or just rent it out, but he *was* sure he wanted to travel. It was time to start living. Seeing the *Wind Dancer* gliding so freely upon the water, he could only nod in approval at the simple wisdom of this idea. He trained his eyes on the water to see if he could still pick out its masts, but it was too late.

Another person who would have liked to have waved good-bye but missed his chance was Billy Carter. He had been on the beach all morning, toting the bag and pointed stick that had become his constant companions over the final two weeks of August. He roamed the beach, spearing the plastic bags, napkins, wrappers, cans, and other debris left by the tourists in their carelessness. The chief had said that next summer, once he'd paid his "debt to society," the town's public works department would give Billy eight dollars an hour for this labor. That sounded pretty good to him.

Billy imagined that by then, he wouldn't be living in the chief's spare room anymore, but hopefully with someone else, maybe a family in town. Anyway, Chief White seemed to think it would work out that way, because when he talked about next summer, he spoke as though Billy would still be in Old Orchard Beach, and when he talked about the community center that wouldn't be ready until sometime after the following summer, he talked about a job there for Billy, too—cleaning the pool, or reading to senior citizens, or doing any number of things—as long as he kept up with his schoolwork. The chief talked about a college fund that had been anonymously established for Billy, too—a generous sum that would one day deliver him from town. But only for four years. After that, it would be up to Billy to return or not.

Billy's mother had already left. She was living in Biddeford at a place that might help her quit drinking, and might help her in other ways, too, Chief said. Billy didn't know exactly what that meant, or how long she'd be there, but he didn't think she would be coming back anytime soon. There was a FOR RENT sign in the front window of their house and a padlock across the door. Billy didn't miss living there, but in a strange way he did miss his mother. Chief had told him that when he was ready to visit her, he would drive him.

When the *Wind Dancer* passed, Billy was off the beach. He was inside one of the condos, knocking on a door.

"It's me," he said. "Open up."

When the door opened, he said, "You should be on the beach."

Sally shrugged.

"Here," Billy said. "I found this." He started to hand Sally a green plastic ring, but right before she took it in her fingers, he squeezed the little rubber bulb that sat where its jewel should have been, sending a stream of water squirting into her face. She flinched as he giggled. She made an unhappy face, but he knew she was amused. An instant later, she put out her hand, impatient for him to give it to her. This time he did. She spent the next half-minute entirely consumed by it, holding it close to her eyes and squeezing the little bulb, which was empty now, to see how it worked. "You need to fill it," Billy explained, but she continued to squeeze the air in and out of the soft plastic.

"Why aren't you wearing the shiny one I gave you?" Billy asked.

Sally shrugged and turned away from the door. Billy followed her to the orange bucket in the corner. It was heavy, but she managed to hoist it up. She shook it a few times, then held it against her stomach with one hand so that her other hand was free to move inside. After a moment of digging, she set the bucket down. Then, she slid a ring onto her finger. It was costume jewelry, but it looked a lot like Marisol's diamond. Billy wasn't sure if he'd fooled her, or if she'd merely pretended that he had, to make him happy.

Now, she stood wiggling her finger back and forth in the center of the room so that the ring's sparkles danced on the wall. She moved her finger, watched the reflecting light, and smiled. Then she slid off the ring and dropped it back into the bucket, filled with so many others, each unique and special, yet each one forgotten, left behind, or lost, and then, recovered.

About the Author

Shortly after moving to Maine in 2002, Josh Pahigian took a part-time job with the Old Orchard Beach Recreation Department. That job lasted just long enough for Josh to fall in love with the town and its residents and helped give him special insight into the seaside community's inner workings. It is his ongoing affection for the well-known seaside resort community that has  prompted him to use the town as the backdrop for his first novel, *Strangers on the Beach*.

Pahigian has previously written several non-fiction books, including *The Ultimate Baseball Road Trip* and *101 Baseball Places to See Before You Strike Out*. His writing has also appeared in a variety of magazines and on ESPN.com. Since 2004, he has worked as an adjunct writing professor at The University of New England in Biddeford, Maine. Josh holds a bachelor's degree in English from The College of the Holy Cross, and a master's of fine arts in Creative Writing from Emerson College. He lives in Buxton, Maine with his wife, Heather, and son, Spencer.

Acknowledgments

Upon the completion of my previous books—all nonfiction sports titles—I used the space afforded by the acknowledgments section to thank those who contributed more or less directly to the work that led to their publication. This cast of worthy individuals included friends and family members who helped me to cover the other bases in my life while I found time to travel, research, and write, as well as fellow travelers, writers, and experts from the amateur and professional sporting ranks.

The publication of my first novel, however, affords an opportunity of a different sort. As *Strangers on the Beach* sprang entirely from my imagination, I believe that nearly all of the life experiences I accrued in the three-plus decades prior to its completion were not just helpful, but necessary to the development of its characters and themes. Of course, some of my life experiences were more instrumental than others in shaping the worldview and imagination from which the book evolved, and so, too, some of the people I've been fortunate enough to know have had more to do than others in my development as a storyteller. I wish to acknowledge those individuals here.

So let me begin where this writer's work has always begun—with my family. My wife, Heather, is amazingly generous with her time, patience, and love, in allowing me the space to complete whatever book I'm writing. For this book, Heather played an even greater role than usual—as my first reader. After each chapter rolled off the keyboard and onto the computer screen, Heather read it and provided instant feedback. This was not always an easy role to play, and indeed, we had some spirited discussions during our daily walks afterwards, as I often defended what I'd written and tried to make my best case for its existence before more often than not coming around to agreeing with Heather's assessment and getting back to work. So for her editorial help, but especially for her love and never-ending kindness, my first thanks go to Heather.

Our son Spencer also earns special thanks for inspiring me to keep at it when it appeared the book might never see the light of day. As a previously childless writer, I always imagined that creating books was something akin to fathering a child; after all, a writer's books are his babies, hopefully living on after he is gone, preserving his name and some small part of who he is. But I see now that the two are pretty different, and I'm not just talking about the diapers. A child loves you back, something a book never quite manages. For the special gleam in Spencer's eyes when he says "Daddy," I am unendingly grateful.

Another important early reader of *Strangers on the Beach* who deserves mention is my good friend and literary agent, Colleen Mohyde, at the Doe Coover Agency. Colleen's editorial suggestions were extensive and spot-on. The story and characters came into clearer focus in the drafts following her critique. For her help with the book, and her friendship, too, thank you, Colleen.

My brother Jamie Pahigian played a special role as a later reader of the manuscript. He was at his nitpicky best when poring through these pages, looking for whatever liberties I had taken with the English language. Even English professors are prone to the occasional throwaway sentence, and this writer was fortunate enough to have his younger brother around to clean up his messes.

While Jamie is my only brother, he is one of several family members whose encouragement and love make my life full. I am especially grateful for those who have maintained an interest in my writing, and I thank them for reading my books and buying them as gifts for their friends, and for always asking what I'm working on. I particularly thank my parents, Richard and Cathy, for raising me to have a strong social conscience; my in-laws, Judy and Ed Gurrie, for being such enthusiastic promoters of my books; and my in-laws, Butch Razoyk and Lynn Pastor, for reminding me that many of their favorite authors spent years paying their dues before making it big. Special thanks also go to my many wonderful aunts and uncles, especially Lucy Pahigian, Vartkis Pahigian, Theresa Lindsey, Janet Capowski, and Jane Hernandez.

Wherever my travels have taken me, I have been surrounded by wonderful friends, and I wish to thank them, too, beginning with my friends in Old Orchard Beach. When I arrived in town a decade ago to assume a part-time position at Town Hall, I had no idea I was forging friendships that would last a lifetime. For accepting a Massachusetts transplant as one of their own, I thank Dean Plante, John Regan, George Shabo, Heath "Tippy" Floyd, Vinny Mattia, Curt Chretien, Steve Labbe, Mike Pulsifer, Nikki Duplisea, and the larger-than-life Jason Webber.

I also offer special thanks to the Scarborough Pahigians, for welcoming me and Heather into their family when we first moved to Maine. Thanks to Cary, Barbara, Brendan, Amanda, and little Bentley, too!

I thank the Scarborough Stagno/Platzman clan for their company on the beach each summer, and for their well wishes. I especially thank George Stagno for his encouragement of this book over a series of summers.

Thanks go to my good friends in Buxton: Roger, Susan, Brianna, and Kendra Ramsey. Isn't it funny how life works? When a neighborhood vandal stole those lawn signs, it turned out he was laying the groundwork for what would become a lifelong friendship between our two families. I also thank Buxton friends Lindsay, Brent, and Parker Havu for bailing us out of at least a couple of fixes so far. Heather and I are both thankful to have you in our lives. We're also thankful to have met Buxton friends Heidi, Chris, Max, and Lily Carter.

From the University of New England, which has been my academic home since 2004, I offer my sincere appreciation to Matthew Anderson, Elaine and Roland Brouillette, Michael Cripps, Anouar Majid, Camille Vande Berg, George Young, Jesse Miller, Lisa Giles, Eric Drown, Cathrine Frank, Susan McHugh, Ali Ahmida, Elizabeth DeWolfe, Dick Buhr, Olga Skorapa, Bistra Nikiforova, John Cooper, Helen Drown, and Brenda Austin. I also thank the wonderful students I've had through the years.

I offer a raucous "Mamie Reilly" to the Holy Cross crew, including Kevin and Sarah Larsen, Ernie and Mary Larsen, Chris and Alyssa Stagno, Matt and Pam Guilbeault, Joe and Carol Bird, Matt and Danielle Jordan, Evan and Raegan Chekas, Chris and Jennie Perrotta, Pat and Carlin Sweeney, Rich Hoffman, Jay McCarthy, and all the rest. And although I haven't done a very good job of keeping in touch through the years, I thank the professors who made differences in my life's path: Anne Bernays, Justin Kaplan, Helen Whall, and David Schaefer.

Likewise, I thank my graduate studies professors from Emerson College, especially Pam Painter, Jessica Treadway, Margot Livesey, Chris Keane, and Joe Hurka. I also thank my development department buddies: Chris DeChellis, Michael Charewicz, Tom Hanold, and Barbara Rutberg.

Another Emerson friend who deserves acknowledgment is my former and surely future collaborator Kevin O'Connell, with whom I published my very first book, *The Ultimate Baseball Road Trip*, which was rereleased in a fully revised and updated edition in 2012. Kevin, we may not always see eye to eye on all things hardball, but I do treasure your friendship. Thanks also go to Kevin's lovely wife Meghan, for letting her hubby leave home to watch baseball games with me every so often.

Speaking of my past publications, I would be remiss if I did not offer a hearty tip of the cap to some of the wonderful editors with whom I've had the chance to work through the years. They include David E. Nathan, George Donahue, Tom McCarthy, Rob Kirkpatrick, Keith Wallman, Gary Mitchem, Brett Pauly, Harry Keyishian, and the late Leo Hamalian.

Finally, special thanks go to Dean Lunt, Michelle Lunt, Amy Canfield, Carole Fallon, Melissa Kim, and the rest of the dedicated professionals at Islandport Press for believing in this book and agreeing to publish it.